THE CURIOUS CASE OF FAITH & GRACE

DAVID B. LYONS

Print ISBN: 978-1-9160518-5-0

❀ Created with Vellum

PRAISE FOR DAVID B. LYONS

"Lyons is the master of the twist" – BooksFromDuskTillDawn

"A devastating twist in its tail" – Irish Independent

"Gripping and high-octane" – Irish Daily Mail

"Smart, dark and fascinating" — Reading Confessions

For my favourite sister...

Debra

✝

Grace pinched her tongue between her teeth and lifted a knee towards her chest. Then she stamped down as hard as she could.

The squelch was so loud and gross that it caused Clive to twist his head in disgust. He stood upright, strode towards his daughter and picked her up by the underarms.

'What have you done?' he shouted, spraying spittle into her face.

She didn't answer. She was too busy trying to squeeze tears from her eyes.

Clive dropped his gaze beneath his daughter's dangling feet, then baulked.

The sight was gross; the frog now a splattered mixture of green and purple slimy mounds. He knew only half of the frog was on that path; the other half likely stuck to the bottom of his daughter's shoe.

Clive placed Grace down, ensuring she missed the mess, then ordered her to take off her shoes before following him in to the kitchen.

She continued to force out the tears as she unbuckled her shoes, only pausing when she noticed Faith pull the net curtains of the living room window across to stick her tongue out at her. Grace sucked up the wet snot that was about to run onto her top lip, then shrugged a shoulder towards her twin. Faith laughed, but she wasn't sure why she was laughing exactly. It might have been because Grace had just splattered the frog to death—or perhaps it was just funny to see Daddy all up in a rage.

The twins had only just turned four years of age then, but splattering that frog to nothing remains Grace's earliest memory. It's not so much the punishment she got from her old man that sticks in her mind. It's that noise. That squelch. She can still hear it today—seven years on. And she can still feel that sensation under her foot no matter what shoes she's wearing on any given day. There was something strangely satisfying about that squelch.

Clive and the twins had just been to Phoenix Park earlier that morning to catch some pinkeens from the Doggy Pond. And when the frog hopped up on the bank next to them, both Faith and Grace insisted in unison that they take it home and treat it like a pet. So they did. Expect they didn't—treat it like a pet, that is. Grace killed it within a half an hour of them arriving back at their bungalow.

'You will spend the next hour kneeling and praying to our Lord —asking him to forgive you, do you understand?' Clive said, staring down at the top of his daughter's head. She was minute by comparison, wiping her eyes in front of his crotch. 'Well... let me hear you,' he said.

She sucked more wet up her nose, then looked around herself in the hope of catching her sister's eye. But Faith was out of sight— hiding behind their bedroom door, and peering through the crack.

Grace slowly placed each of her knees — one at a time — onto the carpet, brought the two palms of her hands together, and stared up at the giant crucifix hanging from the wall.

'Dear almighty Lord Jesus, please forgive me for killing Grebit. It was a accident. I was just walking in the garden and—'

'Don't you dare! Don't you dare!' Clive grunted. He adjusted his *footing so he was standing even more dominant over his daughter. 'If you attempt to lie to our Lord Jesus Christ, you will end up in Hell. Do you understand, Grace Tiddle?'*

Grace and Faith had been made well aware of Heaven and Hell ever since consciousness. Religion was driven into them from day one; Clive and Dorothy hovering above their cribs as soon as they were born to chant prayers at them.

Grace, her face blotchy from all of the rubbing, opened one eye to stare at up her father's tall frame, then closed it quickly again when she noticed him peering down over his rotund belly at her.

'Okay. Jesus... I stamped on Grebit, but I am so sorry. Please forgive me. I want to go to Heaven, not Hell. I want to be with you. Not burning. I will never kill another frog again. I pwomise.'

Clive snorted, then stepped over his daughter.

'One hour. Keep asking for forgiveness. If I hear you stop, you will be given further punishment.'

Then he headed into the kitchen for his usual mid-morning nap. He'd sit at the squared table, his back against the wall, and close his eyes for half-an-hour before getting back on with his day. He got up early, did Clive Tiddle. Always at five a.m. He'd have breakfast, plan his sermons, then do a spot of gardening before taking his little kitchen snooze. He'd follow that pattern almost every morning. But not on Saturdays. Because that was when he'd skip the gardening to spend time with the twins. Which is why the three of them had ventured out to the Doggy Pond that morning. Though Clive would have much rather have been doing gardening. He loved gardening. Probably because he had the look to carry it off. He was massive; six-foot, five inches tall, and he almost always wore a gilet — autumnal in colour — over a plaid shirt. His sandy hair was greying but the straw-orange moustache that covered his top lip hadn't lost any of its colour. The hairs of his 'tache hung over his mouth in a thick, stunted length when he talked, like the bristles of a broom. He looked much older than his years—at least a decade older. So did Dorothy. It wasn't that their skin was particularly weathered, worn or wrinkled. It was more to do with how they dressed. And acted. They were both old-fashioned. Frumpy.

'...and I pwomise I will take good care of everything my mammy and daddy buy for me, like dolls and rosemary beads and other things...'

'Psst.'

Grace held her eyes closed firmer to rid herself of her sister's distraction.

'Psst.'

Then she sighed, opened one eye again and peered over her shoulder.

'Go 'way,' she said.

Faith was standing in the doorway, giggling.

'You killed Grebit.'

'Shh... Daddy will be cross at both of us. Go away. I need to pray. For an hour, Daddy said.'

'That was naughty.'

'Shhh.'

Faith continued to giggle, holding her hand to her mouth. She often giggled by means of communication. Faith — second born by twenty minutes — developed slower than her sister from the outset. Grace instantly fell into line; abiding by the routine Clive and Dorothy had put in place for their twins. But Faith could never handle it. She would often be awake when she was supposed to be asleep, asleep when she was supposed to be awake. And she would talk when she was supposed to be quiet, then fall mute if anybody ever asked her a question. She might've been ever-so-slightly prettier than her sister — though there's really not much in it; they're identical, save for the fact that Grace has a small freckle under her left eye and a slightly wider nose — but in terms of intellect, Grace has always been atop that podium.

'I can't hear you!' Clive's voice boomed from the kitchen.

'...and our Lord Jesus Christ,' Grace raised her voice, 'to whom I owe my life, I promise to always abide by your teachings and to read the Bible every night.'

She wasn't sure what she was saying exactly. She was just repeating phrases and sentences she'd heard time and time again—either in church, or at home.

She loved her daddy. And her mammy. Both twins did. Their parents gave them everything they had ever needed; a comfy bed to sleep in at night; a church in which to pray; food; sweets—on special occasions. And a big back garden in which a one-hundred year old huge oak tree stood that they would run around all day, every day if their parents allowed them to. The Tiddles house itself wasn't huge. It was of decent size. A three-bed detached bungalow on the foothills of the Dublin mountains. But that bungalow was placed inside seven acres of land; a small split garden to the front where Clive would prune his rosebushes, water his plants and mow his lawn every Saturday. And to the back, a rough expanse of green field that seemed to travel as far as the horizon.

Dorothy was actually a stricter parent than her husband but Clive did possess a stern growl every now and then that would rush dread into the twins. Grace knew well that he would be furious with her if she stamped on that frog. But she just couldn't help herself. Kneeling down in front of the crucifix would be worth the satisfying sensation of splattering Grebit into the garden path. Or so she thought. Five minutes in, she was beginning to get itchy. She kept lifting her knees — one at a time — towards her chest so she could scratch at them for a little relief while she continued praying.

'Whatcha doing there, love?' Dorothy said, coming out of her own bedroom, a basket of washing gripped tight to her hip.

'I eh... Daddy told me to pray for an hour because...'

'An hour? Because what, love?'

Dorothy's brow sunk. And her big brown eyes bore into the back of her daughter's head.

'I, eh... I stood on the frog.'

'Oh Mary, mother of God,' Dorothy said, blessing herself with her free hand.

'Did you kill it?'

Grace swallowed, then slowly nodded.

Dorothy blessed herself again and whispered something towards the ceiling.

'Silly girl,' she hissed when she looked back down. Then she trotted across the hallway, the basket of washing still stuck to her hip, and into the kitchen. She didn't notice Faith hiding behind the twins' bedroom door as she stormed past.

'Uuugh,' Grace said into her hands when she heard her mother strike up the conversation about Grebit with Clive.

And then Faith giggled from behind her. Again.

'Hail Mary, full of Grace, the Lord be with you...'

Grace turned to see her twin walking towards her.

'You're better off doing prayers we know, rather than just saying sorry to Jesus all the time,' Faith whispered as she knelt beside her. 'It helps the time go quicker.'

Grace beamed a smile at Faith, and then both of them closed their eyes tight and began chanting a Hail Mary in unison.

Even though Faith was slow to learn, she never had any problem rattling off prayers. Both of the twins had been chanting Hail Marys and Our Fathers since they were two years old. It was as if prayers took priority in their development. They needed to learn prayers first, before they could learn anything else.

Though it seemed apt for Clive and Dorothy that their babies would be immersed in prayer. After all, it was prayers that brought the twins into the world.

It took seventeen years of trying for the Tiddles to fall pregnant. And when a blue cross finally appeared on one of the hundreds of white sticks Dorothy had peed on over those years, they immediately fell to their knees and thanked the Lord Jesus Christ. Not the science that led to them undergoing a dozen rounds of IVF.

They were abuzz with their miracle.

And that was before they had learned they were getting two at once.

ALICE

I've mastered the art of stifling yawns. The trick is to let the yawn manifest itself at the back of the throat while keeping your lips sealed together, then allowing the air to slowly and quietly seep out through the nostrils. It makes my eyes water every time I do it, and I'm certain that if anybody was staring at me they would be able to tell I was stifling a yawn. But nobody's staring at me. At least I hope not anyway. But best I don't gape my mouth open like a hippo incase I'm seen to be finding this tiresome. It's not boring—far from it. It's fascinating, really. But the silences are long and plentiful. Way too plentiful.

I twist my left wrist a little and strain my eyes down. 4:21 p.m. The judge seems to be wrapping everything up. I should be home around five-ish again today.

I find myself glancing up at them as the judge continues to rattle on. I can't help it. If anybody *was* staring at me through the course of this trial, they'd have noticed me do this plenty of times. I just find them so intriguing to look at. Identical. And charged with the most horrendous crimes possible. Imagine bludgeoning both of your parents to death; repeatedly stabbing them with a kitchen knife until they gasped their last breath. I don't know whether they're more cute or more creepy looking to be honest. I've never made up my mind on that. There *has* to be some dark stuff going on behind those big brown eyes, though. I bet that's why I can't stop looking up at them; I'm trying to find that darkness—to justify the verdict I have come to. I'm certain they're guilty... no doubt about it.

The judge stares up over the rim of her glasses at the twelve of us and coughs politely into her fist. It's her regular cue, to let us know she's about to address us directly.

'Members of the jury,' she says. 'I know this has been a tiring and testing two weeks for you all. We have now heard from the last of the witnesses in this case and you will no longer be offered any further evidence. Tomorrow we will hear final arguments from both the defence and the prosecution, after which I will release you to deliberate your verdict.'

Some of my fellow jurors sit face on, nodding back at Judge Delia McCormick, others glance around sheepishly at their peers. I can't keep my eyes off the twins. I've desperately wanted to witness how Faith and Grace have reacted to each and every word spoken during this trial, even if it was only a case of the judge addressing us jurors as a matter of protocol. Grace glances straight at me, meets my eye. It's not the first time she's done this over the past fortnight, but this is the first time I don't blink my gaze away. I stare straight back at her until Imogen — one of her defence lawyers — leans over to whisper something into her ear and our moment is gone. I've often played around with the theory that it was perhaps just Grace who killed Clive and Dorothy. Maybe Faith had nothing to do with it. She's too quiet. Too... what's-the-word... lacking. As if she wouldn't have the wherewithal to kill. Though I've read that can be a common trait amongst murderers.

The jurors to my right stand and suddenly I'm standing too, without me hearing the judge dismiss us. Then we do what we usually do—walk to the side door in two straight lines of six, cloaked in total silence. We've done this every day for the past two weeks, but it always feels uncomfortably awkward; as if the whole world's eyes are bearing into us.

It's relaxing though, to hear everybody's breathing return to normal as soon as we reach the corridor. We must all hold our breaths longer then usual when we're seated in that dock.

'Gee, looks like we'll be starting to deliberate tomorrow,' the obese guy says, turning to me.

I turn my lips downwards in mock dread.

'I know, we've… we've a lot to discuss,' I say.

He nods his chins at me and then uncomfortably places the palm of his hand on to my left shoulder.

'I can't wait to see which way each of the jurors have been swayed, can you Alice?'

I really want to shrug his hand away. But I'm more polite than that. So I answer his question while he's still touching me.

'It'll be interesting alright. I think I know which way I'm going to vote already. Do you?'

He raises an eyebrow, then looks about himself before leaning closer to me.

'We're not supposed to discuss this without the other jurors… but,' he looks about himself again, 'not guilty.'

Not guilty. Who else does he think did it?

'What about you?' he says, inching his face even closer to me, his breath stinking in a sickly warm way.

I shake my head while subtly blowing away the stench.

'I'm undecided,' I say.

I'm not undecided—not at all. I'm certain they did it. But I just don't want to explain myself to him, not with his nose just inches from mine.

'Okay, okay... listen up, members of the jury,' the young woman dressed in all black calls out while clapping her hands. Obese Guy leans away from me, and I inhale again. 'Your day is over. You are all free to return home. May I remind you that it is vitally important you stay away from any news items about this court case, regardless of the medium. Please do not listen to any TV news channels which may discuss this trial, nor radio stations. Please do not read any newspapers. Stay away from your mobile phones and computers so as not to be influenced in your deliberations by anything that may occur outside of these courts.'

She feeds us this script every afternoon before we leave. As she does, I look around at my fellow jurors to try to read their reaction to it. I'd love to ask each of them if they have broken any of these rules. I bet they have. I find it impossible to stay off my phone.

'How long will final arguments take?' the blonde with the bad acne asks, interrupting the young woman dressed in all black.

'Well, that's impossible to say. Different trials call for different levels of argument and it will be totally dependent on what each of the legal teams have planned.'

'But is it safe to say we will begin deliberating tomorrow?' the young woman with the braces asks.

The young woman dressed in all black clicks her tongue against the top palate of her mouth while slowly swaying her head from side to side.

'I would guess so,' she finally answers. 'Final arguments shouldn't take up the whole day. Just don't quote me on that.

But, eh… I can see you beginning your deliberations tomorrow, yes.' She offers a sterile smile. 'Now… as I was just about to say, you will each need to be here by nine a.m. tomorrow. Court will resume at 9:30 a.m. Does anybody have any further questions?'

I observe the shaking heads before me and then without waiting, the young woman dressed in all black steps aside and we are all free to go.

As soon as the fresh air hits us, we each politely mumble a goodbye to each other—and then we're gone. Mostly in different directions. Two of us—me and the middle-aged woman with long red hair whose name I *think* is Sinead— pace towards the taxi rank outside the entrance to Phoenix Park.

'Go on, you first,' she says to me in her posh Dublin accent.

'Are you sure? You were here before me,' I say, smiling back at her.

'No, go on. I got the first taxi yesterday. Your turn to go first today.'

I tilt my head at her. She's posh. But she seems lovely. We've had this kind of exchange almost every evening; me insisting she takes the first taxi, her then reciprocating the following day. But that's been the extent of our conversations. I'd love to ask her about the trial, about what she thinks of Faith and Grace. I've often wondered if I should ask her where she lives, for if we were heading in the same direction we could share a taxi, and then during that taxi ride we could have a right ol' yarn about the trial. But all of that is frowned upon. Legally. We're not supposed to discuss the trial until all twelve of us are in a room together, seated around a table. It's just the gossip in me that wants to break the rules. I'm too impatient. Though there's not long to wait now. Tomorrow we'll all be finally sitting around that table.

She smiles her lovely teeth at me as I wave out of the side window and then suddenly I'm off. On my way back home. Back to my sanctuary where I can forget about the trial for the evening and concentrate on my family, save for the odd time I visit the loo with my phone and inevitably hop on to Twitter to search for tweets on the Child X and Child Y trial.

I can tell my husband has been a little put out by me being on this jury, but he doesn't huff and puff. Ever. He's way too nice to huff and puff. I married well. *Extremely* well. Noel may not be anything close to a George Clooney look alike. But he's a sweetheart. Genuinely the nicest person I have ever met in my life. I say that all the time. And I don't mean it in any sort of cheesy way; the way most married wives would describe their husbands. I actually mean it. Noel Sheridan is as genuine and nice as humans come. Certainly any human I've ever come across anyway. He has treated me the way every woman dreams of being treated; with respect. And he's as good a dad as he is a husband. Zoe and Alfie's relationship with Noel is what gives me most satisfaction in life. I can't wait to get home to them; tell them the jury will be starting deliberations tomorrow and that our household should finally be returning to normal. This could be all over by tomorrow. I'm sure most of the jurors feel the same way I do: guilty. It's odd the obese guy told me he is going to vote not guilty, but perhaps the rest of us are all singing from the same hymn sheet. All twelve of us are supposed to agree. Though I've read that Judge McCormick can come back to us at any time if a verdict hasn't been reached to tell us that a ten:two ratio in favour of any particular verdict would be enough to put an end to the trial.

As the taxi crosses the bridge over the River Liffey, I swipe my phone from my pocket and tap into Facebook. I don't know why my thumb automatically goes to the Facebook app… but it does. Because I'm pretty sure I actually hate Facebook.

There doesn't seem to be much going on. Annie Clavin posting up more pictures of her grandkids. Cute. I tap a like on that one. Jessica Murphy posting more pictures of her lunches. Not cute. Scroll. Davey Lynch posting more political bullshit as if he thinks anybody is paying attention. Scroll.

'Rough day?'

I glance up and smile into the rearview mirror.

'No. No. Not at all. Just tiring.'

The taxi man cocks his head.

'Not you on trial is it?' he says, grinning.

'Gee, no. I'm, eh… I'm a juror on a case.'

'Ahh,' he says. 'Then I better not probe any further.'

I laugh out loud. A fake laugh. But enough to put an end to the conversation so I can return to Facebook.

Michelle Dewey showing off her wealth by posting up pictures of her perfect home. Again. I like Michelle. In the flesh Michelle. But Facebook Michelle's a bit of a bitch.

'It's not the… eh… you're not a juror on that Child X and Child Y case, are ye?' I look up into the rearview mirror again and silently sigh through my nose. 'Ah no. Don't tell me. You can't tell me. Don't mind me,' he says, waving his hand in the air.

I offer a wide smile and as I do, my phone vibrates in my hand. A text message. From a strange number.

I open it and then crease my brow. That looks familiar. A still of what I'm certain is the same wallpaper they use in the bedrooms of the Hilton Hotel.

And immediately my heart drops.

I press at the play arrow and without pause I hear my heavy panting. Followed swiftly by my loud squeals of ecstasy.

Holy fuck!

I thumb at the pause button and then look up into the rearview mirror. The taxi man must be pretending he didn't hear that. But he had to have. That was loud. *I* was loud.

I mute the sound on my phone, press the play button again and stare at myself, my eyes rolled back in euphoria as Emmet pounds at me from behind.

Who the fuck sent me this?

DAY ONE

I jarred my forearm into his throat, forcing him to look up at me. He was only a kid; greasy skin, a poor attempt at a moustache and gelled down flat hair.

'Empty your pockets.'

'Alright, alright,' he shrugged.

I released my grip and took a tiny step back to give him room to unzip his coat. What a giveaway; a long coat on a hot summer's day.

'Careful,' I said, eyeballing him as he reached for his inside pocket.

He tutted, then held a balled fist towards me. I placed my palm under his and he dropped about a dozen light bags into it. Pills. I could tell by the weight.

'I know you've got more,' I said.

He shoved his hand into his opposite inside pocket with a scoff and then dropped a few more bags into my other palm. Heavier. Weed.

I leaned closer to him, almost nose-to-nose.

'That's everything, I swear,' he said. 'Go on. Search me.' He stretched his arms out wide.

I took two further steps back so I could peer up and down the full stretch of lane way.

'I believe ye,' I said, curling both of my hands into a ball. Then I stared into his spotty little face. 'How old are you?'

'Fifteen.'

'Fifteen…' I shook my head. 'You could get eight years for carrying this around with you. That's more than half of the life you've lived already… think about that.'

He didn't say anything. He just stared down at his expensive trainers. They always wear expensive trainers. And brand new ones almost every time, too. I've often joked that sports stores must have more drug money running through their tills than all the dealers in Ireland combined.

'Off you go,' I said, cocking my head.

His brow dropped and his bottom lip hung out.

'You're not… you're not going to…'

I shook my head. And he ran — not a jog, a sprint — to the end of the lane way, skidding to a fall as he tried to turn the corner.

I pushed a laugh out of my nose before I opened my hands. Six quarter bags of weed and about twelve wraps of what looked like that pink MDMA shit that was doing the rounds back then.

I waddled straight over to the big bin at the end of the laneway and lifted the lid. Then I baulked backwards as a butterfly — a giant of a butterfly — flapped its way towards me and perched itself on the edge of the bin. It frightened the shite out of me. I stared it at, noticed it had four wings, and two heads. I'd never seen anything like it before. Then it just flew directly upwards and lost itself in the glare of the sun. I puffed out a laugh, then dropped the bags of pills into the bin and slammed the lid closed.

It was hot that whole week; the sun unusually high in the sky. So I rested my hand on top of the car when I got back to it and took a good look around me—just to take a breather after chasing that spotty little shit down the laneway. It always looks stunning around this neck of the woods when the sun is shining; the green in the Dublin mountains seems to turn luminous.

After I got in and turned the ignition, I pushed at the cassette tape, feeding it into the radio and, after a weird clicking sound, the piano of Billy Joel started to play. I u-turned to head for home; to give Sheila the little surprise I had gotten for her when my other radio started to spit at me, just as I was about to sing along. I immediately stabbed a finger at the eject button of the cassette tape, then grabbed at my radio.

'Say again,' I said, squinting into the sun.

'BA99, can you hear me?'

'Yes. I can hear you loud and clear.'

'BA99, there has been an emergency call to the St Bene-dict's Bungalow which is at the end of Barry Lane.' I squinted even more. 'You there, BA99?'

'Yes. Yes. It's eh… St Benedict's Bungalow? Isn't that the church people… the eh… Tiddles?'

'I'm not sure, Detective. I don't know the address. And I've not been made aware of any names. There's been a, eh… homicide called in. A double homicide.'

I skidded the car into another u-turn, placing the radio on the passenger seat, and when the car was back straight on the road I picked the receiver back up.

'Children or adults?'

'I'm unsure, Detective. Are you on it?'

'Two minutes from the scene.'

I whistled a sigh through my lips after I placed the radio back on its cradle. It's a maze of windy roads that lead to Barry Lane. But I didn't have to make too many of those turns. I was only a mile and a half away.

I swerved into a line of gravel that splits an otherwise perfectly-maintained garden. And as I did, little Johnny came to greet me, puffing out his cheeks. He looked pale. As if he was about to throw up.

'Jesus, Quayle,' he said before I was fully out of the car. 'I'm sorry to blaspheme... especially here.' He looked around himself, then back at me. I thought he was going to pass out. 'Two bodies. Cut up. Cut right up. Sliced, I would say.'

I held my eyes closed and shook my head.

'Adults?' Johnny nodded. 'They've two twin girls, right? Little ones.'

'They're nine, yeah,' Johnny replied, looking down the length of his tie. 'They're in the, eh... sitting room now... with Sully.'

I scrunched up my face, then we both turned and headed for the front door. As soon as I stepped inside the hallway, the large crucifix hanging on the back wall took my attention, even though in my peripherals I could already make out a body laying just inside the kitchen door frame. When I took my gaze away from the crucifix and finally looked to the body, I immediately knew it was him.

'Clive Tiddle,' I said, almost in a whisper.

'You know him, Detective?' one of the paramedics kneeling beside the body asked.

I shook my head as I stood over the body and counted twelve stab wounds.

'I just know of him; he runs that church at the community centre.'

The two paramedics mumbled to each other, something about their realisation of this being 'the church family'. But I wasn't paying much attention. I was bending over the wife's body, counting the stab wounds in her. Seven.

'Dorothy Tiddle,' I said whilst staring into her eyes. They were still wide open.

'You, eh... wanna talk to the twins?' Johnny said.

I sucked a cold breath in through the gaps in my teeth and stood back upright.

'Sure.'

The paramedics pursed their lips at me as I walked past them, to follow Johnny back down the hallway and into the living room. That's when I saw them for the first time. They were both wearing floral-patterned dresses which seemed to disappear into the floral-patterned couch they were sitting on. Sully was next to them.

I noted they weren't crying. Not then.

Sully cocked her head up when she noticed me and then stood.

'Detective Quayle, this is Faith and Grace Tiddle,' she said. 'They're both nine years old—and about fifteen minutes ago, Grace here called 999 to report... eh, what it is we have found here today.'

I dropped myself to a one knee lunge. For some reason. I'm not sure why. Perhaps to match them for height. But I felt uncomfortable immediately.

'Faith... Grace,' I said as softly as I could.

'I'm Grace,' the one on the left said, 'and she's Faith.'

I reached a hand towards Grace and she looked at it before gripping it. Then, almost immediately, she started crying. And so did Faith.

I didn't know what to say.

I looked over both shoulders to see Johnny and Sully gazing down at me. Then I turned back to the twins and reached a hand to Faith.

'I know you are both shocked right now and... and... grieving, but I think it's really important that you tell us everything you have seen today, so that we can catch the people who... who did this.'

Grace sniffled up the end of her crying. And then

Faith did the exact same thing. It was eerie how they started crying and ended crying right in sync with one another.

'So… can you please tell me how you discovered… how you discovered… whatever it is you discovered?' I asked.

Faith turned to Grace.

'We were at dance class,' Grace said, and then she swallowed. 'We go to a dance class every Saturday at Ms Claire's. And when we got back we walked into the kitchen to get a glass of water and…'

Grace paused. And looked at her sister.

'We found Mommy and Daddy with lots of blood. They are dead. We know they are. They are not breathing,' Faith said. And then she started to sob again. And so, too, did Grace.

I held my eyes closed and said, 'I'm sorry.' Again.

I didn't know what else to say.

'Did you see anything else, any*body* else?' I asked.

They shook their heads in unison.

'Has, eh… has anything gone missing from the house that you've noticed?'

They both shook their heads again.

'It doesn't look like a robbery, Detective Quayle,' Sully said, whispering over my shoulder. 'No sign of a break-in. Though the back kitchen door wasn't locked.'

'Was the kitchen door open when you found your parents?' I asked the twins.

Faith turned to Grace again.

'No. I don't think so,' Grace said.

'Well, let me put it this way… have you — or you, Faith — closed the back kitchen door since you came home from dance class?'

Their two heads shook again.

I stood back up from my lunge and turned to eyeball both

Johnny and Sully, then I cocked my head subtly for them to follow me into the hallway.

'Looks like somebody just stabbed the parents to death and then...' Sully whispered to me as soon as we were out of earshot.

'What?' I whispered back. 'They just came in the back kitchen door, stabbed two people to death and then left through the back kitchen door.... closing it behind them?'

Sully shrugged as an answer to my question. So I stared at Johnny. And he shrugged too, his face still sickly pale.

I began to walk away from them, slowly. It was like a corridor of a hallway; two doors on either side of it. One of the doors had a mini blackboard hanging from it, that had the names "Faith & Grace" scribbled across it.

I twisted at the handle of that the door, took one step inside and then back out. I did the same in the next three doors; one a bathroom, one a spare bedroom and another which was Clive and Dorothy's bedroom. It had an oversized bed in it, with a framed photograph of a white Jesus above the bedposts, staring back at me. When I stepped out of that room I turned to the large crucifix on the back wall for a while before I heard a shuffling behind me.

'Y'okay, Quayle?'

'This is fucking mental,' I whispered back to Johnny. 'I've had a look in each room. All the windows are closed. Are you certain the only way in and out of here is through that back kitchen door?'

'We were only here a few of minutes before you, Quayle... But, eh... I checked all the windows too, and had a look at the front door. It locks from the outside.'

'Jesus,' I said, staring at the man himself nailed to a large cross right in front of me.

'This is gonna be some case, Quayle,' Johnny says. 'Have

you ever done anything like this before? Where are you even gonna start?'

I placed my hands on my hips, my eyes still glued to the blue eyes of the white Jesus. And then I sighed.

'I have no bloody idea, mate.'

✝

Clive Tiddle spent almost every single one of his school days being bullied. His height didn't intimidate the other boys at all. He was extraordinarily tall but he was gangly and thin with it back then. Awkward looking, it would be fair to say. Between his appearance and his surname, he never really stood a chance in his teens.

In primary school they called him 'Lanky' just because he towered above the rest of them and that was the default slagging in school for whoever was the tallest. He didn't really mind that name. But by the time he got to secondary school he'd been christened 'Tiddly Wanks' —a cryptic nickname that was a play on his surname, mixed with a well-known board game and a huge slice of immaturity. That nickname did get him down, literally. His shoulders slumped and he became very insular through his mid-teens. But it didn't get him down as much as being called 'Gombeen' did. That's the nickname he was stuck with for the last three years of secondary. Nobody in school could ever remember quite where that nickname originated from, and nobody ever figured out that it made absolutely no sense whatsoever, but boy did it stick. Even years after Clive had graduated, he would still hear the odd 'Gombeen' being shouted at him from across the street. He was an outcast; as out there as outcasts can find themselves. He had no friends. And a family who never seemed to notice — nor care — that he had no friends.

He didn't lick his aloofness from a stone, though. His parents were similar. Well, his father moreso. Brian Tiddle worked on the rigs in the north of the Irish Sea and would be gone for more months than he was home while Clive and his sister Janet were growing up. His mother had quite a few jobs over the years; from working at the local dry cleaners to packing boxes at a factory on the outskirts of the city. She often worked two jobs at once. It meant Clive and Janet rarely spent time with their parents; though it wasn't a huge concern—they were both wise enough to look after themselves. And they did. They looked after themselves—not each other. They stayed as far apart from each other as you can in a small three-bedroom terraced house. It wasn't that they hated each other or would wind each other up; it was just a case of that's what the Tiddles did—they looked after themselves.

Not having a friend certainly led Clive to assuming a girlfriend was well out of the question when he was growing up. He wasn't wrong—he didn't get a sniff of the opposite sex. But that all changed when he literally bumped into Dorothy Wyatt on a random Tuesday evening. He was rounding the corner of George's Street whilst looking behind himself and crashed into a girl he couldn't stop obsessing over for the next week.

'It's my fault, I should have been looking where I was going,' she said, all embarrassed and coy. 'I'm running late to catch my bus, s'why I was in so much of a hurry.'

He smiled at her, soaking in her large brown eyes.

'No... don't be silly. It was my fault,' he said.

She touched his shoulder — an actual touch — and then turned on her heels and paced away.

He visited the scene of that chance meeting every evening for the next week, at the exact same time. Until, the following Tuesday,

*he looked up from staring at his shoes and there she was...
squinting at him.*

'*You!' she said, pointing.*

'*Oh,' he mocked surprise and then held out his hand—a gesture
he'd rehearsed.*

'*My name is Clive. Clive Tiddle,' he said.*

'*Tiddle? That's a name that'd make you laugh.'*

*She actually did laugh when she said that. And he tried to
mirror her, only his laugh sounded fake. The joke was far from
original for him.*

'*Dorothy Wyatt,' she said, placing her hand loosely inside his
and allowing him to shake it.*

*Dorothy had just finished a class. She was doing a night course in
Accountancy at Dublin Business School; studying because she was
starting to fret she may need a career given that no member of the
opposite sex had shown much interest in her. That's painful for anyone
when they're heading towards thirty, but certainly so if you live within
a strong Christian family, given that it's quite uncommon for Christians to go unmatched. Everybody is always fixing folk up through
different 'family' contacts in the church. 'Oh, y'know Linda Brady's
son... he's single'—that kinda thing is rampant among 'families' of
faith. It was rare for a churchgoer to reach their late twenties without
getting married. And if that was the case, the major worry was that
they might end up with somebody who doesn't believe. That's mostly
why Dorothy's father didn't mind when she approached him with the
idea of doing a night course in Dublin Business School. He'd rather his
daughter have an actual career — even though it wasn't ideal for a
church woman to have a career — then to marry outside of their faith.*

*Dorothy hadn't been bullied as much as Clive had been at
school. Though her faith didn't exactly make her Little Miss
Popular either. She wasn't hated, but she was certainly considered
odd; given that she used to mention Jesus Christ's name in conversation way more than any teenager wanted to hear it.*

She got through school mostly unscathed, considering. Though she was happy to finish her Leaving Cert because it gave her more time to spend with her mother and her aunties. She always felt she was a bit too mature for the girls at school, much preferring the company of those the generation above her. Not many would have considered Dorothy pretty, even though she had round chocolate-brown eyes, because her style reflected that of somebody much older; choosing to wear floral patterned summer dresses with lace collars almost every day as if she was living in a previous century. But Clive did indeed find her pretty. In fact, he thought she looked even prettier the second night he 'bumped' into her. It was the eye-contact. Nobody had ever held his stare while talking to him before.

He walked her to her stop that night and by the time her bus arrived had plucked up enough courage to ask her on a date.

'Sure,' she beamed at him. Then she turned to wave the bus to a stop before snapping her head back at Clive. 'Oh...' she said, 'you are Catholic, aren't you?'

His gaze flicked downwards, to the crucifix hanging from a thin chain around her neck, and then he nodded confidently.

'Course, yeah,' he said.

He wasn't lying. Not technically. He had been christened and so his registration on the census all through his life confirmed him as a Catholic. Though he hadn't been to church for over a decade; not since his school required him to go. But his lack of church experience never became an issue because he fit right in with Dorothy and her church 'family' from day one. He really began to feel, quite early on, that he hadn't just found himself a girlfriend when he bumped into Dorothy Wyatt, he'd found himself a whole new life.

As soon as he met Dorothy's mother and father he went about pleasing them in any way he could. He even started to dress like Dorothy's father; never quite realising over the years that the reason Noah Wyatt dressed in gilets and plaid shirts was because he was a keen flyfisherman. Clive never flyfished in his life, because he couldn't swim. Nor could he do boats. But he dressed like a flyfisherman every day for the rest of his life after meeting Noah for the first time. New life. New look.

Clive and Dorothy married in the spring of 1995 in front of three hundred and fifty guests—a lot of whom they had never even met. 'Course you can bring your cousin,' is the way invitations are handled for mass Christian weddings. The more the merrier. As long, of course, as the guest was Catholic. No point bringing an atheist along. They just think we're all crazy.

That's not to say the wedding was totally starved of sceptics. Clive's parents and Janet were in attendance. They hated the day though, constantly rolling their eyes every time the name Jesus Christ was brought up—almost as if it was his special day and not necessarily the bride and groom's. It was the last day the Tiddles ever spent together, though. Clive would lose both his parents not long after he and Dorothy wed. His father collapsed with a massive heart attack as his mother was undergoing cancer treatment. She died three months after him. Both aged fifty-two. The same age Clive would be when he'd meet his death.

Clive and Dorothy couldn't wait to begin trying for a family. In fact, they literally didn't wait. They did it for the first time on their wedding evening, not night. They left their reception not long after their beef dinners and headed straight to the bridal bed to much wolf-whistling from their 'family'.

'We'll get better at it,' Clive said as he lay beside his bride after their first attempt. And they did get better. Not necessarily in a sexual way. Just in a practical way. They figured out when the best times were to try to conceive and they read manuals on what positions could prove best for conception. Dorothy particularly liked doggy-style. But despite their studious approach to baby making, nothing ever seemed to work for them. They were always disappointed when Dorothy would inevitably receive her period cramps each month. Yet deep down she was convinced that this was all part of the plan—that Jesus would deliver them what they wanted in time. But one year fell into two and then four years

*seemed to become five years really quickly. Then it was a decade...
and more.*

*Visits to the Rotunda Hospital for tests didn't really get to the
heart of the problem. It couldn't be determined who was at fault.
Clive's sperm counts were mostly high, but quite often inconsistent.
And Dorothy's ovulations weren't particularly predictable. But the
specialists couldn't pin-point exactly why it hadn't happened for
them, given that they had been trying so much, for so long. As they
rounded the bend into their forties, they decided they had to go the
IVF route... that perhaps Jesus was leading them that way. It was
an expensive way he was leading them, if indeed he was leading
them at all; certainly expensive if you try it twelve times which is
what the Tiddles did over the course of a ten-year period. Until one
day Dorothy peed on a stick... and finally that blue cross that she'd
only ever seen in her daydreams appeared before her eyes like a
miracle. Three months later they'd learn that it was a double
miracle.*

*'This one's Faith. And this one's Grace,' Clive would say, intro-
ducing his bundles of joy for the first time to 'family' members. 'We
wanted their names to reflect our gratefulness to our Lord Jesus
Christ.'*

ALICE

I grip the top of Mrs Balfe's garden wall as I lower to my hunkers and try to force the bile from the back of my throat. But nothing comes. Just a horrible retching sound. I spit. And then hold a hand to my mouth to mop at it.

After I steady my breaths, I reach into my jacket pocket and take out my phone again. My fingers quiver as they hover over the screen. But I manage to press into the text message again. I don't know why, though. It's not going away. Maybe I should ring whoever this is back; ask how the fuck they got their hands on my video. I hover my finger over the number, then instantly feel a need to clasp my hand to my mouth again, dropping my phone to the concrete. The bile retches from me, splashing just outside Mrs Balfe's garden gate. Jesus. If she saw me here like this the whole neighbourhood would know about it by the end of the evening.

I hold my eyes closed and try to breathe steadily before I press my hand against Mrs Balfe's wall to help guide me back to a standing position. Then I pick up my phone and check the message again... It's still there.

Maybe I should ring Emmet. See if he knows what the hell this is about. He can't have anything to do with it, though... surely? Can he? Course not. Jesus. My brain is frying.

I click into my contacts and without hesitation press at Emmet's number.

'Hey,' he answers.

'Emmet—listen,' I say and then I breathe out a long, shameful sigh. 'You need be honest with me, you hear me?'

'Alice…. you okay?'

'Emmet,' I sigh again, 'do you — or do you not — have a recording of that... that...'

'What? The me and you video? No. Course not. I've told you a hundred times. You made me promise that you'd be the only one to ever have the video. That's why you agreed to... y'know... do it.'

I scratch furiously at the side of my hair, then begin to yank at it. I know he doesn't have a copy of the video. We recorded it on my phone. I saved it. Then hid it in a draft email so I could be the only one to ever watch it.

'Alice? What's up? You sure you're okay? Why you asking about the vid—'

'I'm just... eh... I'm just being paranoid,' I say, pulling my hair tighter. 'That's all. Just… just one of those days.'

'You sure?'

'I'm fine. Fine. Just… y'know I'm serving on this bloody trial and the pressure... and—don't mind me. I'll see you soon, right? Next Friday we're doing that night at the Hilton.'

'Yeah... yeah. Looking forward to it. But I think I'll probably be seeing you—'

'Okay, bye, bye, bye,' I say, hanging up.

Of course Emmet doesn't have anything to do with this. Why would he?

My weight gives way and I'm back to my hunkers again;

my breathing growing sharp. I can't cope. I seriously can't cope with this. Somebody knows about the video. Somebody *has* the fucking video!

I spit again; the last remnants of the bile that was swimming in my mouth and then groan as I push against the wall to get back to a standing position. Again. I've been like a fucking yo-yo here.

I have to find out who has this video. I need to know what they plan on doing with it.

I begin to text the number back. Then tut and delete it. I rewrite another text. And delete that too. What the fuck am I supposed to ask? There's just too many questions. I shake my head, and as I do I just jab my thumb at the number and bring the phone to my ear. My heart rate rises with each ringing tone.

'So you decided to ring, not text,' a voice says. It's a woman. A woman's distorted voice.

'Who the hell is this?' I ask.

'Calm down, Alice... Then listen *very* carefully, okay? I will send this video to your husband's phone unless you do as I say.'

'What... what...' I circle the pathway outside Mrs. Balfe's house, my hair tightly twisted around my fist.

'It is your job to ensure the twins are not found guilty. If they are, I'm gonna text this video straight to your loved ones with one push of a button.'

'What… this is all about the trial? Who is this? How did you get my video?'

'Oh Alice. That wasn't very difficult. The draft folder of your emails? Tut, tut.'

'Hold on… what... you hacked my phone? What do you want me to do? I can't... I can't...' I stop pacing when I hear her laugh back at me. 'How the hell do you expect me to convince eleven other jurors to vote not guilty, that's... that's...' I whisper-shout into the phone.

'Oh Alice. It's more simple than you think,' she says. 'You don't need to convince eleven jurors... just two.'

I stop pacing and squint.

'Two?'

'Anything but a guilty verdict and I will destroy this phone. And everything that's on it will go away. All I need is a hung jury. If you and two others hold out and don't vote guilty, the trial collapses. And your life is spared.'

I pause.

Everything pauses.

My voice.

Her voice.

My breathing.

My squinting.

My hair-pulling.

'So I need to... I need to...' I stutter.

'You know exactly what you need to do, Alice.'

Then she hangs up.

And I drop to my fucking hunkers again. Spitting. But spitting out nothing. Not even saliva. My mouth's gone all dry.

I knew I shouldn't have recorded that bloody video. I just... I just wanted it to masturbate to. Me and Emmet only get to meet up once every month... or even two months, sometimes. It's not easy. And because I was finding the whole experience so thrilling and... horny, I asked if I could record a video of us together, just so I could get my own kicks out of it in my alone time. I thought it was safe, locked away in a hidden folder in my email account. I'm a fucking idiot.

'Everything alright, Alice?'

I look up, and when I see her I release the grip on my hair.

'Evening, Mrs Balfe,' I say, beaming a fake grin in her direction. 'Just having one of those days, y'know?'

She stares back at me from her front door, her eyes narrow, her brow sunken, her arms crossed under her fat boobs. She's eighty-two now, Mrs Balfe—our neighborhood's chief curtain twitcher.

'I, eh... gotta get home. Noel will have dinner almost ready,' I say.

She doesn't respond. She just stares at me, as if she's never seen me before. Maybe she's finally going senile. I hope she is anyway; well... I certainly hope she didn't see me panic attacking outside her home.

I pocket my phone and stroll on as my mind begins to swirl again. It must be that Gerd Bracken fucker. He's a slimeball. He must have something to do with this. That's why he always wins his cases—the bastard must be blackmailing jurors all the time. Though it can't be him. It's a woman. Maybe it's that Imogen one who works with him—though I can't imagine that. She's as quiet as a mouse.

I chew on my bottom lip and try to think of all the women who have been involved in this case—wondering who benefits the most from the Tiddle twins being acquitted.

By the time any of my thoughts have made sense I'm at my hall door; my key already inside the keyhole. I pause and take a deep breath. Noel will be home. With Alfie. Noel's been getting off work early for the past couple of weeks while I've been in court, just so somebody's here when our son gets in from school. I let the breath slowly seep out of my nostrils and then I turn the key and finally walk myself inside.

'Hey, Alfie,' I say when I see my son half way up the stairs. 'How was your day at school?'

'Fine,' he says with a grunt. I'm used to it. It's how kids his age communicate when they're asked questions they don't want to answer. I went through it all with Zoe. It's not easy.

'Hey love,' Noel says, sidling up to me while wringing his hands in a kitchen towel. He kisses me on the cheek, then pulls at the lapel of my coat, taking it from me. 'How did you get on today?'

'Grand. Grand. Eh… yeah, grand.' I say.

I look at him. And his face immediately creases.

'Jesus, you okay?' he says. 'You look like you've seen a ghost.' I open my mouth to say something, but nothing comes out. And suddenly my knees collapse and I'm on all fours. Just like I am in that bloody video. 'Sweetie… Alice…'

I can hear Noel. I just can't bloody answer him. The oak floorboards in our hallway are spinning and I need them to slow down before I can even try to settle myself to open my mouth.

He reaches under my stomach and lifts me to a kneeling position.

'You're white,' he says, placing a hand on my forehead. He blows out his cheeks. 'No temperature, but maybe you should take a lie down. Here, let me help you to the sofa.'

I shake my head. And as I do I feel my cheeks fill.

The bile roars out of me, slapping onto the floorboards.

'Mam, mam, what's wrong?'

Alfie runs back down the stairs. I try to smile up at him, but when I do, I feel more bile reach my throat. I managed to swallow it down though, then swipe at my chin with my forearm, mopping up the streams of spit that were hanging from it.

'She's okay, Alfie,' Noel says. 'Here son, take her arm and help her to the sofa.'

'Ye know what,' I say, blinking my eyes so that I can refocus. 'Just take me to bed. I wanna go to bed.'

Noel steadies me by leaning into me and taking my

weight. Then he leads me up the stairs without asking any further questions.

When we reach our room he perches me carefully on to the edge of the bed.

'It's nothing, Noel,' I say, holding my hand to my face. 'Just a bloody ham dinner I had for lunch at the courts, I think. A little bit of food poisoning is all.'

He kneels down in front of me so he can stare up into my face.

'It can't be food poisoning, sweetie,' he says. 'You haven't thrown up any food. Just bile. That's your stomach lining splashed all about our hallway.' He places his palm on my forehead again. 'Still no temperature.'

I kick off my shoes and lie back.

'It's just this bloody trial,' I say to him, a burst of emotion forcing its way out from the middle of my face. Tears. Snot. The lot. 'It's so much pressure. So much pressure.'

He lies beside me, rubs at my arm.

'Oh sweetie,' he says. 'I'm so sorry you have to go through this. Must be almost over now, though?'

I sniff.

'Last witness was called today. It's closing arguments in the morning and then... then it's up to us.'

'Ah... so that's all this is... it's just a bit of anxiety floating around in your little tummy,' he says, rubbing around my navel. 'You have a big decision to make tomorrow. That's all this is.'

I turn to face him and stare into his eyes. I haven't stared into his eyes from this close in ages. Probably years. I love him. So much. So, so much.

'You're right. Just a bit of anxiety. I'm sorry.'

'Don't be sorry,' he says. 'I'm gonna go clean up the hall-way. You, eh... you get yourself some rest. Call out for me when you need me. Do you think you'll come down for dinner in an hour or so?'

I suck in through my teeth and shake my head.

'Not sure, Noel. Think I'll just, eh… think I'll just play it by ear. I don't feel up for eating.'

He holds his hands to his hips, creasing that sorrowful look at me again.

'Okay. Get some rest, sweetie. Big day tomorrow. It's just, eh… Zoe rang earlier. Her and Emmet are coming over for dinner.'

DAY ONE

Even the sound of the gravel crunching under the wheels of a car didn't take my gaze from that white face. I'm not sure how long I'd been staring at it for or even why I was staring at it; perhaps I was willing Jesus to tell me what he had witnessed inside that house that morning.

'Quayle,' Johnny shouted from the doorway, 'Tallaght are here.'

I puffed a long, loud sigh out through my nostrils, then formed my fists into a ball and stormed down the hallway— as if I was on a mission.

'This is *my* investigation, Tunstead,' I said as soon as my shoes touched the gravel. He creased his eyebrows at me, glanced at his partner, Lowe, and then sniggered.

'Wow, calm down, Quayle,' he said. 'Jeez… have some respect. I doubt the bodies have even cooled yet and you've already got twisty knickers.'

I looked at Johnny as he stood alongside me, then back at the two detectives.

'Two bodies, adults,' I said, softening my tone. 'I'm certain

I know their names. Clive and Dorothy Tiddle. They run the church around here.'

'Cause of death?'

'Stabbings. Multiple of them.'

Tunstead and Lowe exchanged another glance.

'Sign of a break in?' Tunstead asked, struggling to remove a notepad from his back trousers pocket. His suits are always way too skinny for detective attire. Not that I'm an old prude or anything. It's just this prick thinks he's acting in a movie; skinny suits, skinny tie, shiny shoes—a thick head full of Brylcreemed black hair.

'Listen, I'm in charge here, Tunstead,' I said, stepping closer to him and placing my hand over his notepad.

'Relax, Quayle,' he said. 'I'm only taking some notes. Listen… I get it. This is your patch. We're just here to assist. Support.'

I looked to Lowe, and she nodded her head at me.

'No,' I sighed out of my mouth. 'No sign of a break-in. But the, eh... back kitchen door was unlocked.'

'Was it open when you got here?'

'Nope,' Johnny piped up, popping the p sound out of his mouth. 'The twins say the kitchen door wasn't opened when they found the bodies.'

'Twins?' Lowe said, shifting her stance on the gravel.

'Two nine year old girls,' I said.

'Did they ring it in?'

I nod.

'So, eh…' Tunstead took a step closer to me and leaned his nose towards my ear. 'It's not the twins who killed them, is it?'

'Pfft… course not,' I said, almost laughing. And suddenly I could feel all three of them staring at me. As if I'd just said something outrageous. 'No. No. Course not,' I repeated. 'They're only nine, for crying out loud.'

Tunstead scribbled something on his notepad, then cocked his head at Lowe before turning back to me.

'Well,' he said, 'let's have a look then, shall we? You got some gloves? Foot protectors?' I stared straight into his eyes before I felt a need to look at my shoes. 'Jesus Christ, Quayle.' A cringe churned inside my stomach.

'I didn't have gloves with me,' I said. 'All I did was take a look in the kitchen at the bodies, then checked for any sign of a break in. That's all. I'll make sure it's all reported it in the log book. It'll be fine.'

'Make sure that's logged, Quayle,' Lowe said, nodding at me, a pinch of sympathy etched in her expression. She's nice, Lowe. At least I think she is. Too nice to be working with that prick anyway. But sometimes even she looks at me like I don't know what I'm doing—and I've been on the force close to two decades longer than she has.

Tunstead walked to the back of his car to pop the boot, then carried back four plastic packages. Gloves. And foot protectors. He handed a pack of each to Lowe, and then me and Johnny stood there in an awkward silence as they both slipped them on.

'How long are SOCO gonna take to get here?' Tunstead asked as he snapped on his second foot protector.

I swallowed, then stared at Johnny.

'Eh... shall I ring them now, Quayle?' Johnny asked, looking confused.

'Yes, yes! Of course. Quick as you can,' I barked back at him.

I could feel Lowe and Tunstead glare at me with disappointment again.

'SOCO will have gloves and protectors for you when they get here,' Tunstead said. 'Don't go inside that house again until you're wearing them. I don't want you contaminating the murder scene.'

'That's my murder scene,' I said, almost too loud. Maybe even so loud the twins might have heard me.

'Well, get your arse in to your murder scene as soon as you get the right gear on, yeah?'

I held a clenched fist to my mouth as Tunstead and Lowe stepped inside the bungalow. I was cringing that I hadn't thought to ring SOCO as soon as I got there. I just wasn't used to taking control. I should have been taking action—not staring at that bloody crucifix. It wasn't as if I hadn't been at a murder scene before. I had. Lots of them. It's just I'd never been the lead detective at a murder scene. Murders just don't happen around here. It's just too quiet… too remote…. too peaceful. I'd been at murder scenes in other jurisdictions. Especially in Tallaght. But I was normally the one assisting those two pricks who had just entered my murder scene. It had never been the other way around.

'SOCO will be about half an hour,' Johnny said, pocketing his phone and walking back towards me. I liked Johnny from the moment he joined our station. He'd only been there about a year before the Tiddle case. It was just me, him, Fairweather and one other uniform — Sully — working from the station then. Rathcoole was always being rumoured to be facing closure. Not a lot happened around our area, and as a result our funding was constantly culled. We hung in, though. A small station on a small budget, looking after the small communities dotted around the foothills of the Dublin mountains.

'Shit, we'll need to get Sully out,' I whispered to Johnny. 'She's no gloves or foot protectors on in there either.'

'But, eh…' Johnny paused and began to tug at his ear, 'who'll stay with the twins?' I didn't answer him; I just stared up into the cloudless sky. As if the answers to the thousands of questions that were circulating my head were just going to rain themselves down on me. 'Quayle…' Johnny took a step towards me. 'You sure you're okay with this? Why don't you let Tunstead and Lowe run the case. They've a lot more exper—'

'Fuck no,' I said to him. 'This is our case. Our station's jurisdiction. It's up to us to find who did this.'

Johnny thinned his lips and nodded his head.

'And we will, Quayle,' he said. 'I'm with you all the way, boss.' He looked over his shoulder, then back at me. 'So, eh... what'll I do? Do you want me to take Sully out? Surely we should have somebody with the twins at all times. The shock they must be under—'

'Bring them outside with Sully,' I said, rolling my shoulders, feeling as if I'd finally made my first decision of the case. I made an instant pact with myself there and then that I would always make the twins' welfare my priority. 'We need to get somebody here to look after them. Who in the force looks after child welfare... who do we ring for that?'

Johnny pushed his chin into his neck and shrugged.

'Haven't you got one of those smart phones?' I said. 'Look it up. Who should we ring?'

As he removed his phone from his trouser pocket again, I mirrored him and stared at my screen, wondering whether or not I should ring Fairweather. I knew she was on the golf course. That was nothing new. I always liked Fairweather. She took me under her wing when I joined Rathcoole Station and we worked closely together for twenty-five years; keeping the streets of Rathcoole and the surrounding mountainside free of crime, save for the odd drug deal and car theft. She semi-retired the year prior to the Tiddle murders and by that stage spent more time on the fairways of the K Club than she did at the station. I was always fearful of when she would fully retire because I didn't fancy running the station all by myself. I liked my working life just as it was.

Well... just as it was before I answered the call to the Tiddle's bungalow that morning.

I turned when I heard footsteps shuffling behind me. It was them. Moving in unison like two dolls that had just come to life. It was such a surreal moment, because I could see Tunstead behind them bent over the body of their father.

I got down to my hunkers and held out a hand to each of them just as Johnny and Sully joined us outside. Grace grabbed a hand first. Then Faith. I stared at them, right into their big brown eyes; shifting my gaze from one to the other.

'I'm so sorry,' I said. Again. And then, from behind me, I heard the crunch of gravel under wheels. I turned to see a large white van; a big-ass aerial on its roof. It skidded to a stop behind my car. And then two men clambered out; one with a camera balancing on his shoulder, the other wide-eyed and almost excited looking. As if murder was a drug to him.

'Sully,' I said, 'get the twins in the back of my car. We need to get them out of here now!'

ALICE

I stab my finger at the elevator button, then step back and wait.

'Morning,' the red head says, startling me.

'Morning,' I say back. 'Sorry... I'm away with the fairies here.'

She smiles her lovely teeth at me.

'Why wouldn't you be?' she says. 'I'm the same. This trial is....' she shakes her head, '...I was awake most the night thinking about it.'

I snort out a laugh.

'Oh, me too. Me too.'

I actually spent fifteen hours in my bed last night and still didn't get any sleep. At all. I went to bed at twenty past five straight after I puked all over the floorboards in our hall and stayed there until seven o'clock this morning when my alarm finally beeped. I was sitting up by that time, staring at the digits; waiting on 6:59 to turn into 7:00 so I could justify getting myself out of bed.

I glance at Red Head out of the corner of my eye as we

ride up the elevator in silence. I wonder what verdict she has going on inside her head; perhaps I can convince her she should vote not guilty. That was specifically what consumed most of my thoughts when I was awake in bed last night: which jurors I can convince easiest. The obese guy already told me he would vote not guilty, so I only need to convince one other, once he doesn't change his mind of course. Red Head is definitely an option for me. So is the guy with the ridiculously high quiff. And maybe the short girl with the braces. They're the youngest, so probably the most naïve and impressionable. But hopefully I don't need to influence or convince anyone. Maybe two or more are going to vote not guilty anyway.

I can't even begin to imagine how Noel would react if he found out me and Emmet have been having sex. His whole life would just deflate. He'd evaporate into a heartbroken mess. I know he would. I can't be quite so certain how Zoe would react. I tortured myself trying to wonder if I'd ever have a relationship with my daughter again if she saw that video. Though that specific torture has been going on a lot longer than just last night. It's been with me ever since me and Emmet started our fling. I couldn't help it. I just couldn't. He's so... so well-built. Like one of those Dreamboys or whatever they're called. A six pack and all. When was I ever gonna be taken from behind by a hottie with a six pack? That was not the kind of offer I'd ever gotten. Not even when I was eighteen. No hot guy ever wanted me. None of the rugby players at my school even gave me a second glance. And now I have a semi-pro rugby player giving me orgasms I would never have had my whole life had he not started dating my daughter a year and a half ago.

I didn't think anything of it when I first met him. I certainly never thought I wanted to fuck him. Or that I wanted him to fuck me. Of course I didn't. He was my daughter's new boyfriend. All I was concerned with then was whether or not he was polite. That's all any parent looks for in their offspring's partner. Having an affair never crossed my mind. Ever. I was totally faithful to Noel. Until... until that first night. I just couldn't help myself. I still can't. Even last night, when I heard Emmet coming up our stairs to go to the bathroom, my body tingled. I was hoping he'd poke his head around my door, ask me how I was. Give me a quick kiss. But he didn't. He washed his hands, went straight back down to have dinner with the rest of my family. Probably for the best, though. Zoe came into me twice. Just to hold her hand against my forehead and give me assurances that all will be okay once this trial is finally over.

'Oh, we're going in already,' Red Head says nudging me.

I look up, see the young woman dressed in all black opening the door to the courtroom, and suddenly we're all filing inside one-by-one, enveloped in that awkward silence yet again.

I form a diamond with my fingers on my lap as soon as I sit down and bow my head a little. This has become a routine. A ritual. I never know where else to look. But as soon as the door on the far side of the room clangs open, my head shoots up. I can't help it. Grace walks in first, followed by Faith; both of their faces void of expression. Just as they are every day. They plonk themselves into the same seats they always occupy: Grace next to Gerd Bracken's assistant Imogen, Faith on the far side of her sister. Imogen whispers to Grace every now and then through parts of the trial. But Faith never says anything. Not a word.

'All rise,' a voice shouts.

And the whole court gets to its feet to welcome Judge Delia McCormick in the most formal way imaginable. I wonder if she feels awkward coming in and out of this court-room drowned in that awkward silence like I do.

She peers up over her glasses at the benches in front of her when she sits.

'The court will hear final arguments.'

And that's it. That's all she says.

After the long silence that follows, Jonathan Ryan, who's done quite a decent job as lead prosecutor even though he must be only in his late twenties, clears his throat nervously, then strolls ever-so-slowly towards us. I'm certain he's staring straight at me.

'Ladies and gentlemen of the jury,' he says. His head swivels up and down the two rows of jurors, taking each of us in. 'I am under no doubt that Faith and Grace Tiddle murdered their parents Clive and Dorothy Tiddle in cold blood on the morning of the day dated fifteenth of August, coming close to two years ago now. And you should be under no doubt too.'

I look over his shoulder at Gerd Bracken, hoping — *wishing* — that his closing argument trumps whatever the hell Jonathan Ryan is about to produce here.

'You are lucky—as jurors,' he says, taking one step back from us and beginning to gesture with his hands, 'because this is a very straight-forward trial in terms of judgement. Yes, it has been chilling and I'm aware that a lot of the content would have been difficult for you to digest over these past two weeks. But in terms of arriving at a verdict... this couldn't be simpler.'

I whisper 'shit' to myself, then stare up the row of faces to my right. The woman with the overly big bust catches my eye and squints at me—so I flick my gaze swiftly back to Jonathan Ryan.

'You don't have to be a legal expert or indeed a crime scene expert to understand the facts of this case. There was zero evidence. Zer—ro,' he says, rolling his 'r'. 'None. Nada. Not a thing. Not a strand of evidence, that suggests some-body else entered that house on the day in question to kill Clive and Dorothy. Somebody inside that house carried out that murder. Only somebody from inside that house could have done this. And, as you have heard through expert witnesses, only somebody of miniature stature could have done this. Unless, of course, you believe the sensational story the defence have tried to spin. That a Hollywood movie-esque contract killer arrived in Rathcoole, broke in to the Tiddle house unnoticed, stabbed two people to death in the manner in which a child — or children — would stab some-body. And then left. Without leaving a trace of their own DNA—or *any* evidence whatsoever. Not a trace. Pufff…. gone.' He gestures an imaginary disappearance with the flick of his fingers. 'And even if you believe that somebody so intelligent and stealth-like and genius at killing people without leaving a spickle of evidence could exist and wanted to target Clive and Dorothy, do we really think that *genius* would forget to bring a weapon with him—that he just happened to use a knife from the Tiddles' kitchen?'

He puffs out a silent snigger. Then he takes a step back towards the desk he had spent most of the trial sitting at and perches his bum onto the corner of it, staring up at us, his arms folded.

I find myself looking around the room during his rehearsed silence. I wonder if the bitch who's blackmailing me is in here. I glare at the defence table first. Gerd and Imogen. Maybe they hired somebody to hack my phone. It was definitely a girl I spoke to last night, so it's not him himself. And it couldn't be Imogen. She's just too… quiet… too fragile-looking. She looks like a female Harry Potter; round glasses, pale, oval-shaped face. I shake my head a little then look into the gallery at the glum faces in the crowd. The court has been full every day of this trial. I look at Kelly McAllister and then at Janet Petersen, wondering if they're the ones who got their hands on the recording of me and Emmet. I guess they might benefit from the twins getting off in some way. But would they even have the means to do this? Would they even know what hacking a phone is? I shake my head more firmly this time, trying to get rid of my thoughts. I shouldn't be playing detective. It doesn't really matter who it is. What matters is that I convince the people sitting beside me here to let these twins go.

'...The defence will attempt to tell you the girls couldn't have done this. That nine year old girls couldn't be so cool and so calculated as to strut off to dance class minutes after killing their parents, acting as if nothing happened. But this is simply not true. Claire Barry, their dance teacher, clearly said when sitting in that witness stand in front of you, that Faith was "particularly quiet" that day. That the defendant was acting out of sorts.'

I sniff my nose at this a little. Faith is always quiet. From what I can make out anyway. I'll convince the jurors that this part of the prosecution's argument is bullshit.

'It's normally the little things; the little things, members of the jury, that ensure guilty people are convicted. When Grace Tiddle dialled 999, she didn't even sound upset that her parents had been killed. When Detective Denis Quayle attended the scene minutes later, neither of the girls were crying. They went and had a McDonalds... *a McDonalds*! Imagine that? You find your parents stabbed to death, lying in pools of blood, and then you go out and have a Happy Meal. Those are the types of 'little things' that will convict a guilty person. But this trial isn't even about the little things. You — members of the jury — don't have a tough decision to make. Your decision doesn't even need to come down to the little things. You've been a lucky enough jury to have big things to discuss. Such as the fact that there is simply no evidence that anybody else was inside that house that day; that the Tiddles were killed at the hands of a child or children; that the Tiddles were killed with a weapon from inside their own home. A home in which only four people live.'

He leans up off his table and takes a couple of steps towards us again.

'Let me repeat something I said there again, members of the jury... There is *no evidence* that anybody else was inside that house that day. Clive and Dorothy Tiddle were killed *inside* their own home, by somebody already *inside* their own home, who used a weapon — a kitchen knife — from *inside* their own home.' I swallow and then strain my eyes to look up the row of faces to my right again. 'Let me ask you this, members of the jury,' Jonathan Ryan continues. 'Which tale is more likely to be true? That a Hollywood movie-type hitman crept into the Dublin mountains one day to murder two innocent church-goers in cold blood without bringing a weapon and then left without leaving so much as a jot of DNA or evidence, or...' he tilts his head, puffs out a tiny snigger. I hope the other jurors are finding this as arrogant as I am. I don't think it's going to do him any favours. He wasn't like this during the trial. 'Or two kids, who finally came of age to realise the abuse they were receiving at the hands of their parents—'

'I object!' Gerd Bracken stands to his feet, his balled fist slamming onto the desk in front of him.

Judge McCormick brings down her gavel, and then... silence.

'Mr Bracken, you are an experienced enough lawyer to know you do not get to object during final arguments.'

'But, Your Honour, he can not stand there and just lie like that. The prosecution brought miniscule evidence to suggest

Faith and Grace suffered any sort of abuse at the hands of their parents.'

Judge McCormick knocks her gavel against her table again, then turns to Jonathan Ryan.

'Mr Ryan, I would ask you to be very careful with your use of language in your final arguments.'

'Your Honour,' Ryan says, almost bowing at her. 'What I was basically getting at… members of the jury,' he says, turning back to us, 'is… are you more likely to believe that a made-up Hollywood creation swept into Rathcoole to murder two innocent people, or that a set of twins who had religion bombarded at them from day one of their lives finally rebelled by putting an end to that bombardment? When all reason and all common sense and all logic is considered in this case then — you will have to agree with me, members of the jury — only one version of those two events could possibly be true.' He steps forward and grips the bench in front of the first row of jurors. 'It is a fact that Faith and Grace Tiddle killed their parents. It is now your job — and your responsibility — to confirm them guilty of that crime.'

He turns to the judge, almost bows again and then strolls back towards his seat.

Is that it? Five minutes telling us stuff he already said during the trial. I thought it'd be longer than that. Though I'm not quite sure what I expected… a PowerPoint presentation or something? I thought a final argument would be a lot more detailed than a small summary.

Though what he said was quite convincing. Jesus… I wonder what all the other jurors are thinking right now after that. I'd definitely find the twins guilty. No doubt about it at all. What Jonathan Ryan said makes perfect sense. Nobody else could have done this.

Bracken needs to nail his closing argument now. He

needs to trump Ryan's. It's not just Faith and Grace's lives that depend on it. Mine does too.

'Mr Bracken,' the judge calls out.

Bracken stands, opens the single button of his suit jacket as he walks out from behind his table and then grins at us.

'Ladies and gentlemen of the jury…'

DAY ONE—DAY TWO

I knew she was in bed as soon as I turned onto our street. There were no lights on downstairs.

I checked my watch as I strolled up our garden path and noted it was five to twelve. The last minutes of the day. And what a day it was!

As soon as I got inside, I shuffled out of my blazer, hung it on the bannisters and made my way up to her.

'You're ever so late,' she called out before I had even made it to the top of the stairs. I smiled. The first smile I'd smiled since I began listening to Billy Joel just before my Garda radio spat at me.

'You won't believe the day I've had.' I held a hand against our wardrobe for balance as I kicked off my shoes. Then I loosened the belt of my jeans, for a little relief, before bouncing up on the bed beside her. She placed the book she was reading onto her lap and leaned a little towards me, just so I could kiss her forehead.

'Go on,' she said.

'Well, first things first... as always,' I said, grabbing her hand. 'How have you been today?'

'Never mind me,' she replied, gripping my hand tighter. 'I've had a day like all the rest of my days recently. You, clearly, haven't. Why are you getting home at darn-near midnight… somebody get killed?' I scrunched up my face, and as I did she removed her hand from my grasp and held it to her mouth. 'Oh no, somebody did get killed…'

I sat more upright in bed and turned to face her.

'Two people actually. D'you know the couple who have the twin girls… they run the church in the middle of the mountains?'

She squinted, her head shaking ever so slightly.

'Have they a silly name?'

I nodded.

'Yeah. Tiddle.'

'That's right… It's not them who were killed… was it?'

'Afraid so. The parents. Both stabbed to death inside their own home.'

Sheila covered her bottom lip with her top lip.

'How old are they?' she asked.

'We found out he was fifty-two—Clive Tiddle. The wife, Dorothy, she was fifty. I thought they were much older, but…' I shrug. 'I guess the twins are only nine, so—'

'Jeez, how are they… the twins?' Sheila asked.

'They're fine… well, physically anyway. They weren't part of the attack. They were at a dance class when it happened. Came home just after midday and found their parents lying there… in the kitchen. Lots of blood. Pools of it.'

Sheila leaned a little closer to me.

'You think *they* did it… the twins?' she asked.

'Not you as well.'

She crinkled her nose up at me.

'No, no. I'm just… just…'

'You're reading too many of those books,' I said, slapping

at the paperback on her lap. 'Starting to think you're a detective yourself, huh?'

She smiled. I love it so much when she smiles—even if it's just a sorrowful smile like that one was. She was producing a lot of sorrowful smiles back then. But at least it was better than no smiles at all, which is the state she had been in for the nine months prior.

'But you, eh... you did verify that they were at a dance class, right?' she asked.

'Course I did. They were at dance class between eleven and midday. Their dance teacher confirmed it.'

'Sweet Jesus. That's some case,' Sheila said.

'Yeah, a case I'm lead detective on,' I spat out. 'It happened on our patch.'

She rubbed at my arm as if she was congratulating me, then offered me another one of those sorrowful smiles.

'You'll nail it,' she said, holding a hand to her mouth to cover a yawn.

'Hey,' I said, swinging my legs over the side of the bed. 'I almost forgot, the day that was in it. I, eh... picked you up a little something this morning.'

I hopped off the bed, paced across the landing and then headed down the stairs to snatch at my blazer . I took the small bags from my inside pocket and tossed the blazer aside when I got back into the bedroom.

'Here you are, my lovely.' I threw the bags of weed to her lap and jumped back on the bed.

Sheila made on 'O' shape with her mouth.

'Six quarter bags... That's about two months' worth, right?' she asked.

I winked at her.

'How did you get your hands on this?' she said as she opened up one of the small bags to take a sniff.

'Ah...' I waved my hand, knowing she wouldn't ask again.

'Thank you.'

'Do you wanna do some now?'

She took another sniff from the bag and then shook her head.

'No. Thanks. I'll take some in the morning. With a nice cup of tea.'

She pinched each of the quarter bags from her lap and then dropped them beside the lamp on her bedside table. I love looking at the profile of my wife in that kind of dim light. It makes her look like her old self. When she was more beautiful.

'So where are the twins now?' she asked, turning back to me.

'It was a crazy day,' I said before I blew out my cheeks. 'The media turned up before the Scene of Crime Officers. We had to get the twins out of there as soon as possible. I didn't know where to bring them. We brought them to the station, then... we ended up in McDonalds.'

'*McDonalds?*' Sheila made a face at me.

'It's just... they were hungry.' My heart dropped a little. Even my wife seemed to be questioning everything I'd done in the case up until that point. 'It's alright now, though,' I said. 'Tusla arrived at about three p.m. They sorted the twins out.'

'Tusla?'

'A specialist child welfare agency. That's what they do... look after kids who are subjects of crime.

'How are they, though—the twins? They must be inconsolable.'

'They seem fine one minute. Then they start crying the next. It's a little bit spooky. Once one cries, the other follows. And when she stops the other one does the exact same thing. As if their batteries get switched off at the same time. You can't help but feel for them though. They're... they're...' I hesitate.

Sheila shrugged at me. 'They're what?'

'Cute, I guess. Two little cuties. They're only nine and... Jeez, can you imagine finding your parents stabbed to death at that age?' I patted at Sheila's knee and then kissed her forehead again. 'Sorry, love. Not the kinda news you want to hear right before you fall asleep.' She yawned again. 'Go on. Knock off your lamp. I'm going to go downstairs, see if I can let my mind unwind.'

I was as excited by the case as I was frightened by it as I sat at our kitchen table, my hands clasped atop of it, my mind whirring. I knew this story would be all over the news the following morning and was already starting to worry that the press would come down hard on me; that I'd be under pressure, under scrutiny. I'd already made some bad fuck ups even though the case was barely half a day old. I couldn't believe I traipsed into a crime scene without gloves or protectors on. And I couldn't believe I forgot to call SOCO straight away. Or Tusla. Though I didn't even know who Tusla were before Johnny checked it on his smart phone. And then I went and brought them to bloody McDonalds. Jesus. McDonalds! It just seemed like the right thing to do at the time. They were hungry. I was hungry. Johnny said he was peckish, too. And I thought it'd be better for them to be out and about, rather than sitting in our pokey little police station while we waited on Tusla. I didn't think it'd be such a big deal; certainly didn't think the press would get hold of it.

ALICE

Bracken's a sleazeball. No doubt about that. There's been an arrogance emanating from him that has bordered on cringeworthy throughout the entirety of this trial. But he seems to have softened his face for his closing argument—is tilting his head a little, squinting at us as if we're twelve teeny-tiny puppy dogs.

'What Mr Ryan here has just shared with you is pure fabrication. A weak prosecution argument, if I may be so bold.' He steps towards us. 'Your only options aren't whether Faith and Grace did this, or some Hollywood movie-esque contract killer did it. That's absurd. And quite a fictionalised analysis of a very real tragedy. Does Mr Ryan genuinely believe that two nine year old girls, who loved their parents so much and who were about to go on a dream family holiday, killed those parents for a reason he has only ever speculated about? Then these nine year olds just hopped off to go to a dance lesson as if nothing happened? Arrived home from that lesson, rang the police and have — for the past twenty months — manage to hide that dark secret from the many experts who work in the police force, who work in child welfare and who work in law? Talk about a Hollywood tale... that's a Hollywood tale right there, ladies and gentlemen. I don't think Mr Ryan does genuinely believe what he preached here this morning. It just happens to be his job to try to make *you* believe it. That's all. That's all his closing argument was—Mr Ryan simply doing his job.'

Bracken places his hands in his pockets, as if this is a breeze for him. And as he does I feel adrenaline spinwash inside my stomach. Go on, Bracken. Nail it!

'Faith and Grace didn't murder anyone,' he says. 'I have spent twenty months getting to know them. Trust me. They are not murderers. They are sweet little girls who are still grieving the loss of both of their parents. Mr Ryan is right in one way, though. He says the facts of this case are simple. I agree. I do. They are. Just not the "facts" he shared with you.' Bracken does that air-quotes thingy with his fingers. 'Put in front of you over the past fortnight — ladies and gentlemen — was a case in which the lead detective is on record admitting that he *doesn't* think the defendants are guilty. Let me say that again... the *lead* detective — Detective Denis Quayle, twenty-five years on the force — is on record as saying he doesn't believe Faith and Grace had anything to do with this double homicide. His own words — said directly to me and recorded on my tape were, "You can take it from me, Mr Bracken—the twins didn't have anything to do with this." But besides that little fact that I would like you to keep in your minds as you consider your verdict, the biggest factor you, as jurors, need to consider before it leads you to acquitting these innocent girls is that this court—that prosecution,' he points at Ryan, 'did not provide any evidence whatsoever beyond doubt that my defendants are guilty. There is plenty of doubt about the case they have brought to this court. There is *doubt* whether or not the investigation was handled correctly. There is *doubt* that Faith and Grace had any motive whatsoever to carry out this crime. There is *doubt* about the contents of that safe. There is *doubt* that Faith and Grace even had the wherewithal to act out this level of crime.'

He steps closer to us.

'And when there is doubt — jury members — it is your job to acquit. You know — as much as I do, as much as anybody inside this courtroom here today knows — we simply do not have the answers to this case. The answers to this case were not proven in front of you over the past two weeks. We don't know the answer as to why Clive and Dorothy had so much cash. We don't know the answer as to why anybody would want them dead. We don't know the answer to where the murder weapon is. And without all of the answers — jury members — it would be remiss of you to find Faith and Grace guilty. Thank you.'

He returns to his seat swiftly. I'm shocked. I thought closing arguments would last most of the day. I flick my wrist. 10:21 a.m. That's it? Are we going to start deliberating right now?

The whole courtroom falls silent except for the sound of shuffling as Judge McCormick sifts through her paperwork. Maybe lawyers don't want to bombard a jury with too much during closing arguments. They just want to sell us the verdict they want us to buy. I guess both Ryan and Bracken did that equally well in the few short minutes they tried to sell to us. But I don't believe Bracken for one minute. I've no doubt those twins are hiding some sort of crazy behind their eyes. They definitely did this. I just need to convince these people sitting beside me that they didn't.

'Okay, members of the jury,' Judge McCormick says, staring over her glasses at us. 'You have now heard all of the evidence, all of the witness statements and all of the arguments of this trial. You will hear no more, though you can — of course — request transcripts of any aspect of the trial during your deliberations. Before I give you some orders and release you to begin those deliberations, I want to say something to you.' She removes her glasses and rests them on the desk in front of her before staring back up at us. 'I want to thank each of you for your service during this trial. In all my years as a Judge I have never been involved in a case quite like this one. It was not easy for my experienced ear to hear some of the facts of this case and so I am certain it was not easy for you to hear some of the facts of this case. It has been a mentally tough two weeks for you all, I'm sure. On behalf of the legal and judicial arm of our nation… thank you. Your job, now, is to come to a unanimous verdict based only — *only* — on the evidence you heard in this courtroom.' She bounces the butt of her paperwork off the desk. 'I now dismiss you to begin your arguments.'

I'm the last of the jurors to stand. And then we all shuffle out, one-by-one in that awkward bloody silence again, to be met by the young woman dressed all in black. She leads us down a long corridor and then stops at a door — a door just like every other inside these modern courts — then removes a large bunch of keys from her pocket and unlocks it. The young guy with the quiff sits to one side of me at the conference table. Red Head sits on the other. Again. I notice then that all of the jurors seem to have taken the same seats they took when we were first in this room two weeks ago, discussing who our Head Juror should be. I was tempted to put myself forward for it, but chickened out at the last minute. Only Obese Guy and the rough looking guy with the scar across his forehead put their hands up. Men. They have so much more confidence than us women. Or arrogance. I'm not quite sure what it is. I could kick myself now for not putting myself forward. I would have had a lot more sway and influence if I was Head Juror. Though I probably wouldn't have won the secret ballot for the position. Not against Scarhead. He trounced Obese Guy eleven to one. Obese Guy must've been the only person to vote for himself.

'Okay,' Scarhead says when we've all settled around the large oval table. 'Well... that was an intense couple of weeks. Don't know about you all, but I've been dying to find out what you think about this case. I don't know how I've stopped myself from asking you about it every day in those bloody corridors.'

'Me too,' I burst out of my mouth. A few turn to face me, some with smiles of agreement, some with a hint of impatience because I talked over the Head Juror mere seconds in to him opening deliberations. I hold my hand up in apology, then signal for Scarhead to continue. 'So, eh...' he says, looking around the faces. 'Where'll we start? I looked online to see how these types of thing are supposed to be dealt with but, eh... there is no manual, I have come to realise. Every case is different. Every deliberation is different. All I can gather is that we have to come to one of two conclusions... we either need to come to a unanimous conclusion that finds Faith and Grace either guilty... or not guilty.'

'Well,' I say loudly. The jurors all turn to face me. Again. 'That's not strictly true. It doesn't have to be a case of us definitely getting a unanimous verdict. We could be a hung jury. Easily. Not all of us have to agree. If we don't, we shouldn't beat ourselves up about it.'

'That's true. I believe the judge might come back and take a vote of ten to two either way if she wishes,' Red Head next to me says. I turn to her. And smile.

'You're right,' I say. 'That can happen. And may happen. But I would just like to say that we shouldn't beat ourselves up even if we don't come to a ten:two agreement in some way. If people are unsure or undecided, that's perfectly okay.'

I can feel Scarhead stare at me. I've taken control of his deliberations.

'I know… eh… sorry, what's your name again?' he asks.

I look back up at him.

'Alice.'

None of us really exchanged names throughout the course of the trial. In truth, we rarely got a chance to speak to each other. Once, early on in the trial, Obese Guy leaned in to me in the corridors and asked for my name. And so too did Red Head. I asked for their names too, out of politeness, but I didn't log them in the memory bank. I'm just no good with names. There are badges that we could fill out and stick to our chests during the deliberations, but nobody has brought up that option. Besides, I'm fine not knowing. Though now everybody knows *my* name, because I'm the only one who has been asked for it at the table. And it hits me. Maybe somebody in here is the one blackmailing me. Maybe somebody in this room has hacked my phone. I pivot my head to take in each of the six other women around this conference table, then shake my head. No. Course it's nobody in here. Why would it be a bloody juror? I think I'm starting to go a bit crazy.

'You're right, Alice,' Scarhead says. 'But perhaps we should at least aim for getting a majority decision or a unanimous decision. After all… that is our job here.'

I nod at him.

'Why don't we see if we have a majority one way or another already?' I propose. 'I think we'd benefit from an early verdict vote… just to see where everybody stands.'

'Good idea,' Red Head says, rubbing at the arm of my blouse. 'The trial is fresh in our minds right now. Fresher than it'll ever be. Why don't we find out how each of the jurors feel? Instinctively. I mean, we've all been dying to find out what's going on inside each of our heads, haven't we?'

Nobody objects. A few nod their heads and, as they do, Scarhead stands up.

'Right… yeah, okay. I agree. We'll just go around the table. This is obviously not a final verdict vote… just an indication of how we feel instinctively following the trial.'

Perfect. I'll know what the playing field is like within a matter of seconds. I'll know which jurors I have on my side, and which ones I might need to work on. I need at least two other people in this room to help save my life. And Zoe's. And Noel's. They don't deserve any of the shit that will hit them if this jury return a guilty verdict.

'Why don't we start with you then, Alice?' Scarhead says, sitting back down. 'In terms of instinct only: do you think the twins are guilty or not guilty?'

'Not guilty,' I spit out of my mouth, leaving no pause between his asking of the question and my answering of it.

'Okay, okay,' he nods again. 'I like it. No hesitation. Maybe we should all do that. Next…' he says. Red Head looks up at him.

'Not guilty,' she says. And as soon as she does I feel a bubble of excitement form in my stomach.

'Next.'

'Guilty.'

'Guilty'

'One hundred per cent guilty,' the blonde with the acne scars says.

Holy shit.

'Guilty.'

'Guilty,' Scarhead says when it comes around to him.

Bollocks.

'Not guilty,' Obese Guy says. I nod. He's definitely on my side. He won't waver. I'll make sure he doesn't.

'Guilty.'

'No doubt they're guilty,' the guy with the thick-rimmed glasses says.

'Guilty.'

'Not guilty. Not yet anyway,' says the last juror—the young guy with the stupidly-high quiff. 'There's a long way to go. And I could be convinced they're guilty, but for now, it's too early for me to commit to that.'

I try to do a quick count in my head... but seem to have lost track.

'Eight guilty, four not guilty,' Scarhead says, answering my math problem for me. Shit. I've only got three on my side from the outset. I need to make sure two of them don't change their minds while we're in here. And sure that idiot with the stupidly-high quiff has already admitted he could easily be persuaded into the guilty camp.

I've got Red Head, Obese Guy and Quiff Boy here to work with. Four. Four of twelve. Jesus. It would be only three of twelve voting not guilty if I actually voted how I wanted to vote. These deliberations would be practically over before they'd even begun. My stomach turns itself over and my hands instantly begin to sweat. This is not good. I've wanted to know all the way through this trial what the other jurors were thinking. And now I finally know. The majority in this room, like me, think the twins did it. That would have been great news yesterday morning. But now it's a fucking night-mare. My actual, genuine nightmare coming true.

I stand up, hold a palm to my forehead, then suddenly find myself on all fours, panting heavy breaths into the squared patterns on the carpet.

DAY TWO

I was really groggy the next morning; had no idea much sleep I'd managed to catch. Only about one hour, though. Maybe two. Max.

I showered, put on my crispest white shirt, my favourite navy blazer and a pair of jeans before I joined my wife at the kitchen table, sitting on the same seat I'd spent hours numbing my bum on the night previous.

'You're going to nail this,' she said to me exhaling cannabis vapour towards our ceiling. I grabbed my toast on the go, kissed my wife's forehead, then drove to the station and waited — and waited — for Fairweather to arrive. She was supposed to meet me at eight a.m., but didn't arrive till gone half nine.

Fairweather was as supportive as my wife was that I could nail the case. Though she did let me know on quite a few occasions that I hadn't handled anything of this magnitude before. Tallaght Station had been on to her numerous times since the murders, demanding they run the case. But Fairweather stayed strong; told them they could count on me.

In that meeting, on that early morning of day two, she looked me straight in the eye and asked if I was as suspicious as she was about the twins.

'It's not the twins,' I said almost laughing with the absurdity of it all. 'I spent most of yesterday with them. They are not killers. No way.'

Fairweather cancelled her game of golf that day but she didn't accompany me on my investigation. She stayed at the station, handling the multitude of questions coming her way not just from the media, but practically the entire community. Everybody wanted to know what had gone on. I was adamant I wouldn't stop until I had the answer for them. Though I was still kinda cringing about a couple of the missteps I'd taken on day one.

Fairweather wasn't that concerned that I approached the scene without protectors on, nor that I took my time ringing SOCO and Tusla. But she was somewhat baffled that me and Johnny took the twins to McDonalds. I still don't get the furore over that. They were hungry, for Christ's sake.

I rang SOCO as I drove to the church, just to get an update on when they'd be able to deliver results for me. The next day, they said, though they did give me a little insight during that call; informed me that there was certainly nothing obvious found that pointed in any direction. They said whoever did this was very careful not to leave any evidence whatsoever.

I was surprised how many people had packed into the church that morning. Though it's not technically a church; it's a community centre. A basketball net hangs above the stage and the straight lines of a basketball court are still taped over the pale floorboards. Though they did do their best to dim the lighting to mainly candlelight and decorate the walls with framed biblical paintings. More white Jesuses.

The congregation were a mix of not only generations, but cultures. From teenagers to those close to retirement. And from pale skin to black skin. But every face was drawn with the same sombre expression. Some looked as if they'd been crying non-stop since they'd heard the news.

Kelly McAllister did most of the speaking. She looked me straight in the eye, made me promise that I'd find out who killed their leaders. I found it odd that these people saw Clive and Dorothy Tiddle as the people who should be worshipped. They were so frumpy and ordinary.

I stood on the stage to make a little speech, to calm each of the churchgoers down as best I could. I promised I wouldn't rest until the killer was put behind bars.

My phone vibrated a few times while I was in that church. Tunstead was desperate to get hold of me. But I wasn't giving in to him. My main focus was the investigation. Him and Lowe could wait.

I spoke with so many people in the church that morning individually—over sixty of them. I wanted to know if they were aware of any people who didn't like the Tiddles. I learned there had been whispers of unrest around some residents of Rathcoole; complaining that the church seemed to be taking over the mountainside. The Tiddles were bringing people in from all corners of the globe to the local area every Sunday—but nobody I spoke to in the church seemed to believe that complaining stretched beyond anything other than a slither of unconscious racism. One name kept coming up, though. Repeatedly.

Tommo Nevin had let it be known in no uncertain terms that he didn't want 'darkies' strolling the laneways of the Dublin mountains.

'He's not the nicest man I've ever come across,' Kelly told me. 'But I don't believe he's a killer.'

She was in a state of shock the whole time I was there, shaking her head constantly as if she couldn't quite fathom what had gone on.

'Well, if it wasn't Tommo Nevin,' I said to her, 'who else could it be?'

She looked up at me, through the tears in her eyes, and shrugged ever so slowly.

I placed a hand to her shoulder.

'You look after these people,' I said, nodding towards the grieving parishioners around us, 'and I'll look after the investigation.'

I gave her a long hug, then left them all to it to grieve for the loss of their leaders.

The sun almost blinded me when I finally pushed open the double doors and stepped outside.

'Get anything useful in there?' a voice said from beyond the glare.

I held a hand above my eyes as a visor. Tunstead was wearing another skin-tight suit—this one tanned brown. Lowe had on a light navy blazer, like me. But she matched hers with pants. Not jeans.

'Y'know,' I said, leaning against my car, 'people around this neck of the woods didn't like the Tiddle family. Mainly because they were bringing foreigners up here. Some folk don't like seeing dark brown faces among the bright green fields.'

Lowe stuck out her bottom lip and placed her hands into her pants pockets.

'Anybody in particular?' she said.

'Yep. A Tommo Nevin. Apparently he had it out with Clive Tiddle a couple of months ago. Didn't hide his racism either, from what I understand.'

'Tommo Nevin's not a murderer,' Tunstead said, sniggering at me like a prick. 'He's just an old-school man with old-school views.'

I turned to Lowe.

'Well, I'm gonna go talk to him now. See what he was up to yesterday. What are you guys—'

'Quayle, we need to talk to the twins,' Tunstead interrupted. 'There's a whole load of questions they need to answer. Let's get them to the scene and have them walk us through what happened when they got home from their dance class yesterday. We could end this case today.'

I scoffed.

'You think it was the twins?' Tunstead and Lowe looked at each other. It always irritated me when they did that right in front of me. As if I couldn't bloody see them. 'Well, you're wrong. It wasn't them. It couldn't have been them.'

'They had time to do it, then go to dance class, then come home and ring 999.' Tunstead said. 'They bought themselves an alibi by going to dance class, but it's not going to prove enough.'

'What… and then they just lied to the paramedics, lied to unformed cops, lied to us detectives, lied to Tusla and have been able to hold in the fact that they killed their parents in cold blood ever since? You saw them yesterday. You think they're capable of that much calculation?' I asked.

Tunstead shifted his standing position.

'That's why we need to talk to them… we gotta find out what they know,' he said. 'It's been almost twenty-four hours since they called in the homicides and they haven't been questioned thoroughly.'

'Well, I'm off to interview Tommo Nevin first,' I told him. 'Then I'm going to visit the twins at Tusla.'

'Quayle,' Lowe said, taking a step towards me. 'Let's start with the twins. Please. Arrange for Tusla to bring them out to the scene. Me, you and Tunstead can meet them there and... look, you can lead the questioning. This is your investigation, after all. We just want to assist you. Support you. But I agree with Tunstead... we need to start with the twins. Find out what happened at the scene... then we can start elaborating on other theories.'

The three of us barely said a word to each other as we stood on the Tiddles' graveled drive, waiting on the twins to arrive. Though I spent most of the time internally kicking myself for giving in to Tunstead's request. It was only because Lowe approached me in such a nice way that I decided Tommo Nevin could wait till later. Besides, I hadn't seen Faith and Grace since I handed them over to Tusla the evening before, and I was keen to see how they were holding up.

They weren't crying when they got out of the car. But they looked as if they had been. I strolled towards them, bent down and squeezed them both with a one-armed hug.

'I'm so sorry to do this to you,' I said. 'But as I told you yesterday, I am going to find out who did this to your mammy and daddy and I just need some help from you, okay?'

Grace looked as if she was about to sob, but she managed to hold it back.

'But... but we don't know who did it... we don't know anything,' she said.

I rubbed her back.

'Everything will be okay,' I said. 'But there could be something, anything that you may be able to tell me and the other two detectives over there, that will help us find out who did this. So just tell us everything you know, no matter how small you think it is. Okay?'

Grace nodded her head and rubbed her eye at the same

time, and then Faith mirrored her movements almost perfectly.

I stood back up, then motioned for them to walk towards Tunstead and Lowe.

'Thanks for getting them here on such short notice,' I whispered to the two Tusla staff who had been introduced to me as Joe and Dinah the previous evening. 'How've they been?'

Joe blew out his cheeks.

'Okay,' he said. 'Considering.'

Dinah leaned towards me.

'Are they suspects, Detective Quayle?' she whispered.

I shook my head.

'No. No. Not at all. This looks like a professional job. Whoever did this knew what they were doing. We just need the girls to walk the scene, see if they can come up with something — *anything* — that'll help us out.'

They both looked at each other and shrugged.

'Okay, Detective,' Joe said.

'What... not you guys as well. Do you think they did it?'

'Ohhh.' Dinah held both of her palms towards me. 'That's not for us to say. That's your job.'

I squinted, then glanced over my shoulder to see Lowe and Tunstead spark up conversation with the twins and decided I had to join them.

The bungalow was really cold when we walked inside. Bizarrely cold. As if we had just walked outside from being inside.

'I'll lead,' I whispered to Tunstead. He took one step back, then waved his hand down the hallway.

I strolled to the end of the hall where Faith and Grace had stopped in front of the giant crucifix, and crouched down to my hunkers.

'Okay, Faith and Grace,' I said, slowly. 'Can you tell me

what happened the moment you arrived home from dance class at about 12:15 yesterday afternoon?'

Faith looked at Grace. And as soon as she did Grace started to cry. Not a sob. A full-on howl. And without any haste, Faith followed suit.

The 'family' members of Clive and Dorothy's church, which had expanded well beyond five hundred people by the time Faith and Grace arrived, were equally as intrigued as they were infatuated by the twins when they were born.

They were undoubtedly cute; their little button noses complemented either side by the same large chocolate brown eyes their mother had. There was often, in their very early days, a queue of people lined up the aisle of the community centre all waiting to coo at them in their double pram. Clive and Dorothy would stand on the stage during those processions, basking in their miracles. Even folk from the neighbourhood who had never set foot inside the church prior to their arrival popped along to offer cards and gifts. Both parents were high as kites; for the first three weeks anyway. But Faith's refusal to sleep when everybody else was trying to sleep soon increased tensions. Even Clive, who had never so much as raised his voice in all the time he'd been with Dorothy, began to fume. Though he'd do so as quietly as he could; gurgling his frustrations in the back of his throat while Dorothy would try to rock Faith back to sleep. It was always Dorothy's responsibility to get up in the night to whisper lullabies to Faith—the job of the mother.

Adapting quickly to the tiny progresses humanity makes doesn't seem to come naturally to believers of faith—any faith.

Dorothy didn't mind getting up anyway; never even thought to suggest that Clive's sleep should be ruined to see to their daughter. Dorothy was tired, but not overly-tired—could still function. Which was just as well, as their growing church needed her as much as the twins did. Both Clive and Dorothy had done incredibly well from starting out as regular parishioners at St Benedict's Church at the bottom of the Dublin mountains as soon as they moved into the area, to running the whole parish eighteen years later. Through their struggles to conceive, the Tiddles decided their calling must be to preach God's message rather than parent. So... they immersed themselves even further in their local church. Though they were pretty much the only ones who did. By the mid-nineties, when Clive and Dorothy moved into the area, the traditional church had had its day—certainly in Dublin. The Irish capital was by then abuzz with new money and becoming way too liberal to be bothering itself with two-thousand year old books. The attendance in churches in Ireland dropped by over one thousand percent in 1995 compared to the figures from the decade previous. And St Benedict's Church was one of the old-school churches that suffered. It suffered gravely, in fact. The numbers attending any of the regular Sunday sermons was practically making its way to single figures. So they cut down from four masses each Sunday to three... and then two, until they were eventually only running one sermon at eleven a.m. each Sunday. And even that one sermon was in danger of hitting single figures for attendance.

The parish priest at the time was Fr. Frank Munro. He was just beyond middle-aged but still brightly and filled with character — as well as Guinness — when he died. He adored the Tiddles because they did their utmost for the church. They started as regular parishioners attending services, to helping to bring up the offerings, then passing out Holy Communion and eventually even reading gospels. They inched their way onto the altar over the years and became a key part of the church's mechanism.

They were probably the closest people in the world to Fr Frank as he withered from life. He didn't know he had a tumour pulsing at the side of his brain. It must have been growing for at least two years prior to diagnosis, the professor at Tallaght Hospital had told him. He died ten weeks later. Gone. Just like that.

A lack of newly-ordained priests, by now down to just one per year in the country, made filling the vacancy at St Benedict's Church impossible. In the end the Catholic church chose to close it down, which was an unusual position for them to ever take. The feeling was that the church-goers in that specific small area of the Dublin mountains were a dying breed, and the statistics of Mass attendances over the previous decade had firmly illustrated that. The church building, over three-hundred years old, still sits high in the Dublin mountains, but the natural habitat around it has over-grown, making it look like something out of a graphic novel.

Clive had kept the church going initially after Fr Munro had passed by giving sermons. But only because a few parishioners begged him to. He immediately loved it; standing on that altar with everybody listening to what he had to say. It was the total opposite of what he had been used to his whole life.

'We have to keep this church going,' he would often repeat to Dorothy.

She agreed; but couldn't see how it was even possible. Clive wasn't ordained—the Catholic church would not allowed it. And they didn't.

But their insistence on closing the church down didn't deter Clive from his longing to be on an altar, preaching. He approached the local community centre and asked if they could give him use of their facilities for two hours each Sunday afternoon. And they agreed.

By that stage he hadn't even thought about money. Though, out of pure traditionalism and instinct, they did pass around a collection basket during their first mass. Two hundred and forty pounds they took in—and there was only thirty-one people in attendance.

Clive wasn't sure what he was supposed to do with the cash. But he didn't hesitate in quitting his job as a customer service rep for Eircom to become a full-time preacher.

The numbers attending Clive's sermons were rising even before the twins came along, but their birth gave it a huge shot in the arm. It was mainly to do with how cute they were; that and the fact the story often told was that they were conceived by miracle at the hands of Jesus Christ. They were always dressed to the nines—in perfect Sunday wear, even on a regular Tuesday morning. They wore ribbons in their hair consistently and they always adorned a floral summer dress—just like their mother. And her mother before her.

It was incongruous that Clive ended up becoming a church leader though. When he first started dating Dorothy and was introduced to her extended 'family', he instinctively went along with playing the role of a Christian. He knew the answers to almost all the questions. School had saw to that. Bible was the first thing studied every morning at the Christian Brothers Schools in Ireland when he was growing up—and prayers were rostered to be said at least twice a day. He knew the parables, knew the Ten Commandments, knew the rough outline of the story of Jesus' life. So he fit in straight away; nodding away in agreement with everybody's ideologies. But he was lying to everyone as much as he was lying to himself. Believing in a God who created the world a few thousand years ago made absolutely no logical sense to him. But going along with that narrative afforded him a life, afforded him friends, an extended family, a wife, God-damn it! And as a result he became so convincing in his role as a man of God that he almost convinced himself.

Though the lie he was living, as influential as it was in shaping who he was, was really the only negative trait Clive Tiddle possessed. Yes, he was an odd man to look at; almost stand-offish *given that he was so tall and had a rotund belly that ensured it was difficult to ever literally get close to him. But all of the 'family' found him really sincere and genuinely polite. Possessing those two traits were particularly important to Clive. Because he was bullied at school, all he'd ever yearned for was for people to be sincere and polite to each other. So he spoke sincerely and politely to everyone who ever crossed his path.*

Except for one man, on one occasion. A local fella by the name of Tommo Nevin.

ALICE

'Here,' Obese Guy says, taking my hands and bringing them towards the sink. 'Let the cold water run over your wrists… it'll help you wake up.'

'Oh my God, I'm so embarrassed,' I say, eyeballing myself in the mirror as he twists my wrists left and right under the running water.

'Don't be a silly woman,' he says. 'We're all feeling the stresses and strains of this trial. It's not just you. I barely slept a wink last night.'

I look at his reflection, and when he catches my eye I whisper a "thank you" to him.

Then he turns and whips three sheets of paper towel from the plastic dispenser hanging on the wall before taking my hands again. He pats down my wrists for me, like I'm a four-year-old girl, and as he is doing so the bathroom door opens and the red head peers around it.

'You okay, Alice?' she whispers, taking a step inside and then closing the door quietly behind herself.

'Embarrassed.'

'Don't be silly,' she says.

'That's what I said,' Obese Guy says.

Red Head approaches me and holds me in a light embrace. I hug her back, even though Obese Guy wasn't quite finished drying me off. It'll probably leave a wet stain on the back of her top, but I feel as if I need this hug.

It hits me as I'm resting my chin on her shoulder that I may not be the only juror being blackmailed. These two in here are also not guilty voters. Maybe one of them is being blackmailed too. Or both. It could be both. I release my hold on Red Head, and stare into her pale face.

'You sure you're okay?' she asks again.

I nod, because I feel I may cry if I open my mouth.

'Why don't we take a seat at the table… when we get into the deliberations you'll probably feel yourself again,' Obese Guy says. I look to him and nod again, and suddenly Red Head is linking my arm and leading me out of the bathroom and towards my seat at the far end of the jurors' table. The silence in the room is really awkward, even more so than it is when I'm walking in and out of that courtroom.

I huff an embarrassed laugh across the table when I sit, and then raise a hand.

'Apologies everybody,' I say.

'Don't be silly,' Scarhead says. And then both Red Head and Obese Guy say, "That's what I said" in unison.

'We, eh… didn't discuss anything while you were in the bathroom, Alice,' Scarhead says. 'So the last we all discussed was the result, just before you, eh... fell. The result was eight jurors voted guilty, four jurors voted not guilty. I guess that gives us all a good understanding of where everybody stands. It's a platform for us to begin our arguments, I guess. Though I'm sure minds can and indeed will change as we strive towards a unanimous verdict.'

I sit back in the chair and try to breathe as steadily as I possibly can, to give my panic room to pass through.

'I'll start... I just find them undoubtedly cold,' Scarhead says. 'They are the oddest girls I have ever laid my eyes on and I am convinced they killed their parents. I think their defence team did a great job, and why wouldn't they? Bracken is about the best and most expensive defence lawyer in the country. But he didn't do enough to convince me. And if *he* couldn't do enough, nobody could have.'

'Hold on a minute,' I say, 'it is not our job to judge the lawyers. What you are saying—'

'That is *exactly* our job,' the man with the thick-rimmed glasses says, interrupting me. 'Our job is to judge how the defence did and how the prosecution did. Our job is to determine whether or not the defence team did a good enough job suggesting Faith and Grace are innocent. Or whether the prosecution did a good enough job to convince us that they are guilty.'

I want to argue back with him, but I agree with him so much that I'm not sure where to even begin debating against that.

'Nothing was proven. They're innocent,' is all I can muster up.

'I disagree with you,' the elderly woman with the over-sized bust says. 'They are cold and creepy. And, let's be honest, they had the time to do it. They planned this. They stabbed their parents to death just before heading out to use that dance class as an alibi, and then they came back and rang the police. They thought they were being clever. But they didn't realise forensics would be able to determine an exact time of death.'

'But forensics didn't specify an exact time,' Red Head pipes up. 'They said it could have been any time between ten-thirty and eleven.'

'Yes, which tells us the twins *could* have done it. They didn't leave their house until about ten forty-five... they arrived at dance class at ten fifty-five. That gave them time to do it.'

'No, no!' I slam a hand to the table. 'It only gives them a very narrow window. These kids can't be as calculated as you are suggesting.'

'They fuckin are,' the man with the thick-rimmed glasses says.

'Hey, no need for that kind of language,' Obese Guy says. And then everybody begins to talk over each other.

Jesus Christ. This is exhausting. And we're only about ten minutes into deliberations. I just need to hold on to my not guilty verdict and make sure at least two other people do, too. Red Head and Obese Guy seem to be supporting my arguments already. Hopefully they're as stubborn as I am and hold out until the judge determines our time is up and declares us hung.

I can't imagine how my life would change if I got home this evening to find Noel and Zoe had watched that video. I stab my fingernails into my palms and cringe. I'm a fucking idiot.

It was all because of Alex and Lyndsey's wedding. Me and Emmet were both drunk. He stopped me in the corridor as I was making my way to my hotel room, where I knew Noel would be snoring his head off.

'You looked absolutely gorgeous today, Alice,' Emmet said, his tie all loose around his neck. He was swaying a little. And slurring. But I still took it as a huge compliment. Especially coming from him. A twenty-three year old with shoulders practically the width of the corridor. He leaned in to kiss me, and I moved away.

'What are you doing?' I gasped. He apologised. And apologised. And then apologised some more before he slumped his way back to the bedroom he was sharing with my daughter. Two days later he texted me to meet him for a coffee. He wanted to explain himself and apologise even further. Which is exactly what he did. I could see the sorrow etched on his face as he told me he *did* find me attractive but that he was so glad nothing had happened because he couldn't live with himself if he hurt Zoe.

I left the café that day almost buzzing. I hadn't been paid so many compliments in years... not since me and Noel started dating. I couldn't stop thinking about Emmet after that. And then two weeks later he called around to see Zoe when she wasn't in, and we ended up sitting across from each other at the kitchen table. We were just shooting the breeze, talking shite, when he rested his hand on my knee. And I instantly got wet. *Instantly*. I could feel the juices practically foaming inside of me.

I kissed him. Leaned forward, threw my tongue in his mouth and we made out, grinding up against each other on our kitchen counter tops until I realised Zoe might walk through that door any minute. And so I got up, put my coat on and went for a walk to nowhere. I had to calm my whole body down.

That night, after Noel went to bed, I played with myself on our sofa, imagining what it would feel like to have Emmet make love to me. As soon as my orgasms were over, I felt really bad. Guilty.

The following day Emmet rang, told me he couldn't stop thinking about me and asked if I would be interested in meeting him at the Hilton Hotel that weekend. I said "no" at first, even shouted at him for leading me on. But five minutes later I rang back, told him he should wear that tight-fitted white shirt he looked so buff in at Alex and Lyndsey's wedding and that I'd see him at eight p.m on the Friday.

The sex was mind-altering. Better than I'd ever had by miles. Better than I ever will have. I came nine times that night. *Nine!* My whole body shook so hard, it took minutes for it to actually stop. I was just lying there in a sweat, my hand over my face, my mouth grinning from ear to ear.

I have lived, ever since, balancing the highs of those orgasms with the lows of the guilt.

'Alice!' I look up, and notice everybody has turned to face me.

'Sorry. Was away with the fairies there.'

'We were discussing McDonald's, getting everybody's view on it,' Red Head says.

'Oh,' I say, readjusting my seating position. 'Eh... McDonalds... well, as in, eh....'

'Alice, you really need to be paying attention to everybody's points.' Scarhead is talking down to me. Literally. He is stood at the top of the table, peering at me with his eyebrows dipped. 'We've all shared our opinion on the twins eating a McDonald's three hours after they found their parents lying in pools of blood. What is your take on it?'

I shift my seating position again, stare at Red Head who offers me a sympathetic smile, and then slowly lean both of my forearms, one at a time, on to the table.

'It's not as if they just headed off for a McDonalds, is it?' I said. 'The detective and an officer took them there because there was no food for them at the station—and they were hungry.'

'I agree with you, Alice,' Thick-rimmed Glasses says. 'Detective Quayle has been the main problem with this case from the very beginning.'

I shake my head.

'No, that's not what I'm saying. What I mean is... I don't think he's the problem at all. I believe he is the only one who has had this right from the get-go. What if he is right and we all put two innocent children behind bars for the rest of their lives? Think about it. He doesn't truly believe that Faith and Grace killed their parents. And he was the lead detective on the entire case!'

DAY TWO

I t took a glass of Ribena each, an ice-pop and a dozen hugs from Joe and Dinah before the twins finally settled down.

Dinah and Joe suggested abandoning the walk-through there and then, to which I agreed. But Lowe talked me around. She said the sooner we did this, the sooner we'd find whoever it was that murdered Clive and Dorothy—and that it was imperative we did it while everything was as fresh as it could be in the twins' minds.

I started by apologising to Faith and Grace. Again. Then I asked about their welfare; how they were getting on at Tusla. They shrugged and nodded their heads. I had to inform them that we were trying to track down their aunt Janet. Johnny had found out she was their closest living relative. Clive's sister. She was living in Carrickmacross in Monaghan; had moved there over twenty years ago. But she was proving difficult to get hold of.

When the twins had finally settled I asked them to talk me through exactly what happened when they arrived home from dance class the previous afternoon. Without prompt,

Grace hopped off the sofa and beckoned Faith into the hall-way. They walked to the front door, and me, Tunstead, Lowe and Joe and Dinah looked on as they opened it.

Then they turned to us and Grace sighed.

'We came in and shut the door like this,' she said. Then she slammed the door behind them both. 'We were really thirsty from dancing and so we walked straight into the kitchen to get a drink.'

She strolled past us, towards the kitchen, Faith following.

'Was the kitchen door open when you came in?' Tunstead asked.

The twins paused… hesitated, until Faith looked at Grace.

'Yes. Open,' Grace confirmed.

'Okay,' Tunstead said. 'So, really as soon as you opened that hall door, you would have seen your father's body, isn't that right?'

I flicked my hand at Tunstead, signalling for him to hush. He didn't react—he just stared back at Faith and Grace, waiting for their answer.

'I, eh... saw it when I got to about here,' Grace said, circling her foot on the carpet a few yards short of the kitchen door.

'And you, Faith?' Tunstead said.

She circled her foot in the exact same place as her sister without saying a word.

'And then what?' Lowe asked, in a much more calm manner than her partner had been firing off his questions.

'Then we… we looked inside and saw mammy and daddy were lying there with blood all over them.'

'Okay, and tell us more,' Lowe said. I was getting a little peeved that I wasn't the one in control. Tunstead and Lowe were doing all the questioning. But I didn't say anything. Because I was fascinated. I wanted to know the answers to all of the questions they were asking too.

'We didn't stay in here long, we just went out to the hall and rang—'

'Actually,' Lowe said, lowering down to her hunkers. 'I would like Faith to answer this question for me. Faith… what happened next, sweetheart?'

Faith looked at Grace, then at Lowe.

'Then we rang 999,' she said, as she rubbed her eye.

'The back kitchen door was not locked,' I said. 'Is this unusual?'

'It's always unlocked,' Grace said. I nodded at Tunstead when she said this but he didn't seem to notice.

'See this right here?' Tunstead said, picking up the knife block. 'We believe the knife missing from here is the weapon that was used to kill your parents.' He pointed at an empty slit, then swiped another knife from the block and held it up, twisting it ever so slightly.

'Alright, alright,' I said, stepping in. 'That's enough questioning in here,' I said.

I ordered them all to follow me to the living room where we sat the twins on the sofa. I asked them to talk us through their morning routine of the day previous; specifically in the lead up to what happened before they left for dance class. Grace answered most of my questions, but I did use the tactic Lowe had used earlier by asking Faith to specifically chip in every now and then. I felt really guilty questioning the two of them. It didn't feel right. Every part of me was sorrowful. They had literally become orphans in the most horrific manner possible just twenty-four hours prior. And here we were demanding answers of them; not letting them grieve.

They said they had their usual breakfast at about eight-thirty a.m. that morning. Grace was able to tell me what each of them had eaten. Then she said both her and Faith played in their bedroom for an hour or so while Clive and Dorothy spoke in the kitchen.

'So you didn't see your parents for an hour during that morning?' Tunstead chipped in with. 'Do you know if they were definitely alive by the time you left for dance class?'

Grace started to cry. Faith followed. And I made a face at Tunstead again, making sure he noticed my annoyance this time. After the Tusla guys had consoled the twins with a light rub to the back, Grace confirmed that her parents were definitely alive when they left at ten forty-five, because they had kissed them goodbye.

When the Tusla guys suggested we put an end to the questions after that one was answered with a further sob, I agreed. I could tell Tunstead was a little pissed off with me, but Lowe had a quiet word with him and minutes later the twins and Joe and Dinah were skidding the tyres of their minivan off the gravel.

'What's your gut telling you now, Quayle?' Tunstead asked.

'I feel guilty,' I told him. 'Those poor girls. It's a sin to bring them here... questioning them like that.'

He glared at me.

'You don't think they did it?' he asked.

'Detective work isn't about thinking, it's about knowing,' I said. I actually said that instinctively. But it sounded good. As if it should be a quote framed on a wall in a Garda station.

I'm sure him and Lowe shared one of those stares they always share, but I didn't take the time to notice. Because I had turned to walk back down the hallway.

'The kitchen door was always unlocked and we know that there was a man in the community who had a problem with the family,' I said back over my shoulder. 'We need to explore Tommo Nevin.'

'Jesus, Quayle,' Tunstead said as his designer shoes

clacked after me. 'You seriously don't think there's anything creepy about those twins?'

'Karl,' Lowe said, grabbing at Tunstead's sleeve.

He sucked in a deep breath.

'You follow Tommo Nevin if you want,' he said, 'we're going to follow up other lines.'

'Well you need to tell me what lines you are following. I'm in charge of this investigation. And I don't want you two going off gallivanting—'

'Quayle. Why don't you just let us take control here… this is a massive case.'

'No,' I spat back at him.

He flared his nostrils. The prick.

'Right,' he said, 'I'm going to take a look in the bedrooms.'

After he'd entered the first bedroom, Lowe followed me to the end of the hallway; where we both stood staring at the white Jesus.

'When you, eh…' she said, 'when you spoke to the church people this morning, what did they say about the twins?'

'They said their hearts went out to them and that they were praying for them.'

'No,' she said, taking a step closer to me, 'that's not what I mean exactly. I assume you asked their opinion on the twins.' I looked at her, then back at the crucifix. 'You didn't ask that question, huh?' she said.

I didn't answer her. I just stared at Jesus' blue eyes.

'Hey!' Tunstead shouted, cutting through the awkwardness of my silence. Both myself and Lowe paced into Clive and Dorothy's bedroom, where he was knelt down in the corner, lifting up a square of floorboards. 'A safe,' he said. 'A pretty big one. I wonder what the hell's in here.'

Lowe looked at me.

'Okay, Quayle,' she said, 'why don't you order somebody to come and have a look at this safe. Whatever's inside it could be of big importance. Then go question Tommo Nevin and follow your gut.'

'What are you guys going to do?' I asked.

'Well, we're going to speak to SOCO, see if they can get a hurry on. This investigation is all over the news, so I'm sure somebody in the higher echelons can put a word in so we can get those results as quickly as possible. Let's get this investigation motoring.'

'I'll do that,' I said. 'I'll make that call to SOCO.'

'Quayle,' Lowe said. She walked right up to me, placed her hand on my arm.

'You are the Detective Inspector of Rathcoole Garda Station. And you are in control of this investigation. We get that. We are here to support you. This is a huge case. A massive case. And even when cases aren't this big, me and Tunstead have each other to lean on to solve them as best we can. Together. But at Rathcoole, there's just you. You are the only DI from your station. You need to lean on us. If you try to tackle this all on your own, you'll go crazy.' She smiled at me. 'You've things to do. Important things. Let us ring SOCO, we have contacts there and we'll get this hurried up. We'll tell them to ring you first, with whatever they find.'

It was unusual Lowe would talk to me like this. With respect. I relented, by nodding my head and replicating Lowe's touch by placing my palm on her arm. Then Tunstead stepped forward.

'Lowe and I have ordered a sweep of the area, we are on the lookout for one of these knives.' He held the kitchen knife aloft; had been holding it all the while questioning Faith and Grace. The prick. 'And I've asked SOCO to take all of the twins' clothes in for analysing.'

'Now hold on!' I shouted.

Lowe patted her hand against my arm.

'Quayle, listen… listen. These are the most practical procedures. This goes without saying.'

'Well, wait until I order the procedures,' I replied. My frustration was flaring up again.

'We *were* waiting,' Tunstead said before he swiveled and walked back up the hallway.

It was Lowe's touch that stopped me from pacing after him. Though I didn't really have much to argue. I knew they were right.

'Come on, Quayle—you know this,' Lowe said. 'It's rule one-o-one: the first suspects are always the ones who find the bodies.'

ALICE

A debate ripples around the table. It seems as if Detective Quayle has split us right down the middle. Some jurors are praising him; saying he did the right thing in looking after the children's welfare first and foremost whilst he continued to investigate. Some — especially Scarhead — are slamming him; saying it was totally ludicrous that he would bring them for a McDonalds just hours after their parents had been murdered. I couldn't understand that argument so much. Then again, had my phone not been hacked and my relationships with my husband and daughter not at stake, I'd definitely be siding with them; demanding that Quayle didn't know what the hell he was doing and that everybody should vote the same as me—guilty as charged.

I want to go the bathroom again, run the cold water onto my wrists so that my head stops spinning and my palms stop sweating. But I can't. It's not that long since I was last in there, holding up the deliberations so I could take care of myself like a fucking diva. I'm wary everybody already thinks I'm the snowflake in the room; the one who collapsed. The one who keeps tuning out of the discussions. But I guess I got to stop caring what everybody else thinks of me. I need to show some strength here. I have to have a voice in this room. Otherwise I'm screwed.

'Shut up!' I shout, slamming my hands to the table. 'You are all going round and round in circles, can you please just stop?' I hold two fingertips to my temple as the ripples of chatter drop to a dead silence. I'm aware everybody is staring at me. Again. Even though I haven't fully looked up. 'Listen,' I say, steadying myself by placing a palm to my beating heart, 'we are not here to judge Detective Quayle… we are here to judge Faith and Grace. And I am certain, and my mind will not change on this… there was not enough proof put before us that tells us *without doubt* that they are guilty of this crime.'

'There's loads of proof,' Scarface says. 'There is no forensics that suggests anybody else entered that house that morning. Only the victims and the two defendants. There is also the fact that the knife used to kill Clive and Dorothy was a knife that was in the Tiddle kitchen, and has since gone missing. Only somebody from inside that house could have taken that knife.'

'Now hold on,' Red Head says. I have a feeling she is going to be my hero. 'A missing knife is not proof. If the knife was found… now that would be proof. But nobody found a knife, did they? There was nothing that links Faith and Grace directly to the murders. Besides, we know that the back door to that kitchen was unlocked. Somebody conceivably could have come in, taken that knife, stabbed Clive and Dorothy and left.'

Scarhead sniffs a patronising snigger from his nose.

'Without leaving a trace?'

Red Head parts her lips, then interlocks her fingers atop the table.

'Well… we don't know. In the same way we don't know for a fact that it was Faith and Grace who killed them. This trial needs to be proven beyond all doubt and jurors are going to have a difficult time arguing against all of the doubt that has cropped up in this case.'

Another ripple of debate sparks from one side of the table to the other. Like ping-pong. Scarhead is the loudest; arguing that trials rarely prove anything indefinitely, and that's why there is a need for jurors. But I can't listen to all these voices at once, so I tune out again, eyeballing the bathroom door and wishing my wrists were being soothed by cold water.

'There was no blood,' I say under my breath while everyone is arguing. 'There was no blood.' Louder this time.

'Huh?' Red Head says, turning to me.

'Not on any of the twins' clothes, not on their skin. Isn't that proof enough that it couldn't have been them?' The table falls silent again, all tuning in to my growing volume. 'Right?' I say, my eyes lighting up. 'Police checked all of the twins' clothes; no traces of their parents' blood. The dance teacher... what was her name?'

'Claire,' Red Head confirms.

'Yeah, yeah... Claire. She testified that she didn't see any blood on the twins' hands that day.'

'Yeah but...' Thick-rimmed Glasses says. 'But if they had time to kill their parents before they left for dance class, then they had time to wash their hands. It wouldn't have taken long.'

'And what... dumped their clothes, dumped the knife... they did all this before they hopped off to do a bit of ballet?' I say.

Scarhead bounces the paperwork he has in front of him off the table.

'Alice, if the twins planned this murder — and that's what the prosecution believes because they wanted to use dance class as their alibi — then yes... they would have got rid of the knife, got rid of the clothes they were wearing, washed their hands and went to dance class…'

'I don't believe for one second that two nine year olds would be capable of that much calculation,' I lie. I lie because I genuinely feel as if Faith and Grace *are* capable of that much calculation. They are cold. They are evil. I have felt that way about them since I first heard about this case. I'm actually surprised that there are three other jurors sitting around this table who think otherwise. It's obvious they did it. Evidence or no evidence.

'You are saying, Alice, that Ms Claire's testimony suggests that the twins didn't do it because she said she didn't see blood on their hands? Because that's not the biggest take from her time on the stand.' The old woman with the overly big bust has decided it's her turn to have a go at me. 'What I take from her testimony is the fact that she feels these twins *did* do this. She says they were acting weird that day.'

'No she didn't,' I say, snapping back. 'All she said was that Faith was particularly quiet. But sure, as the defence team said, Faith is *always* quiet.'

'Y'know what?' Scarface says as he stands to attention. 'Claire Barry is a key witness in this case and we are right to be arguing her testimony. But there seems to be disagreement about what she said on the stand.' He rubs at the long scar on his forehead with the tip of his index finger. 'I suggest we ask the court for the transcripts of her testimony, do we all agree?'

I don't answer him. But I don't have to. Because the rest of the jury have answered for me; all of them nodding their heads.

'Great idea,' Big Bust says. And then suddenly our deliberations have paused again while Scarhead pushes at a button on the table to speak with the court assistant, requesting twelve copies of the transcripts.

I sip from my glass of water, noticing that my hands haven't quite stopped shaking. Red Head stares at me, but I don't look back. I just place my glass down, then stand up and take advantage of the small break in deliberations to visit the bathroom. Again.

I stare at myself in the mirror as soon as I've locked the door behind me. I look terrible. As if bags have just decided to form under my eyes in the past few hours. Then I turn on the tap and allow the cold water to flow over my wrists again.

'Hello… you okay in there?' I pause. Then turn off the tap. It's the red head. I know her voice.

I shake my hands dry then walk over to the door and welcome her inside.

'How are you feeling?' she asks, looking genuinely concerned. I scratch at my head, unsure how I can handle this conversation.

'Grand,' I say. 'It's just… it's just the pressure. The tension. I've so much going on.'

She rubs at my arm.

'I understand. We all feel the same. We all just seem to be arguing with each other, don't we? We don't seem to be making any progress. Is it, eh… just me, or do you think the Head Juror is doing a poor job?'

'Who, Scarhead?' I say, and then I hold my hand over my mouth.

She laughs. Not a big laugh. A polite giggle.

'Got nicknames for us all, have you?' she asks. I shake my head, then mouth an apology. Jesus… I'm coming across like a proper bitch. 'He just doesn't have a good rein on the table, does he? He's letting everybody talk over each other. I wish I had have put myself forward to be Head Juror. It's always the bloody men, isn't it?'

'Yes!' I say. 'I was thinking the same. I should have put my hand up too. We'd have handled this a lot better.'

She rubs my arm again.

'I know we're not supposed to talk about our delibera-tions without the others all present, but… you really believe they're not guilty?' she asks me.

I slap my hand on top of hers and hold it firm against my arm.

'I do,' I reply. And in that moment I immediately get the sense that she's in the same boat as I am. She *has* to be getting blackmailed too.

'Do you?' I ask, whispering.

She sniffs up her nose.

'I don't know what to believe exactly,' she says. 'I just think we — as a jury — owe it to the twins and everyone involved in this case to argue this out in as much detail as we can. I hope they aren't found guilty. They really shouldn't…' she shakes her head. 'Kids being tried in Dublin's Criminal Courts… it's not right. They should have been tried as chil-dren in a children's court.'

I stand there staring into her eyes, my hand still clasped on top of hers.

'Yeah, you're right,' is all I can say.

She tilts her chin to her chest and stares at me. I want to ask her out straight if somebody texted her her dirtiest secret last night and is blackmailing her to ensure a not guilty verdict. I wonder what her secret is. Probably an affair as well. Though she's no ring. Must be something else. Maybe she's fucking her boss. Or maybe she's a high-class hooker or something. I don't know.

'Remember I said to you that I've so much going though my mind?' I say, ready to open up to her. She nods. And as she does, I take a deep breath. 'Well it's just, eh… it's just—'

Knuckles rattle against the door.

'Ladies, I really need to use the loo.'

DAY TWO

He looked like trouble the moment I laid eyes on him. The faded tattoos of Chinese symbols on his knuckles and an in-flight swift on the side of his hand gave that away. It was hugely ironic that he would be a racist piece of shit, yet thought nothing of it to brand himself with a foreign language for the rest of his life.

'Whatcha want?' he grunted.

He looked old, weathered. About seventy, with tightly-shaved hair that was so short and so white that it glistened.

I held my badge in front of his face.

'Mr Nevin, I'd like to speak to you about the double homicide of Clive and Dorothy Tiddle.'

Nevin opened his door further, giving me space to walk in, and as I did he tutted.

'Tragic, that is,' he said. 'I hope you don't think I did it.'

His house was tiny. A small two up, two down in a tight cul-de sac estate at the foothill of the mountains.

'Just making inquiries,' I said.

He led me to his sitting room which was mostly taken up by an oversized TV screen.

'Clive and Dorothy invited many strange people to that church of theirs… I guess…' he shrugged.

'You guess what, Mr Nevin?'

'Well, I guess something like this was bound to happen, wasn't it?'

I stared him up and down.

'You mean their deaths were "bound to happen"… as in you knew they were going to happen?'

He shook his head and delivered a slimey snigger from the side of his mouth.

'No, no, that's not what I'm saying at all, Detective. All's I'm sayin' is they hung around with enough dodgy people that I'm really not as surprised as everybody else in this town seems to be.'

I asked if I could sit, and when he signalled that I should with a wave of his hand, he sat too. On the sofa opposite me.

'Funny you say they hung around with "dodgy people"— as that's the reason I'm here, Mr Nevin. I've heard that you had an issue with the types of people Clive and Dorothy invited to their church.'

He sniggered. Again.

'Is that what's bein' said?' He rubbed at the stubble on his chin, then leaned forward, his forearms on his knees. 'Detective, I am not a racist. I am not… what's the word… the one beginning with X?' He clicked his fingers.

'Xenophobic?'

'That's the one. I'm not xenophobic either.'

'Well, that's not what I have heard, Mr Nevin. I have been informed you had a problem with the colour of some of the churchgoers' skin.'

He reproduced his snigger; same puff of laughter from the side of his mouth.

'I don't care about the colour of their skin. I care about where I live. You don't get many nicer areas in Dublin than this one. I've lived here all me life. I like the quiet. I like the people. We just need to keep it that way.'

I sat forward.

'As in, you just want white people walking these narrow country lanes?'

'There y'go again, Detective. Making it all about skin colour.'

'You call the churchgoers "darkies"—that's what I've heard. "Darkies". What are you referring to when you call them "darkies"? The colour of their shoes?'

'I only used that phrase to explain them. To describe them. So people know who I'm talkin' about.'

'So it is about skin colour,' I said.

He stood up.

'Whatever, Detective. Either way, look where hanging around with different skin colours got Tiddle and his Mrs, eh? A first–class ticket to Heaven.'

My phone buzzed in my pocket. But I wasn't to be distracted.

'You think one of the churchgoers did it?' I asked.

'Course they did. It was hardly anyone who lives around here now was it? When is anybody killed around this neck of the woods? Can't remember a murder around here in my lifetime.'

He opened his sitting room door, inviting me to leave. I could tell he was starting to feel uncomfortable.

'Nice tatts,' I said as I stood and made my way towards him. 'Mind if I…' I held my hands out, and after a slight pause he formed two balls of fists and then held them up. The swallow on the outside of his left hand was blue, but it had practically faded into an outline. And the Chinese symbols, I'm sure, were meant to be black, but were now a tired-looking cracked charcoal.

'What do they mean?'

'War,' he replied, flexing his left fist. 'And peace,' he said.

I grinned.

'Clever,' I said, gripping both of his fists so I could stare at them more closely. Then I turned his hands over and asked him to open them.

It was a good gut instinct.

'Mr Nevin, where did you get this cut from?' I asked.

It was a fresh wound, about four centimeters in length, inside his right palm.

'Doing the lawn,' he said. Then he looked at me all funny. 'So you *do* think I did it?'

'I'm just following all lines of enquiries, Nevin.'

'Well, are you arresting me because I have a cut on my hand, Detective?'

I paused and then shook my head before I reached inside my blazer pocket for my notepad. As soon as I took it out he placed his hand on top of it. 'No need for that, Detective. If you aren't arresting me, your time here is up. Send my sympathies to those two young girls they have. Though in my opinion, I'm pretty sure their pain is actually just ending now.'

'Sorry?' I squinted at him.

'No more cult shit for them to go through. They can grow up to be normal. As regular as you can be after finding your parents dead, I guess. But I bet any money in the world that their lives will end up better now than the shitty ones they would've had playing apostles.'

I leaned closer to him.

'You're not the nicest of men, are you, Nevin?'

He sniggered that horrible snigger again, then reached for the handle of his front door and yanked it open.

'Bye, Detective,' he said.

I was fuming when I stepped outside, but the air helped me to slowly breathe it down.

I had missed calls from both Fairweather and Tunstead while I was in there. So I jabbed my finger at Fairweather's name when I got back into the car.

'Hey, boss,' I said.

Silence. I always knew she was going to deliver bad news when she started with silence.

'Quayle… Laurence Ashe has been on to me. He wants Tallaght to take over the investigation. Thinks it's too big for us to handle.'

'I'm right on top of this, Fairweather,' I said. 'It hasn't even been two days; we've not even heard from SOCO yet. I'm pretty sure that as soon as we get results back from the lab, we'll know exactly where we stand.'

There was another silence.

'They seem to think they know who did it. They're leaning towards the twins… and they feel your questioning of them this morning was too… too "protective", they said.'

'Listen. I circled a knuckle around my temple. 'They are two nine-year-old girls who just lost their parents. There is no need for us to start throwing accusations at them, especially when I have another lead… somebody Clive Tiddle had a strong falling out with.'

'What are you talking about?'

'A Tommo Nevin. He's a racist piece of shit. He didn't like the Tiddles overcrowding the area with immigrants. I've literally just pulled away from his house now… fucker is hiding something. And get this… he had a nasty scratch on the palm of his right hand.'

Fairweather fell silent again. And as she did I slapped at my steering wheel. I wasn't frustrated with Fairweather. I never have been. I was pissed off with Tunstead. The prick had been telling me him and Lowe were willing to support me, but they must have been going behind my back and bitching to their boss about how I was handling the case.

'Interesting,' Fairweather finally said. 'But, eh... Ashe is wondering why you haven't yet corroborated the twins' story? They say they were at dance class when the murder happened. And I know two Tallaght Detectives spoke to the dance teacher and she confirmed that they were there between eleven and twelve that afternoon. But why have you not spoken to her yourself yet?'

I rubbed my knuckle deeper into my temple.

'I'm gonna speak to Claire Barry now,' I said. 'I'm not that far from the dance studio. I'll be able to rule out the fact that the twins seemed distracted when they were dancing on Saturday morning.'

'Ms Claire already confirmed to Tallaght that Faith was particularly silent during that lesson. That's what Ashe told me.'

I sighed. A deep sigh.

'See... this is what happens when cops like Ashe make accusations when in truth they don't know the personnel involved in the case. Faith is *always* quiet. She's practically mute.'

'Well, Detectives Tunstead and Lowe seem to think the twins—'

'Fuck Tunstead and Lowe!' I shouted. 'They are the ones supporting *me* in this case. And I'd appreciate support from you, too.'

'Of course. Of course,' she said. 'I'll have words with Ashe and let him know you are confident you can see this investigation through.'

I looked up at the sky through my windscreen and hocked a frustrated grunt at it.

'Listen, Fairweather,' I said. 'I'm sorry. I shouldn't be shouting at you. I'm on this. I've got it.'

By the time we'd hung up, I was already at the gate of the new-built hut that sat on the edge of the mountains about a mile away from the Tiddle bungalow.

I walked up to it, noticed the cheap signage that read 'CDC Dance Studio' and pressed at the buzzer.

Claire was lovely. Pretty. Tall. And slim. Very slim. With long, long hair that went all the way down past her bum. She held an extremely sorrowful, pale gaze all the way through my meeting with her; was shaking almost.

'Ms Claire, I believe you told a colleague of mine that Faith was particularly quiet on Saturday during her class. Faith is always quiet, is she not?'

'Oh Detective Quayle, I don't know what to believe. I've barely slept a wink since I heard the news. I just keep thinking back to how the twins were in my class on Saturday. It's hard to take in that two killers may have been doing ballet and tap just over there minutes after stabbing their parents to death.'

'Hold on... is that what you believe? That Faith and Grace are capable of this?'

'Oh... I don't know what to believe...'

I held my hand to hers. Just to stop it from shaking.

'How long have you known Faith and Grace?' I asked.

'They've been coming to my studio for over two years.'

I pulled the chair I was sitting on slightly closer to Claire.

'And knowing them for over two years, do you believe they are capable of murder?'

Claire raised her shoulders towards her ears.

'The Tiddle family... y'know... they're just... they're just...' She paused and pursed her lips at me.

'Go on, Claire.'

'I don't want to be one of those anti-religious types. People are free to believe what they want to believe. But I always found all four of them quite... *odd*. There's always been something strange about that family.'

'So you knew Clive and Dorothy, too?'

She held a shaking hand to her face.

'One or the other used to drop the girls off to begin with. Then the girls started coming to class by themselves.'

'And you've always found the twins odd, too?'

'Just different. They don't pal around or even talk to the other girls. They just sneak off into a corner during break times and whisper to each other.'

I sat back in my chair.

'I find them odd, too, Claire, I must admit. But being odd or believing in a God doesn't make you a killer.' She began to sob, so I leaned forward and gripped her hand again. 'Claire… don't allow their uniqueness to cloud your judgement. I just want to know what time Faith and Grace showed up here at on Saturday, and what time they left at.'

She looked at me with her glazed eyes and nodded again.

'Yeah, yeah. They got here at about five to twelve, as they always do. Left when the class was over, as they always do. They were certainly here alright… they were here for the full hour.'

'Then it couldn't have been them, could it?'

She sniffed up her nose.

'So Clive and Dorothy were killed while the twins were here?' she asked.

I tapped my fingers against the back of her hand, unaware of the exact answer to her question. Early indications had been the deceased weren't long dead by the time I arrived. But we still hadn't heard from the coroner on the exact time of death.

'We think so,' I said, just to dampen her sobs.

She was too nice to be this upset.

I had more missed calls while I spoke to Claire, but didn't check them until I got back to my car. I immediately assumed a lot of them were Tunstead… again. But they weren't. They were mostly from my wife.

I pressed at her name.

'Denis, Denis.' Sheila sounded panicky, out of breath. 'Come home. Quick. I—I—' Then the line went dead.

ALICE

S carhead picks up the sheets of paper in front of him, then clears his throat.

"'Yes, it is true. I did tell the policeman that I thought Faith was particularly quiet in class that day. But it wasn't just her quietness... I don't know. She seemed a little dazed, though I have to say, she danced for the full hour of that class.'" Scarhead looks up at us, then continues reading.

"'But on reflection, I just can't quite put my finger on it. I've thought about that day, that dance class, a thousand times at least in the two years or whatever it's been and I just...'"

'She shook her head saying that,' Red Head pipes up.

'Yep,' I say, agreeing with her. 'It was like she wanted to say Faith was quiet that day, but the more and more she's thought about it over the months, she's not sure what she believes exactly.'

Acne Girl, who normally disagrees with me, nods her head.

'Yeah, that's the impression I get from her, too. Claire

Barry's testimony was kinda… what's the word… indifferent. It didn't make me believe the twins were guilty at all.'

'So what did, then?' I ask.

'Now hold on here,' Scarhead pipes up. 'We're not quizzing jurors on their reasons for their verdict vote earlier, we are discussing the testimony of an important witness here. Claire Barry spent the next hour in the company of Faith and Grace right after they killed their parents and—'

'That's only if you think they killed them,' I say, as snappy as I possibly can.

I was gaining confidence. Finally sitting upright, finally arguing my side.

Nobody seemed to pay me any attention when Red Head and I walked back out of the toilet. I was glad of that. Because it meant they hadn't been talking about me when I was gone. As soon as we sat down beside each other, Scarface began to read the testimony he had requested from the court. I felt sorry for Claire Barry when she was on the stand. She looked stressed, as if she had been worried sick about her day in court every day for the past twenty months. She constantly sipped from the glass of water in front of her, asking the court clerk for a refill every ten minutes or so. Her hand shook every time she took the glass to her mouth for the full hour and a half she was on that stand. It was almost as if she was the one on trial.

'And then Bracken said to her,' Scarhead continues, '"So you say Faith is always quiet in class, yes?"'

'"Yes."'

'"And you say Faith danced for the full hour of this class… does she always dance for the full hour in your classes?"'

'"Yes."'

'"Well, then… I'm wondering what the difference is… if Faith is always quiet in your class, and Faith is always dancing in your class, what was the difference between this

Saturday and every other Saturday? I suggest, Ms Barry, that when you were asked by police if the twins had acted strange in your class on the Saturday in question, you said Faith was quiet, because she *was* quiet. But I put it to you that on reflection you have realised that what you said to the police wasn't out of the ordinary at all. That is all, Your Honour.'"

'Yeah, he sounded really smarmy the way he ended his questioning of her so abruptly,' Thick-rimmed Glasses says. I agree with him. He did. Bracken oozes smarmy. I didn't think his questioning of Claire Barry went that well for the defence at all to be honest. He came across as if he was bullying her, trying to convince her that she was confused. He didn't let her answer his last point, he just flung an accusation at her and then told the judge he was done.

'True,' the old woman with the oversized bust says. 'I think the whole court liked Claire. And by undermining her, Mr Bracken lost that particular battle.'

'It's not a battle,' I say. And then all eyes turn back to me. 'Listen,' I say, easing the potential tension. 'It's true to say that Claire Barry should have been a great witness for the prosecution. Her witness statement was one of the main reasons the detectives were focused on the twins in the first place. Part of my problem is that the detectives didn't really look into any other suspects.'

'Its not our job to play detective,' Thick-rimmed Glasses says.

'I know that... I know... it's just that it's our job to either suggest that twins did this beyond all reasonable doubt, or simply that it wasn't proven beyond reasonable doubt. And even here... Claire's testimony...' I say, pointing at the sheets of paper in front of me. 'It offers nothing definite, just like all the other evidence offers nothing definite. That's why we need to find Faith and Grace not guilty. The case simply wasn't proven.'

The entire table falls silent. I must have struck a chord. That was my best moment so far.

'Hmmm,' the young girl with the braces says, nodding her head.

'You, eh… you seem to be wavering now,' Red Head says to her.

It's exactly what I had been thinking.

'No, she's not wavering. We all know the twins did this—'

'Hold on!' Red Head says, interrupting the man with the thick-rimmed glasses. 'How are you feeling now, Lisa?'

Lisa. The girl with the braces' name. Doesn't matter that I've just learned her name. I won't remember it. I sit closer, leaning my arms onto the table, willing her to say she's going to change her mind, that she wants to vote not guilty.

'Truth is, I'm pretty certain in my heart of hearts they did this,' she says. *Shit!* 'But, I kind of agree with you and, eh… Alice.' I smile at her. 'I don't think the prosecution really proved the case.'

'Well if you think they did it, then you must find them guilty,' Scarhead says, and then the table goes off on one again. Everybody talking. Nobody listening.

'Hold on! Hold on!' Acne Girl shouts. She's usually mute. Which is why her shouting shuts everyone up instantly. 'I believe they did it too,' she says quietly. 'I — *one-hundred percent* — believe they did it. It doesn't matter to me if Faith was particularly quiet or regular quiet in that dance class, because I am sure that they are cold and calculated enough to dance their little asses off as if nothing had happened that morning. They had the time to do it, too. I know there was a huge argument over timelines. But let's face facts on that. Clive and Dorothy could have been stabbed between ten-thirty and ten forty-five—which is before the twins left the house. They're guilty.'

'But sure, Clive and Dorothy could easily have been killed

between ten forty-five and eleven,' Red Head says. 'The experts said it was any time between ten-thirty and eleven. So, just as easily as the twins could have done it before they left, somebody else also could have done it after the twins left. Timing doesn't win the argument here, either way.'

Scarhead groans into his hands.

'Jeez,' he says. 'The argument is: did the twins have time to do it? Yes, is the answer. They had time. Simple as.'

Red Head looks at me, as if I am the one armed with the rebuttal to what Scarhead has just said. I don't, though. He's right. The timing issue comes down to 'could the twins conceivably had time to do this?' And they could. Conceivably.

'Well, I don't believe they did it,' is all I can say. 'Ye know what… we left something out of the verdict vote we had earlier.' I don't know how I got here. I think I just wanted to change the subject. Or maybe it's because the girl with the braces is on my mind. She sounded like she might be wavering. 'We never made *undecided* an option. We just said guilty or not guilty. I bet some people in here are undecided. Would you all mind…' I say, looking sheepishly around the table at them all, 'if I asked you to put up your hand if you are undecided with your verdict.'

Scarhead tuts. But nobody else says anything. And then the young guy with the high quiff who voted not guilty earlier sticks his hand in the air. Bollocks. This is backfiring on me. I've lost one from my team. But then the girl with the braces reluctantly raises an open palm too. Half-arsedly.

'What does this prove?' Scarhead says.

'Not much,' I reply. 'I wanted the vote to be just and true. We never gave an option for undecided and it is a legitimate stance for any of us to take right now.'

He huffs. Like only one of those blokes who hates it when a woman stands up for herself huffs.

'It's okay,' I whisper to the girl with the braces. 'You can put your hand down now.'

Everybody turns to Scarhead, wondering where he is going to lead us next. He coughs, then sifts through his paperwork.

'We could, eh...'

A knock at the door saves him from his awkwardness. Red Head beats me to it, getting up first and answering it. I watch her nod her head before she turns to us.

'Lunch time,' she says.

Some don't even hesitate. They're on their feet. Though I have to admit, I'm eager to get to that dining room myself. Arguing does work up an appetite.

Braces is the last the leave the room. I hold back at the door, and wait for her.

'Hey,' I say, offering my brightest smile. 'I eh... hope you don't feel as if I put you on the spot asking about undecided jurors.'

'No, no. Not at all,' she says, 'I mean, I'm here for my voice and my opinion, so I gotta speak up. Thank you for allowing me to have a say.'

I place my hand on the small of her back as we walk the maze of corridors.

'You really are undecided, huh? Ye know, if you have any doubt at all, you gotta go with not guilty.'

'I know... I know, it's just—'

'I mean, I'm sorry, I don't wanna tell you what to do...' I'm whispering now because we've just caught up with the others, all standing in a line outside the dining room door. The young woman dressed all in black unlocks it with her overly big bunch of keys and then we all head inside.

'I don't think you're telling me what to do,' she whispers back to me. 'It's just I've thought all the way through this that they were guilty. In fact, every witness who took that stand seems to think they did it.'

'Not really,' I whisper back really quietly as we take our seats across from each each other at the end of the table. It's not like the table from the Jury Room. It's more rectangular, more restaurant-like. 'Detective Quayle didn't think they were guilty, now did he? And he was lead detective on the case.'

Her eyes squint and then her head starts to nod. I think the penny might be dropping with her. I'm doing well at this.

'Perhaps you're right,' she says.

I lean closer to her. Give her my best puppy dog eyes.

'Lisa, think about it, you can not—'

'Hey, you two…' Scarhead shouts down from the top of the table. 'Hope you're not discussing the trial.'

I grin a fake smile at him and shake my head.

'We weren't,' I lie.

'Good. Because I was about to suggest we don't discuss the trial at all. Let's give ourselves a break. To enjoy some lunch. Don't know about you all, but I'm starving.'

The young woman dressed in all black places a plate of ham and mash in front of me, then stretches across to place one in front of Braces. Our eyes meet through the steam of our lunch, and then everything goes quiet.

✝

The two hundred and forty pounds Clive and Dorothy took in the collection basket at their very first mass would be — by quite some margin — the least amount they would ever take in.

Even before Faith and Grace were born, their weekly pull was averaging over the one thousand euro mark. Following the arrival of the twins, that amount instantly doubled, then trebled as Clive really got to grips with marketing his sermons. He had long since given up trying to convince Dubliners that the answers to all the questions they ever wanted to ask lay somewhere within the book he would preach from. Dublin folk had taken too long as it was finally catching their breath after the suffocation brought to them by the Catholic church. They had only just woken up—and weren't remotely interested in falling back asleep.

So Clive had a brainwave. He recruited immigrants; foreigners, lost souls he could find in the city centre. He bought a bus, had somebody brand the side of it with stickers that consisted of a crucifix and the title "The New St Benedict's Church" and then set about recruiting loners in the city. He promised them tea and Jammy Dodger biscuits — which he always delivered — as well as an ear. It was everything these lost souls had ever wanted.

✝

Over the years the Tiddles welcomed over ten thousand people to their church. Christian folk like to come and go. A lot of believers are actually much more liberal than their reputations suggest. They like to travel and often just kip on other 'family' member's sofas — anywhere in the world — as a means of getting around. It's a bohemian, non-conventional way of living. That's one of the most redeeming features of the communities that grow from churches— they really feel as if they are all in it together. The community centre actually packed one thousand people in to the large room Clive and Dorothy had converted in to a church in one day. It was for the double christening of Faith and Grace. Some folk even flew from so far as Melbourne to attend.

Even aunt Janet — Clive's sister — and her husband, uncle Eoin, turned up. She was irked that she wasn't a Godparent, but her complaints fell on deaf ears.

'I'm the only blood relative you've got!' she snapped at Clive. He barely responded, but to say he wanted people who believed in God to actually be Godparents. He never even thought to consider Janet. In fact, he was loathe to even invite her and her husband as he knew they would both turn up in tracksuits. They were never out of tracksuits.

The Godparents to Grace were married couple Corey and Dana Calisis who Clive and Dorothy were really close with at the time, but who had since moved back to California. Faith's Godparents were Paul Doughtery—an Irish guy who was influential in helping Clive and Dorothy set up their church after successfully setting up his own in the outskirts of Cork, and Kelly McAllister—a young Scottish lady who had been one of the early recruits of Clive and Dorothy as they went searching in the city. She practically married herself to The New St Benedict's Church as soon as she walked inside that community centre.

They took in almost one hundred thousand euro on the day of the twins' christening; each invitee told not to bother with presents, that a church donation would be most appreciated. The average donation was a hundred euro; offered up by quite a lot of people who couldn't really afford to offer up that much cash. They genuinely didn't mind though; it was another liberal trait of churchgoers. Money wasn't such a big deal. God would provide no matter what.

The twins were three months old when they were christened and so tiny that they almost looked as if they were drowning in their dresses and bows. Dorothy had handmade their gowns; silk-white meringue-style with lace collars and cuffs; complemented by huge white and pink striped bows that were actually bigger than the babies' heads.

Even by this stage it was obvious that the twins had different personalities. Grace was an extrovert, always trying to create noise, to seek attention. Faith was already in her own world; quite often asleep when there were crowds around so as not to receive any attention whatsoever. Often she would just lie there, not necessarily with her eyes closed, but with them rolled to the back of her head.

Grace was such an attention-seeker early in her life that Clive felt a need to put at stop to it. Even when she was just a toddler she would ask too many questions; was full of wonderment. Sometimes she would even stump Clive or Dorothy with questions about the Bible. And out of fear of her doing so in public, Clive sat her down and informed her of her responsibilities and role within the family. Even though he loved her — adored her – and gave her the attention she was seeking most of the time, he couldn't risk her ever being such an extrovert that she would question all of the beliefs he had spent years convincing himself he needed to believe.

'So why don't you just be a bit more like Faith,' he said to her when she was just three years of age. 'Quiet.'

He was so convincing to his daughter — as he always was — that she practically became the opposite of the person she naturally was. She fell into the role of being an introvert; only speaking when being spoken to. It wasn't as if the twins were always quiet. They would converse constantly when alone. Grace would do all of the asking; Faith would make all the decisions.

'What will we do today, Faith, wanna play teddy bears on the rug?'

'What colour bow shall we wear in our hairs today, Faith?'

'Shall we go to the bathroom and do pee-pee now, Faith?'

Grace offered up all of the questions; Faith would stand there, sometimes rolling her eyes to the back of her head in consideration, and would then make the decision.

They were thick as thieves as soon as they were born and didn't mind being stared at in church. It was all they knew. Daddy would help out churchgoers with some wise words and counselling during the week, in between writing his sermons, and Mammy would bake fresh Jammy Dodgers and make tea for anyone whoever visited the community centre. She was practically there full-time and began acting as Clive's sidekick—being a counsellor of sorts. She was very good at what she did, Dorothy. She would always convince folk that their worries were mainly superfluous. After all, 'this is part of God's plan' is a hell of an ace card to have up your sleeve when you are trying to counsel people. Any grievance anybody could possibly ever have would be temporarily settled and calmed by a visit to Dorothy. She would often contradict herself, but she had learned how to talk her way out of any situation. Besides, she was lovely; a real honest woman who genuinely had everybody's best interests at heart. She might not have looked like the nicest and most friendly person in the world — her hooked nose and dated, short hair not particularly appealing — but she did have a kind heart. And kind eyes. Though when it came to the money being generated by the church, her generosity somehow seemed to evaporate. It wasn't that she actually wanted to hide the money from everyone or even steal it in any way; it was genuinely a case that she didn't actually know what to do with it. Neither of them did.

Dorothy was a little sterner with the twins, certainly in comparison to Clive. It would often be her who handed down *punishments or who raised a voice at them. But it was never anything bad. A shouted 'Girls!' if she heard them practising their tap-dancing too loudly in the kitchen or a 'What are you two up to now!?' if she thought they were talking too much in their bedrooms. She never hit them. Never even considered it. Her punishments consisted of the twins having to do extra chores around the house—or, more often than not, a lengthy prayer session. She pretty much raised the twins how she was raised: stern, fair and smothered in traditionalisms... as well, of course, as old-fashioned floral dresses and oversized hair bows.*

In truth it was mainly Grace who found herself on her knees praying as a course of discipline; she was always the loudest. Not necessarily with her voice, as Clive had well and truly stemmed that, but with almost everything else she did. She couldn't help it. Although both girls were slight and light, Grace running around the house would sound like a refrigerator falling down a staircase; whereas Faith moved with such considered carefulness that often Clive and Dorothy wouldn't even hear her entering a room.

Faith did, one day, get in to a lot of trouble for not listening to her father. He had been trying to tell her that her dinner was almost ready and that she needed to come to the kitchen. But she didn't hear him. She was too busy zoning out, doing that thing she does when she rolls her eyes to the back of her head.

'I called your name five times!' Clive snapped.

Faith turned out her bottom lip as an offer of apology. But she was sent to her bedroom to pray for twenty minutes nonetheless, ensuring the dinner she would eventually eat afterwards would be cold.

'Why do you do that... the eye thing?' Grace asked her that night. Faith squinted at her sister, and tilted her head. 'Y'know... the eye thing,' Grace said, and then she rolled her eyes into the back of her head to show her sister what she meant.

Faith's brow pointed downwards. She was truly confused

'What do you mean?' she asked.

'Well...' Grace threw the covers off her legs and sat on the edge of her bed. 'Sometimes you're praying and stuff... and then you just go all quiet and....' She rolled her eyes again to the back of her head.

'Oh, do I?' Faith said, grinning. 'I guess that's when I'm listening.'

'Listening?' Grace said. 'Listening to what?'

'To him,' Faith replied. 'To Jesus.'

DAY TWO—DAY THREE

I must have paced the corridor a thousand times before the door finally snatched open.

As soon as it did, the rate of my heart slowed, because the first thing I saw was the doctor smiling at me.

Sheila was sitting up in the bed and although she looked paler than normal, she seemed to be back to herself: giving out to me.

'You should've gone back to work, Denis,' she said. 'Y'know he's working on the big case you are reading about in the papers ever day, doctor. He's lead detective.'

The doctor formed an "O" shape with his mouth.

'The, eh... religious family up in the Dublin mountains? What a strange one that is. Anywhere near to finding out who did it?'

I shook my head.

'Sorry doctor... you know as much as I do about confidentiality in the workplace.'

'Of course,' he said, almost embarrassed that he asked in the first place. 'Anyway... Sheila has recovered remarkably well in the past couple of hours. She was just too dehydrated.

That's all. We've run some tests and we should have the results back soon. But seems to me as if she's been starving herself of water. Two litres. Every day. It's very important.'

I inched closer to the bed and pursed my lips at her.

'So... what kind of tests did you run?' I asked the doctor, whilst still staring at my wife.

'It's nothing to worry about. More routine than anything. I wanted to run another ultrasound to the stomach. Just to monitor the tumour.'

'Think you'll have any results tonight?' I asked.

'Earliest will be first thing in the morning,' the doc replied. Then he stepped closer to the bed too. The opposite side of it to me. 'Sheila is adamant she will not undergo any more chemotherapy... said the two of you have spoken at length about this.'

I grabbed my wife's hand and brought it to my mouth to kiss her knuckles.

'Never again, doctor. She's never felt worse than she did during those months. It was fading her away.'

'Well, we're mightily impressed how healthy she's keeping. Without any medication for the past few months, she seems more than reasonably healthy.'

'It's the weed, doc.' Sheila said, laughing. I glared at her, my eyebrows dipped. 'Oh, it's okay, Denis.' She waved her hand. 'Everything said in this room is just between the three of us, isn't it Doc?' She didn't wait for him to reply. 'I've been vaping some cannabis. And I've... I've never felt better. Well, not since I was young anyway. It's a miracle plant. It hasn't only put an end to the cramps in my stomach, it's stopped the misery in my head, too. I'm never in a bad mood. Not anymore. I love it. In fact... I'm gonna send Denis home to pick up my vapouriser so I can have a puff out in that garden there.' She nodded out of the ward window, to the decking below.

The doctor held his clipboard close to his chest, then smiled out of one side of his mouth.

'We've been hearing some eye-opening research on cannabis,' he said. 'But I'm, eh... I'm no expert on it. Far as I know it's still illegal here.' Then he touched Sheila's shoulder and looked at me. 'Detective.' He nodded and made his way to the doorway, where he paused and turned back. 'I've informed Sheila we'll be keeping her in overnight. We want to keep her hooked up to the intravenous so she can rehydrate.' Then he smiled at us both and pulled the door closed.

I turned to my wife as soon as he was gone, my eyebrows dipping again.

'Relax, Denis,' she said. 'You heard him yourself. He's only heard good stuff about the research that's going on.'

I leaned in, kissed her forehead and then sat in one of those uncomfortable blue plastic chairs for the next two hours, telling her all about my day.

We were only disturbed once. By Fairweather. Ringing to tell me the media were constantly on to her looking for an update on the case, and she felt she could no longer palm them off. She insisted I held a press conference the next morning; just to get them out of her hair. So I agreed. Even though I hadn't a clue what I could — or even should — tell them yet.

She also informed me that aunt Janet had been tracked down and would be making her way to Dublin in the coming days. Johnny, who had contacted her, said she hadn't been very specific on when she would make the trip, nor did she seem to be in any rush.

'She sounds weird. And cold,' Sheila said when I filled her in. 'Ye think *she* did it?'

I laughed. Told her again she needed to stop living inside one of her novels.

I did go home. To pick up the vapouriser. Then I escorted

her downstairs, into the vacant garden decking that was reserved for smokers, and stared at her in the moonlight as she exhaled vapour. The weed always has an immediate effect on her mood; her lips turn upwards and her eyes widen. Just like old times. It was cold that night, but we stayed outside on that wooden decking for over an hour and shot the breeze; about the case, about her illness, about the fact that we never had kids, about travelling the world. That topic was bound to come up any time we spoke at length. We love Tuscany. And Florida. We often go to Florida. But just for two weeks a year. Like normal people. Sheila always had dreams of me retiring and us having the freedom to travel. Though that was before she was diagnosed with stomach cancer. Like most folk tend to do, we stupidly planned that the best years of our lives would be for a time a lot of people don't actually get to see.

It was gone one a.m. when I finally crawled into bed that night. Though I still couldn't sleep. There was too much to think about. Clive and Dorothy. Faith and Grace. Tommo Nevin. Clare Barry. But I was mostly tossing and turning with thoughts about my wife's results; fearful the doctor was going to inform us that it's chemo or bust. I didn't want to watch her fade away again.

My biggest fear, ever since I met Sheila, has always been losing her. And I really thought I was going to at the start of that year. She looked awful. Her hair and eyebrows had disappeared and I could almost fully grasp her whole waist with my two hands. But she gained some weight and grew her hair back as soon as she decided to come off the chemo. And her mood picked up. That's because when we went online to find the best alternatives to chemotherapy in order to reduce the size of a cancerous tumour, cannabis kept screaming at us as the answer.

It was Tunstead who woke me up. Constantly ringing. He

rang four times between seven a.m. and seven thirty. But when I eventually sat up in bed, I rang Sheila rather than him.

She was adamant that she would be coming home later that morning, once she got the intravenous out of her arm. She didn't seem as worried about the results as I was; had long since given up caring about how much time she had left. Her mantra had been "quality, not quantity," ever since she sucked in her first hit of cannabis.

'Right, you're doing this at the church, you all set?' Fairweather said to me as soon as I arrived at the station.

'Doing what?' I asked.

'Your press conference.'

'Press conference?' my voice went all high-pitched. 'I just thought you wanted me to release a statement or something.'

Fairweather looked at me, displaying *my* confusion on *her* face. Then she shrugged her shoulders.

'It's a press conference, Quayle,' she said. 'And it starts in twenty minutes, so you need to get your ass over there.'

'Alright… alright…' I said. 'Let's get going then.'

She shook her head.

'I've, eh… I've an eight-thirty tee time.'

I didn't respond; didn't even bother to laugh. Or sigh. I just swiped my keys from my desk and headed for my car. It didn't surprise me that Fairweather didn't disrupt her plans while this investigation was going on. This case was the last thing she wanted. She was used to the quiet life… yearned for the quiet life. I knew she was going to retire once this was over. She couldn't risk her routine being put out like this again. I reckoned Fairweather did more work in those five days than she had done in the two decades I was working with her prior to them. And yet she still fitted in two rounds of eighteen holes.

'Do you not answer your fuckin' calls?' Tunstead barely

waited for me to open my car door when I pulled into the community centre car park.

'Relax, Tunstead. I have more important things going on than making sure I get back to you without hesitating.'

He was about to fume back at me, but Lowe rubbed his arm, calmed him down.

'I was wondering if you wanted me to take this press conference. I've done a dozen of these—'

'I know what I'm doing,' I snapped. I didn't. Not at all. In fact, I really wanted to accept his offer, especially after I'd walked into the church to see an ocean of TV cameras. But I didn't. Because I didn't want him to think I thought he was a better cop than me.

'Just don't use anybody's names. Except the deceased. If you mention Grace and Faith by name, you will damage any case we bring to the courts. They are too young to be named. Don't reduce the chances of us getting a verdict.'

I stared at him, then at Lowe.

'You two still think it was them, don't you?' I tutted. Then I walked down the aisle of the church, and pursed my lips in sorrow at a crying Kelly McAllister before taking my seat at a makeshift table just in front of the stage.

My heart rate definitely rose. I could feel it. Then I went and spilled the jug of water over the table when I tried to pick it up to pour myself a glass. My hands were too sweaty. It just dropped. Then smashed. And the water splashed everywhere.

It took a tiny army of people to come to my rescue before everything was set up and ready to go again. I could see one of the journalists growing with impatience; her director yelling into her ear.

As soon as everything was set back up, she was the first to speak.

'So, Detective Quayle, can you read your statement out before answering some of our questions?'

'Sorry,' I said. 'A statement?'

She stared at me, then at the journalist beside her.

'We were told you would have a statement to make on the double homicide of Clive and Dorothy Tiddle, Detective. The nation is waiting. We are live…'

ALICE

Scarhead made the decision to not discuss the trial without even consulting the rest of us. He just proclaimed that we'd all benefit from giving our minds a rest by enjoying some food. In fairness, I think everybody around the table agreed with him, because nobody questioned his proclamation.

So the twelve of us talked about ourselves instead over lunch; the guy with the thick-rimmed glasses welcoming us all to open up a bit about our livelihoods—asking us about our jobs. We listened to each other as we chewed on our ham. Everybody seemed different over lunch. More relaxed. More themselves. Even Scarhead showed some redeeming qualities. I wouldn't have put him down as a hairdresser. Though after he'd told us he ran his own unisex salon in north county Dublin I did, for the first time, notice he does have a particularly trendy cropped do himself. I hadn't looked at it. My eyes never went above that scar.

The girl with the braces — who I constantly tried to make eye contact with across the lunch table for nothing more than to purse my lips at her and let her know that I've got her back — is an insurance consultant in Fullams Accountancy. Red Head owns her own architectural firm, and she lectures on architecture part-time at Trinity College. Impressive. Quiff Guy is a student, but he's also the lead singer in a band. Sinono, they're called. He said they get thousands of hits on Instagram every day… whatever that means.

I told them I work in catering. Which I do. But I kinda egged myself up a bit; saying I provide for high-end corporate events. I don't really. I provide for the odd party here and there, picking up business through word of mouth. I don't have to work. Not really. Noel's job brings in enough for the entire house to run like clockwork. But I didn't want to be a housewife. I always assumed I'd have a career. That I'd be a chef; working in some super cool restaurant. Maybe even open a restaurant of my own. But ambitions like that are hard to fulfill if you're a woman, and almost definitely if you are a woman who wants a family.

My diploma is in culinary arts. I knew what I wanted to do as soon as I left school. And straight from college I got a job in a cute little restaurant in Malahide. The commute was a bit of a bitch, but I enjoyed the heat of the kitchen and stayed there for four years until just after I'd met and fallen in love with Noel. Even then he was bringing in close to a hundred grand a year. So he constantly asked me why was I bothering to travel all the way to the coast every day to earn myself a measly few quid. And I guess when I fell pregnant with Zoe it just made sense that I would never go back. I had a baby to raise, after all. Between Zoe and the absolute struggle we went through to have Alfie, I set up my own sideline business: Sheridan Catering. Just to stave off the tag of 'housewife' more than anything. I provide for friends' and family's parties. But that's essentially all I do. Every now and then. Whenever the phone rings.

I don't resent Noel in any way for having the high-flying

career while I twiddle my thumbs for most hours of the day. I've just come to realise that that's how it is for women. We always get the shitty end of the stick. But I guess it's just as well we get it—could you imagine the fucking headache it would be for all of humanity if it was men who got the shitty end of the stick?

Scarhead took his time figuring out where we should take our deliberations when we settled back around the jurors' table after lunch—shuffling his paperwork around, trying to appear as if he knew what he was doing.

After a few prompts and inputs from others around the table he eventually decided we should continue to deliberate Detective Quayle's testimony. I guess it made sense. We seemed divided right down the middle on how Quayle handled the investigation from the get-go.

Quayle was an odd one. I kinda liked him. He smiled up at us all when he was on the stand and even bowed to us gently after he was done. But I would certainly question whether or not he is a decent detective. He looked too timid, too nice, to deal with such serious matters. Though maybe the stereotype of a detective being a bit of a wise-guy smar-tarse is only down to the glorification of that profession on TV. I think it was Quayle's moustache that made him look friendly; he kept playing with it, spreading it out with his thumb and forefinger before he answered most questions put to him.

'I think that he looked a little awkward in that press conference the defence team played for us, but that's the only reason anybody is questioning whether or not he did a good job,' says the old woman with the oversized bust.

She, like me, seems to have a soft spot for Quayle.

'It wasn't just the bumbling press conference, was it though? He went on record with Faith and Grace's lawyer a couple days later and said that the twins didn't do it. Then he arrested them and is now not sure whether they did or didn't do it.' Thick-rimmed Glasses was speaking, tightening the knot Quayle seemed to get himself entangled up in through the course of the entire investigation. The detective refused to say on the stand whether or not he felt the twins were guilty. Yet he was the one who went on record a couple of times admitting he didn't think they did it. And that was before he arrested them five days after the murders. He called out to Janet Petersen's house — where Faith and Grace had ended up following the death of their parents — and placed them both under arrest for double homicide. Then he retired from the job. He just said he had enough of it and left. He was asked, on the stand, whether or not he received a handsome pay-off for his twenty-five years of service. But he refused to answer that too, backed by the judge who agreed the answer to that line of questioning was redundant. Quayle was a witness for the prosecution but it was really hard to determine whose side he was on exactly. I think that's why he fascinated us jurors. And probably why our minds were split on his testimony.

He had said, and we all heard it played over and over again in court, at the press conference he did two days after the murders that there was 'just one suspect' in the case. And then we heard a voice recording of him talking to Gerd Bracken two nights after that, insisting the twins were not the main suspects. Yet, he arrested them a little over twenty-four hours later. No wonder we were all confused by his investigation; no wonder we were spending so long discussing him.

My take on it is that those above Quayle knew the twins were guilty from the off, but he wanted to protect them initially. Probably because he's just a nice guy. But I don't believe he doesn't think they did it. He must know they did it. Because they did do it. They had to have done it. I really wish he had have answered that question in court, because it would have made a huge difference in this jury room. I'm pretty sure Quayle's reluctance to admit the twins are guilty is the reason Red Head and Obese Guy can justify their not guilty verdict. I'm sure it's why the other jurors think I'm holding on to my not guilty verdict too. But it's not. I'm only holding on to mine because some bitch has the recording of me fucking my daughter's boyfriend.

'I don't think he believes they did it,' I say when I'm finally asked for my opinion. 'He didn't believe they did it straight after the killings, didn't think they did it while he was investigating the case and I don't believe he thinks they did it now.'

'You don't know that for certain,' Scarhead says.

'Listen,' I reply to him, 'if he thought they did it, he would have just said so on the stand. He would have just said "I arrested them because I think they're guilty." But ye know why he didn't say that? Ye know why he wouldn't answer that question in court? Because he didn't want to let his former colleagues down. Out of respect, he didn't want to step on the prosecution's arguments.'

'It's such a shame he retired straight after the case,' Thick-rimmed Glasses says. 'If he was still a cop, he would have *had* to admit he thought they did it.'

Thick-rimmed Glasses is right with what he's saying. Quayle retiring straight after this case added a huge dollop of intrigue that otherwise shouldn't have any intrigue at all. It should be simple. Faith and Grace are evil and they killed their parents in cold blood. End of. But Quayle's mis-steps along his investigation offer a sliver of doubt to this case—and that gives us three who are voting not guilty justification for our stance.

'We could talk about how Quayle handled this investigation all day... but as I've said before, he's not the one on trial,' Scarhead says.

'I disagree,' I say. 'I think Detective Quayle is the absolute key in this trial. He investigated the case and is hesitant to say the twins did it. In fact, all he is ever on record as saying is that they *didn't* do it.'

'He was surely on record when he arrested them. So by arresting them he is admitting he believes they did it. He hardly arrested two nine-year-old girls, as they were at the time, thinking they were innocent '

'Uuuugh… we're gonna go round and round in circles talking about this guy.' Thick-rimmed Glasses is starting to flare beetroot red, flapping his arms in the air and reeling back in his chair. 'Why don't we look at more evidence, rather than just trying to second-guess witnesses all the time. Can we look at the cold, hard facts of this case... so that we can all surely come to the same obvious conclusion, here? The twins did this, right. The evidence says—'

'The evidence says fuck all,' I say. A few gasps are heard around the table. I don't know why. I'm not the first to swear in this room today. Nobody gasped before when Scarhead swore.

'Well… what about the stab wounds?' Thick-rimmed Glasses says. And then I reel back in my chair, because the stab wounds are the most significant aspect of this trial. They literally point to the twins being guilty.

DAY THREE

I stormed out of the church furious.
Not embarrassed.

Not mortified.

Not ashamed.

Just furious. Why the hell didn't Fairweather warn me I'd to read out a statement?

I slapped both hands to my face when I got back into the car.

Maybe I should have let Tunstead handle the bloody press conference.

I just rattled off some nonsense about the time of the death being "approximately eleven a.m. on Saturday, the 15th of August", then I suggested we are zoning in on a suspect. When another reporter asked me if I was talking about "a sole suspect, not two?" I immediately knew what he was getting at.

'Just a suspect, at the moment,' I said as sternly as I could, then I called for the "next question".

I couldn't wait to get out of there. When there was a slight hesitation after the fifth question, I just stood up and declared that I needed to get back to work on the case.

I didn't look anyone in the eye as I traipsed through the crowd of photographers and journalists and then down the long aisle of the church.

'Fairweather, that was live,' I grunted down the phone as I pulled out of the church car park. She didn't say anything. 'Did you watch? Did I make a fool of myself?'

'I… I… no, I didn't know it would go out live. I wasn't sure what to expect to be honest—'

'You're the bloody station chief, you should have told me what to expect.'

There was a silence for more seconds than there needed to be whilst I cringed inside. Then I heard a golf ball being struck on the other end of the line.

'But… listen, Quayle,' she said, 'Tallaght said you wouldn't be able to lead this case and I was adamant that you wouldn't put a foot wrong. This is the second time you've snapped at me. There are crossed-wires, clearly. But that's because we are a small operation. We don't have the resources and the experiences like the detectives in Tallaght do. Are you sure you don't just want to pass this over?'

I deep sighed into the phone.

'I'm onto something here,' I said. 'I just wouldn't mind a bit more support.'

There was another silence while I imagined her looking around the golf course.

'I'll get back to the station,' she said. 'But I want you to know; I'm all for giving this to Tallaght.'

I thanked her, hung up and then checked who had been miss-calling me while I was talking to Fairweather. I'd heard two different beeps and was hoping at least one of them was from the hospital.

But both missed calls were from the same strange number.

I stabbed my finger at the callback option and held the phone to my ear.

'Hello, Sana Patel,' a voice answered. I knew the name. She's SOCO.

'Patel. It's Detective Inspector Quayle.'

'I have the results you were looking for, Quayle,' she said. 'Not sure you're going to be thrilled. Not much to go on, I'm afraid. The Tiddles were killed with a knife from their own kitchen. One knife out of a set of six is missing from the scene. It fits the murder weapon perfectly. Whoever murdered this couple took that knife from its block, stabbed both deceased multiple times and left. Clive was stabbed thirteen times; three times in the chest, nine times in the torso and once in the upper left thigh. The fatal stab wound was one made to his heart. I believe it was the first stabbing. Dorothy died slower. She was stabbed seven times, all in the lower torso. A stab wound to her liver is likely the cause of her death. But she likely bled out for up to an hour.'

I rubbed at my temple to help absorb everything Patel was saying.

'Any DNA left? Any leads as to what sort of profile we're looking at here?'

'That's the weird thing, Quayle,' she said. 'The killer came and left without leaving a drop of DNA. Whoever did this knew what they were doing. Small. Definitely small. Or certainly whoever killed Dorothy was small. The stab wounds, they're not only low. But delicate. Two inches in depth.'

'Small... as in... you think it's the twins, too?'

'Oh I'm not making any judgements,' she said. 'That's your job. But I will say small doesn't mean kids, per se. It could easily be a short adult. Five foot, three inches—max, I would say. Though this is only a light theory. And a very early theory at that. I should also add, though it's very difficult to know for certain, but it's likely Clive Tiddle was asleep when attacked. First two stab wounds were to his chest, around the heart. Then they were all lower after that. He likely woke, tried to stand and was then downed.'

'Interesting... but that's it?' I asked. 'No DNA at all?'

I could hear suck a breath in through her teeth.

'It's unusual, but not unheard of.'

I gurned.

'What about the time of the killings?'

'I could conclude a half-hour window. When I first examined the bodies it was six p.m. I could determine there and then that Clive likely died somewhere between ten-thirty and eleven. Dorothy sometime later, somewhere between eleven and twelve.'

I squinted, doing the maths. These timings narrowed down the twins' likely involvement to just fifteen minutes. They left the house at ten forty-five to go to dance class, arriving at ten fifty-five. If the murders happened at the earliest possible time — ten-thirty — that means they could only have had a fifteen-minute window. It wasn't them. It couldn't have been them.

'Let me ask you this, Patel,' I said, 'when DNA is absent at a scene, what does that normally tell you?'

'Well,' she said, before pausing. 'It's rare. But it guarantees to mean one of two things: either somebody whose DNA would already be at the scene is the killer... Or...' she paused. Hesitated.

'Or what?'

'Or... somebody who knew exactly what they were doing carried out the murder.'

I had finished the call by the time I'd reached Sheila's ward, then, after I'd hung up, I paused in the doorway, just as

I was about to push it open. I could hear her lecturing the doctor.

'Go on, Doc,' she said. 'Tell me... how many people do you think died in the world since the turn of the century because of alcohol?'

He chuckled.

'Oh, I don't know, Mrs Quayle... hundreds of thousands.'

'Millions. Three and a quarter million to be exact. Isn't that a staggering number? And here... tell me, how many people do you think died since the turn of the century due to pharmaceutical drugs; pain killers, that kinda thing?'

I had to stifle my laughter. I knew this argument off by heart. She says it to almost everybody we ever meet. And now she was lecturing a bloody doctor about it of all people.

'No idea,' the doctor said.

'Over two million.' The doctor whistled in surprise. Then chuckled again. 'And last question,' she said. 'How many people do you think have died since the turn of the century from taking cannabis?' I observed the doctor through the crack in the door. He shrugged both his shoulders. 'Go on, have a guess,' Sheila pushed him. And then I pushed the door open to save him.

'Zero!' I said.

'Exactly,' Sheila smiled at me. 'Zero since the start of this century,' she continued. 'Zero since the start of any century. Nobody has ever died from cannabis intake. It's impossible. And yet that's the one that's illegal. Mad, isn't it?'

I walked over to her and kissed her forehead.

'It sure is, sweetheart,' I said to her. 'You seem in good spirits.'

She was sitting up in bed, her arm free from the intravenous, her smile wide.

'Do you wanna tell him, or will I, Doc?' she said.

'Oh, that news is all yours,' the doctor replied. He matched her smile.

'From a Brussel sprout to a garden pea,' she said to me. I must have looked confused. 'My tumour,' she followed up with.

'Huh?' I said, turning to the doctor.

'That's the metaphor I used,' he said. 'The tumour, it's… it has decreased by about sixty per cent. From the size of a small Brussel sprout when we last measured it three months ago, to a garden pea today.' He pinched two fingers together to show me how small a garden pea is.

Sheila sang along to the radio all the way home, to songs she didn't know the words to. Then I left her on the couch to watch an old Robert Redford movie while I raced back to the station.

Fairweather looked sombre when I got to her; sad almost.

She cocked her head, subtly, towards her office. And I followed her in to see Tunstead staring at me. The prick. As well as another man with a very serious expression etched on his face who was sitting in Fairweather's chair.

'You haven't been easy to track down today, Quayle,' he said.

'Quayle, this is Tallaght station chief Laurence Ashe,' Fairweather said to me. I eyeballed Tunstead, who was leaning his back against the wall as I shook Ashe's hand.

Then we both sat down and he leaned closer to me.

'I'm gonna cut to the chase,' Ashe said. 'We're taking you off the case, Quayle.'

ALICE

'Yeah… the stab wounds absolutely scream guilty to me,' Braces says.

I remain reeled back in my chair as heads nod around me.

'The one thing that really stood out to me was not so much the fact that most of the stab wounds were in the lower and middle torso of both victims, but the lack of depth of the stab wounds. Whoever stabbed Clive and Dorothy was short, most likely weak. Five centimetres… is that right, that was the deepest stab wound? Most of them just two or three centimetres?'

'Yeah… that's what everybody agreed on; the crime scene investigation, the defendants' expert's findings, and the prosecution experts' findings,' Scarhead says.

'Yep, but that's about all they did agree on,' Red Head says. She's really great at pushing back against anything the guilty mob are offering up.

I dart my eyes at her, but leave her to this argument. I don't want to speak up. The stab wounds argument is an impossible one for us to win.

'Okay… well, let's go through it,' Scarhead says, taking the reins. 'So, your point, Lisa, isn't it?' he asks Braces Girl. She nods her head. 'Are you saying the depth of the stab wounds is what mainly leads you to believe Faith and Grace are guilty?'

She stares down at the table in front of her, then begins to slowly nod her head.

'Yeah, I think that is the clincher for me. That and the fact that Clive was likely asleep when he was killed, even though the expert couldn't say for certain.... wouldn't the twins perhaps know if he took a nap on a Saturday at mid-morning? So those kinda things as well as all the psych reports on the girls make me think they're guilty. Everybody seems to find the twins quite odd, don't they? Aunt Janet. Kelly McAllister. As well as Joe O'Beirne and Dinah Dore who worked at Tusla. Claire Barry, the dance teacher. Nobody painted a glowing report of the twins; that's always said a lot to me.'

"Cept for Denis Quayle,' Red Head pipes up. Pushing back again.

There's a slight pause in the proceedings, as everybody soaks up Quayle again... Then they all turn to Scarhead.

'Well, let's stay on the stab wounds while we are discussing them. We all now have a copy of the testimonies given by Doctor Barry O'Hanlon and Professor Eleanor Kane in front of us.'

It was agreed by all of us that we should order these as soon as the issue of the stab wounds arose. Even I agreed. When the last thing I wanted to do was go through these testimonies. I felt one side of these theories absolutely plausible, the other — argued by the defence — was pretty much fantastical. I don't want to argue for the fantastical... it'd make me look ridiculous. But I guess I'm going to have to.

'I'll read some of Doctor O'Hanlon's testimony first..,' Scarhead says. 'So, eh this is when prosecution lawyer Jonathan Ryan asked him, "The Crime Scene Investigation team initially reckoned these stabbings were made by somebody five foot, three inches in height and then they came back on that and insisted what they meant was *at most* the killer or killers were five foot, three. Your findings are somewhat a little different, are they not?", "Inches different,'" O'Hanlon said.' "We believe the attacker to likely be four foot, nine inches to five foot, one inch.'"

Scarface looked up at us when he read that out. We were all aware both twins were exactly four foot, nine. It was repeated to us numerous times during the trial; especially when it came to the evidence surrounding the stab wounds.

'And then, Ryan asked, "'And the depth of the wounds themselves, Doctor O'Hanlon, what did they inform you?", "Well, I don't want to say the word weak. That's not it exactly. Two, three, four up to five centimetres deep is not a weak stab wound. They are stab wounds directed to damage or kill. Especially given that they were all around vital organs... but... my genuine understanding of the impact and locations of these stab wounds points to a child... or children.'"

'That is when Bracken objected,' Thick-rimmed Glasses says.

'And the judge agreed with him,' Braces Girl offers up.

I sit forward and eyeball her a bit. I wonder what she's thinking now. If I can get her over to the not guilty camp, I'd be in a strong position. That'd be four. But she keeps bloody changing her mind. And this argument isn't going to change her mind the way I want it to be changed. I open my mouth to reply to her, but I'm beaten to it by Scarhead.

'Well, that's the golden nugget of the case, is it not?' he says. 'One of the experts is saying children definitely did this.'

'Hold on... he didn't say *definitely*, let's just be clear,' Red Head says. 'He just said his examinations point to the attackers being children. Nothing *definite* about it. Besides, he wasn't the only expert talking about stab wounds, was he?'

She was referring to the defence's expert witness—Eleanor Kane; a professor of Forensic Science at the Coombe Lab. Blonde, sharp bob cut, attractive, impressively confident and one hell of a talker. Except for one little thing. She was talking shit.

'Well, shall I read from Professor Eleanor Kane's testimony?' Scarhead asks. And everybody nods their head. Including me.

'"The stab wounds would not necessarily have come from a child,"' Scarhead reads and suddenly I'm sitting upright again. Even though I know this is all bollocks. '"There is a known disguised stabbing technique favoured among street criminals—it's an old underground Martial Arts Technique called the Mikna Sqay. It's when somebody disguises the fact that they have a knife right up until they stab, piercingly in-and-out, in-and-out repeatedly and in very swift fashion in the lower body, landing in all the major organs down there. The stab wounds suffered by both Clive Tiddle and Dorothy Tiddle hold all the hallmarks of an expert assassin."'

I hear a couple of dismissive huffs, around the table; quiet ones, puffed lightly through nostrils.

'I mean... what do we say to that? An expert assassin?' Most faces turn to Red Head, probably because she's the most vocal of our not guilty camp. The party of three. And a half. If you count the one undecided.

'All that says to me,' Red Head says, glancing towards me as she sharply sits up in her seat, 'is that it can't be considered a fact that this was children.'

'Ah come on!' Scarhead says. And then arguments spark across the table again. This is doing my head in.

'Hey!' I say. Loudly. Cutting through the noise. I hate this part. When everybody turns to me. 'It is not our job to play detective here. But Clive and Dorothy Tiddle were not regular Joes, were they? They were quite strange. They raised quite strange children. In a strange way. They lived very strange lives.'

'They ran a church, Alice, not a cult,' Thick-rimmed Glasses says.

'What's the difference?' I shrug my shoulders as a ripple of groans come at me. 'Okay, okay... okay,' I say, literally cutting at the air with a swipe of my hand. 'I'm just saying that the Tiddles are not like us... they have many, many friends; acquaintances from all corners of the world, built up over many years. I don't want to say anything more than that, other than to let it be known as a fact that they knew people, lots of people from all different walks of life. And we must bear that in mind... they weren't normal.'

'So what... you think one of these many people they met in their lives came back to kill them?'

'That's not what I'm saying at all,' I answer back. 'It's just when you think about the contents of what was found in that safe.... it's just not normal. They had what the rest of us would call secrets. The expert assassin theory, if that's what it is—or the Hollywood movie hit-man theory as Jonathan Ryan called it in court... is it really as far fetched as the other theory on offer?'

A flurry of answers all at once fly at me, but Scarhead shushes them.

'Well, you raise the contents of the safe there, which is fair enough,' he says. 'And we will get back to that. But don't you think it's absolutely unbelievable that somebody — some hit man as you say — came into Rathcoole, up the moun-tains, past dozens of houses along the roads and not one person saw a thing. Not one person that day saw a strange man or woman coming or going. And not a jot of evidence proves that anybody was in that house that morning; other than all four Tiddles. I mean... come on... you can't really believe this, can you?'

'I didn't say I believe it,' I reply. 'I'm just saying that it's not implausible, and if it's not implausible then there is doubt in the other theory. There is doubt that it could only have been children, there is doubt that it was Faith and Grace. And when there is doubt, you gotta acquit.'

'Very good,' Red Head says, rubbing at my arm.

Everybody else falls silent. I bloody nailed it. I actually turned that around. I went from losing what was clearly the prosecution's greatest weapon — the stab wounds — and turned it into a win. At least I think I did.

I look up at Braces. It's hard to read how she's reacted to that. She's just sitting there, nonplussed, staring back up at Scarhead as he decides where to take our deliberations next.

'Well, I guess it's a case that the prosecution have their side and the defence have theirs, right?' he says.

'Well,' Red Head replies, 'I think you'll find that is what a trial actually is.'

She gets a snigger from Quiff. I wonder where Quiff's head is at. He was on my side earlier, but he seemed to be swinging the other way. I'd rather have Braces on our side than him anyway. Me. Her. The Red Head and Obese Guy. That seems to me like it would stay strong. We could easily hold out for a hung jury.

The door rattles again, and as it does I look at my watch. It's just gone half-four. Jeez... that afternoon flew in. I guess we got some arguing done. I certainly did. I'm proud of myself.

I turn my shoulder and see the young woman dressed in all black entering.

'Your Honour Judge Delia McCormick would like to ask if you are near an agreeable verdict?' she asks.

'Eh...' Scarhead hesitates, rubbing at his scar. 'What do we think, guys?'

'No. Jeez. We are not, no!' I say, really snappy. 'There's no agreement at all. We had an earlier verdict vote... four people said not guilty, then this young man,' I say, pointing at Quiff Guy. 'And this young girl,' pointing at Braces Girl, 'are still undecided. So no...'

'Are you?' Scarhead says, looking at both of them. 'Undecided?'

'I, eh... I'm not sure,' Braces says. 'So yes. Undecided, I guess. I'd like to think it through in my head... and then come back tomorrow, argue it out some more.'

'And you?' Scarhead asks Quiff.

'I'd like more time too... but have to say, the Hollywood hit-man thing, it's just so difficult to buy—'

'Alright, alright,' I say. 'No need to enter into deliberations with this lady in the room. Let's just answer the judge's question. No,' I say, turning to the young woman dressed in all black, 'we are not close to an agreeable verdict.'

She looks over to Scarhead, awaiting confirmation from the Head Juror.

'Not very close, no,' he says.

'Okay, I will let her know, though I am sure I will return to you in moments.'

She scurries out of the room, closing the door tight behind her.

'I'm sorry,' I say, holding my palm out to Quiff Guy. I was a little short with him there, cutting him right off. But it was ludicrous to even discuss whether or not we are close to an agreement. We're nowhere near it.

I look over at the Red Head as everybody shuffles in their chairs and I'm certain she nods a nod of approval at me.

I'm about to spark up small talk with her when the door rattles again.

'Ladies and gentlemen of the jury,' the young woman

dressed all in black says really formally. 'You have been dismissed for the day. The court will ask you to return at nine a.m. tomorrow to reconvene your deliberations. We thank you for your time and service to these courts.'

We're all standing in the doorway of the court's side entrance within seconds, the cold hitting us as soon as the door opens.

I walk slowly behind Red Head, unsure whether or not it's appropriate to talk to her now that we've opened up lines of communication, albeit in the company of all the others. But we don't say a word as we cross the road towards the taxi rank, not until we reach the first car and she turns to me.

'You're first today,' she says.

'No. No. I got the first one yesterday. It's you today.'

'Oh yeah.' She laughs. And then she purses her lips at me.

'You seem to be feeling much better this afternoon, Alice,' she says. 'You were really socking it to them there at the end.'

I laugh this time. And then I take one step closer to her.

'You adamant they're not guilty?' I ask.

'We, eh…' she looks up and down the street. 'We really shouldn't discuss it out here.'

I shake my head.

'No. Sorry. My bad. Please… go on. You grab that taxi. I'll see you in the morning. Try to sleep well.'

'You too,' she says.

I hold up my hand in a wave before I spin on my heels and head for the second taxi.

I've barely finish telling the driver where to take me when my phone buzzes in my blazer's breast pocket.

I squint at the number on the screen and as I do my stomach flips itself over.

'Hello,' I say, my voice shaking.

'What's been going on inside that jury room… tell me!' the distorted voice yells.

DAY THREE

I eyeballed all three of them. Ashe. Then Tunstead. Then Fairweather. She just twitched her wrists helplessly at me.

'You can't throw me off this case,' I said.

'Quayle, you do not have the experience—'

'This has nothing to do with experience,' I said, crossing my arms at my chest.

'Of course it has,' Tunstead said from behind me. The prick.

'So you have lots of experience in this, do you, Tunstead?' I said, turning to him. 'Double homicides in the Dublin mountains. Religious family. Twin girls, who you think are the main suspects. You have lots of experience with that type of case specifically, do you?'

'That's not what we mean,' Ashe said. 'And,' he interrupts me as soon as my mouth opens to respond, 'the twins *are* the main suspects.'

I threw my hands in the air.

'It's not your call,' I said. 'This crime happened in the mountains, on St Benedict's Road. That's our jurisdiction.'

'Christ, Quayle,' Tunstead said. 'Jurisdictions? This isn't the 1990s anymore. We are all the one force, we all lean on each other. Especially in cases of this magnitude.'

'I *am* leaning on other members of the force,' I replied, irritated. 'Johnny and Sully are out talking to all of the neighbours and anyone who frequents the area. You and Lowe and a number of other officers are leading a search of the bungalow's grounds and all areas around it. There are twenty-eight uniforms overall helping in that search. The force *is* in use, doing a great job. But it's doing a great job under my orders.'

'Well, they won't be under your orders anymore,' Ashe said.

'You have no right to remove me as Lead Detective. It happened in my jurisdiction, as much as Tunstead here doesn't want to believe jurisdictions are actually a thing anymore. I was first at the scene. I am very familiar with the entire area of the mountains. It's my case, no matter what way anybody looks at it.'

Ashe sniffed his nose, then peered over my shoulder at Fairweather. She didn't say anything. That disappointed me. I really wanted her to stick up for me. For us. For our station. Though I shouldn't have been surprised. I knew she would much rather do without the pressure of all this. It would suit her if we handed it over. I didn't see it as pressure. I never felt any pressure. I just saw it as a case I needed to solve. It happened in the mountains, to people I am tasked with protecting. I wasn't going to give this case up to feed egos.

'Quayle, I'm going to give this to you straight... I like you. I do. I think you've been a mighty fine detective for Rathcoole Garda Station.' I knew that was a sleight, as much as he tried to finely wrap it up in a compliment. *For Rathcoole Garda Station...* as he feels arresting folk for petty crime or drug dealing is about the peak of my limit as an investigator. 'But this murder happened a little over forty-eight hours ago now, right?' I looked around myself, then nodded my head. 'In those forty-eight hours or so, it has become apparent that there are two suspects in this case. Yet they have been under the guidance of Tusla since four p.m. on Saturday afternoon and have only been released once to visit the scene, where you questioned them.'

'I don't agree that they are the only suspect—'

He held a finger up to silence me.

'But your questioning of them was so delicate, it bordered on babysitting.' I leaned back in my chair and gasped. 'When you are questioning a suspect, it is your job to find out what they know, not find out how they are.'

'I just want to stop you there,' I said, pointing a finger just as he had. 'I know this case more than anyone. I was first on the scene and I have spent the most amount of time with Faith and Grace.'

'Yeah, at McDonald's,' Tunstead said. I held my eyes closed briefly to let the disdain wash over me.

'They are two orphans now,' I said. 'Two young girls who lost both their parents in cold blood two days ago. We know where they are. They are in Tusla's care. And from what I understand, they are getting fantastic counselling there. They are grieving and getting the best support they possibly can. While they are grieving, I am investigating the case to rule out any other line of enquiry.'

Ashe scratched at his chin.

'Tunstead tells me you are looking at some bizarre racism angle because Clive Tiddle once had a shouting match with some old geezer.'

I sigh and then look back at Fairweather for support.

She hesitated before taking a step towards us.

'You and I, Ashe,' she says, 'are equals. I insist Detective Quayle remains on the case. You want your station in charge, I want mine…'

She shrugged her shoulders. And Ashe sighed. Then, after leaning back in his chair and twiddling his fingers, he shot back up and swiped at the phone on Fairweather's desk.

'We'll call the Assistant Commissioner, he'll decide who takes the lead.'

I stood up, and as I walked to the door I eyeballed Tunstead just to shake my head at him. Then I strolled straight to the cooler to pour myself a plastic cup of water. I was sipping from it as the ringing sounded from the Fair-weather's speakerphone.

'Hello, Assistant Commissioner Riordan,' Ashe said as soon as the ringing tone stopped. I strolled back into Fair-weather's office, still sipping on my water. 'This is Detective Superintendent Laurence Ashe. I am here with fellow Detec-tive Superintendent Brigit Fairweather, Detective Inspector Denis Quayle, both of Rathcoole Garda Station. And one of my own Detective Inspectors—Karl Tunstead. We are at a, eh... a bit of a standstill over who should run this Tiddle case.'

'Well, whose jurisdiction is it, Rathcoole's right?'

I eyeballed Tunstead. But he pretended not to notice me.

'Well, with all due respect, sir. That is correct. The crime happened at the foot of the mountains. But as you know, sir, Rathcoole Garda Station is a small outfit. Just four employees and they are not used to dealing with crimes of this, eh... magnitude.'

I tilted my chin ever so slightly forward towards the phone in anticipation of Riordan's response.

'Yes, well. I expect Rathcoole are leading the investigation with the full support of Tallaght. The support of the whole force.'

'Yes... well that is supposed to be the case,' Ashe said. He looked at me out of the corner of his eye and began to play with his fingers. 'It's just that my best Detective Inspectors —

Detectives Tunstead and Lowe — they are reporting to me that Lead Detective Quayle is letting his ego get in the way. He is keeping them at a distance.'

'What!' I crushed the plastic cup in my hand and then spun on my heels to face Tunstead. 'You what?'

'Now calm down, Quayle,' he said, backing into the wall. 'All's I — we, me and Lowe — said was that we needed to be more involved in this case. We need to know what you are doing... where you are going. We need access to the suspects and you're blocking us from doing what we need to do. Anytime I ring you I can't get through. You're not answering...'

I huffed and shook my head. The prick!

'Sir,' I said, turning towards the phone. 'Detective Tunstead has a narrow mind in this case. He is solely focused on two suspects in particular.'

'Yeah—the twins, right?' Riordan said.

'Yes,' I replied, just as my own phone began to ring in my pocket.

'Well, isn't Tunstead right though? That's who all the evidence points to. Shouldn't this be an open and shut case?'

'Well, the twins haven't said much, sir,' Tunstead said, stepping forward. 'Because Quayle here won't let us speak to them. He doesn't believe it was the twins.'

'Huh?' Riordan said.

'That's nonsense, sir. Tunstead and Lowe accompanied me to question the twins at the scene of the crime. So please take what this detective says with a pinch of salt.'

'Jesus, can you all calm down!' the phone spat out. 'You are dealing with the biggest case this country has seen in years, don't make me take you all off it. Do you hear me? Grow up. The lot of you!'

The whole office fell silent.

'You don't have another suspect, Quayle, right?' Riordan asked.

'Actually, sir...' I tossed the crushed cup into the bin under Fairweather's desk, then leaned my hands either side of the phone. 'The deceased had rows with one neighbour in particular who lived at the very bottom of the Dublin mountains. It was race related. The Tiddles ran a church and invited a lot of immigrants to that church. They had a small bus that they used to pick people up in and bring them out to the mountains every Sunday. They'd stay for the entire day, coming and going to Rathcoole village. Well, one particular neighbour — a Mr Tommo Nevin — didn't like this. He had a run-in with Clive Tiddle about it.'

'What kind of run-in?' Riordan asked.

'Well, a shouting match. A back and forth. Witnessed by others.'

'That's it?' Riordan said. 'They shouted at each other and now you believe he broke into their house without being noticed and stabbed both husband and wife to death?'

'Well...' I stood back upright and stared down at my shoes. 'I don't have everything figured out yet, sir. But at least I have motive. Tunstead and Lowe have no motive. There is no reason whatsoever to suggest the twins would want their parents dead. Everyone says they were a close family.'

'Everyone says the twins are weird,' Tunstead said.

'Oh shut up you two... acting like children,' the phone spat at us again. My phone rang in my pocket in the resulting silence.

'Ain't you going to answer that?' Ashe asked me. 'You are lead detective on the biggest case in the country. You may need to find out who's trying to contact you.'

I took my phone out and then stabbed my finger at the green button before walking back towards the water cooler.

'Hello.'

'Detective Denis Quayle, this is Robin Deutch of Golden Locksmiths. You asked us to ring you as soon as we managed to open the safe found at crime scene 82033. St Benedict's Bungalow. I believe, eh… it's the Tiddle case.'

'Yes, yes, yes,' I said.

'Detective Quayle, we managed to open the safe almost an hour ago and—'

'Almost an hour ago, what took you so long ringing me?' I asked.

'Well, Detective, we eh… we had to count it all.'

'Count it?'

'Money.'

'Money?'

'Four hundred and forty thousand in used notes.'

I swivelled back into the office and stared at everyone inside. Then I paced towards Fairweather's desk.

'Say that again, Robin,' I said after I'd pressed at my speakerphone button.

'We found four hundred and forty thousand euros in used notes in the Tiddle safe. And, eh… holiday tickets. For Disneyland, Florida. That's the entirety of the contents. The safe was practically packed with cash.'

I looked at Fairweather and offered her a tiny wink. Then I eyeballed Tunstead and Ashe, a grin stretching across my mouth.

'I told you this wasn't the twins,' I said.

'This doesn't change much,' Tunstead piped up.

'Oh, it changes a lot. Know many people with nearly half a million in used notes hiding in their bedroom floorboards, Tunstead? Looks as if the Tiddles weren't quite as squeaky clean as everybody thinks they were.'

I turned to Fairweather's desk, placed a hand either side of the phone again, and bent forward.

'Sir, I had been sniffing around other theories for these

past two days. I knew something wasn't quite right. I implore you to make the right decision and maintain me as lead detective in this case. I am no rookie. I have been in the police force for over twenty-five years. I have an exemplary record... isn't that right, Fairweather?' I said, turning to my boss and then waving her towards the phone.

She took a step forward.

'That's right, sir. Detective Quayle's a fantastic member of the force.'

I winked at her again, and then held my breath.

'You guys have such little experience in this kind of case,' Riordan said. It fell silent until we heard the sound of him popping his lips on the other end of the line.

'Quayle, you're gonna involve Tallaght Garda Station in the case, give them rights access, fill them in on everything you do...okay? You're all working on this together. You need to be a team. We don't need any wannabe-heroes here. We need this case solved as quickly as we can solve it.'

I looked back at Tunstead.

'Of course, sir. Once I am the lead detective and they are following my orders, I am happy to oblige.'

'Well either way, I'm going determine what the next move is on this case. We'll look into the contents of the safe in time, but I want the twins formally interviewed as a matter of urgency. Everyone I speak to says this was the twins. They should have been leaned on straight away. Yourself and the two detectives from Tallaght need to get on that as soon as you possibly can. Do we have a deal?'

'Deal,' I said.

'Well then, Quayle, you've bought yourself forty-eight hours. You don't make an arrest by Wednesday lunch-time, I'm handing this over to Tallaght!'

✝

As the success of The New St Benedict's Church grew, so too did Clive and Dorothy's work load. It actually got out of hand at one point — too many sermons to write, too many parishioners to console, too much money to count — that they decided between them that they needed an assistant.

Kelly McAllister wasn't necessarily the obvious choice, given that she had tendencies, but she had been with the church the longest out of the entire 'family' and both Clive and Dorothy had developed a soft spot for her.

When Dorothy had first recruited Kelly — finding her begging for money on the trams; skinny, spotty, greasy-haired and famished — she instantly knew she could transform her. Though she never would have envisioned Kelly would eventually become their closest confidante. Nobody would have. Kelly had strong issues around addiction. She relied on alcohol, drugs and — on the rare occasions she had cash in her pocket — gambling. It's why she left Glasgow in the first place. She threw all her wages up the wall; betting on anything from televised horse racing to side wagers with neighbours about who would be the next person in their community to die. She couldn't help it; gambling gave her a reason for being. It raised her endorphins as much as the drugs did.

Soon after she'd been let go from her job as a waitress in Clydebank for consistent lateness, she took a ferry to Antrim, which was followed by a long bus ride to Dublin. Just to get away from her old life. She had been living most nights on the streets of the Irish capital for almost a year before a woman with a hooked nose and large brown eyes sidled up to her on a tram one day.

'Jesus will repent all your sins,' the woman said. 'Fancy a hot cup of tea and a Jammy Dodger?'

Dorothy took a shine to Kelly instantly; felt befriended by the melodic lilt of her Glaswegian accent. She ensured Kelly got lodgings, calling on an array of folk who attended the church to sort her out with a spare bed or a couch if and when they could. There was always a welcome mat at the door of these people's homes. Feeling refreshed in life, Kelly began to turn up almost daily at the community centre. She'd often find Clive or Dorothy running through some paperwork for the coming Sunday's sermon or perhaps hosting a counselling session with one of the 'family'. And pretty soon after those daily drop-bys she was right in the middle of that 'family', chanting hymns and songs towards the makeshift altar with her hands in the air during sermons. She loved every minute of it, and within two months had come completely off the drugs; though the alcohol and gambling not so much.

By the time the twins came along, Kelly was a key member of the church; often taking up collections or assisting Clive by handing him different microphones on the stage. Even though she was by then a very good confidante of the Tiddles, she was still genuinely gobsmacked when she was asked to be Godmother to one of the newborns. She is officially Faith's Godmother, but she was insistent she would love them both equally. Though those early visions she had of spoiling two little sweet girls never really came to fruition. Yes, she held them when they were babies, and quite often babysat. But by the time they were two and three years of age —

when they were beginning to communicate with others — they seemed to fall mute and were quite awkward for her to be around. Anytime Kelly tried to talk them, they could barely understand her thick accent anyway. So she just admired them from afar like everybody else did. She'd wave at them when she'd see them at the community centre — or at the Tiddle home — and make a tiny bit of small-talk that wouldn't be reciprocated. And that was about it. There were no hugs, no kisses. Just waves, from about six feet away. She thought them odd, but she never said a cross word about them to anyone.

Although Kelly's mindset changed under the tutorship of the Tiddles, her body never did. Even in her mid-forties, she had the shape of a ten year-old boy. She's barely five foot tall and has the waistline of a standard shop-front mannequin. No bust, no hips, no ass. Her hair is always held back tight by a scrunchy, though she does go to the effort of applying mascara; the only make up she ever wears, save for a big day at the church such as a wedding or a christening when she might also apply some lipstick.

She had been part of the 'family' for over almost eighteen years when Clive first leaned in to kiss her. She had no idea it was coming. He just inched his face down to hers and pressed his lips to her mouth—then he leaned away and held a finger to his lips to shush her.

'Jesus put us in this place,' he said. And then he leaned back in; his lips ajar, his tongue poised.

Clive hadn't been looking to have an affair; family, for him, was always priority—both his immediate family and his church family. But Kelly had sort of grown into a more mature woman at that point and he was genuinely getting the distinct impression she was courting a come-on from him. He felt she'd hold hugs with him a little too long, or that whenever she was supposed to kiss his cheek, she would press her lips ever so close to his mouth. This wasn't actually the case at all; that was how Kelly began to greet everybody as she grew in confidence as her status in the church progressed. The first day Clive noticed her lips went dangerously close to his, he hesitated and leaned away from the embrace in shock. He masturbated thinking about Kelly that night, and a lot of nights afterwards for the next three months. Until he finally picked up the courage to act on his desires.

The first night he leaned in to kiss her properly they made love behind the stage of the church; him thrusting into her from behind with his trousers around his ankles, his gilet and plaid shirt still on.

Guilt often niggled at Clive, but by this stage he was now a minor celebrity amongst his own people and felt as if he was owed this extra gift in life. Kelly genuinely saw the affair as her duty; though she enjoyed the orgasms—had never really had proper adult sex before.

Dorothy was the right mix of too busy and too naive to notice that the two people she saw the most throughout the day were actually riding each other when she wasn't looking. Clive would often make excuses that he was giving sermons in other churches around the country when he'd usually be shacked up in a city-centre hotel having sex with Kelly.

'Listening to who?' Grace said, squinting back at her sister.

'Him. Jesus.'

'Jesus?' Grace placed her hand over her mouth. 'Why do you listen to him?'

Faith looked confused.

'Because we're supposed to talk to Jesus.'

'Yes, silly,' Grace said, giggling. 'But we talk to him, he doesn't talk to us.'

The confusion didn't dissipate from Faith's face. And then they both fell silent as they perched on the edge of their twin beds and faced each other.

'Faith...' Grace finally said, scratching at her temple. 'Does Jesus speak to you?'

Faith tilted her head again, then shook it slowly from side to side.

'No. Course not,' she replied. Grace giggled, but Faith — who normally mirrors her sister's emotions; whether laughing or crying, or huffing in anger — kept her lips turned down. 'He doesn't talk. He just kinda... sends me signs.'

'Huh?' Grace said.

Faith looked at her sister.

'He sends me signs.'

'He what?'

'He, eh... sends me signs. He would leave the light on in the bathroom, or something on the floor. Or something would knock off the cabinet in the living room... signs.'

Grace gasped.

'Signs... what do you mean? He, he... hold on!' Grace swallowed, then inched closer to her sister and placed her hands on her shoulders. 'You know when I killed Grebit last week, what did Jesus say about that? What sign did he send you, because I've been... I've been...' Faith shrugged her shoulders as Grace tried to find her words. 'You mean you didn't ask him?' Grace said, sounding disappointed.

'I don't... I don't ask questions. He just—'

'Well ask him now, ask him now. I want to know what he thinks of me killing Grebit. I want to know if I am going to go to Heaven or Hell... please... please, Faith. Ask him. Do it for me.'

ALICE

Noel's been perched on the edge of our bed for the past five minutes, brushing a hand gently up and down my thigh.

'Are you sure, sweetie?' he says. Again.

'Of course,' I reply, smiling. 'I've told you a thousand times. I'm fine. I feel much better than I did last night. Don't put yourself out. This case might be all over tomorrow. We can get back to normal. You go have fun.'

He leans in and kisses my nose.

'Love you,' he says.

Then he stands up and *finally* leaves the bedroom. I hear him jog lightly down the stairs and scoop up his car keys from the hall table before the front door swings open and then clangs shut behind him.

I sit more upright, my back against the rail of our bed and finger-tap the screen of my phone back to life. I told her I'd ring back at seven forty-five. It's two minutes past that time now. When she rang earlier, demanding to know what happened in the jury room, I had to whisper down the line to her that I was in the back of a taxi. She insisted I ring her as soon as I got home, but I told her I wouldn't be alone until about quarter-to-eight... because that's when my husband leaves every Thursday evening to participate in a quiz night down our local pub. She paused. For ages. Then agreed.

I'm not strictly alone. Alfie's here, playing computer games in the back room downstairs. It's where he spends way too much of his time. I know we really shouldn't let him play those things for so many hours, but it keeps him quiet. And isn't that the goal of every parent in the world: quiet. I love my kids. To death. I really do. But I've been a mother for over twenty-three years now. It's been a long old stretch. It just didn't seem to ever stop for me... not when there's a nine-year age gap between them. It took us two years of trying naturally, six years of IVF and four miscarriages before we had a successful pregnancy with Alfie. He was our little miracle. But by this stage I don't mind admitting that I wish he was at the age Zoe is now; where he is about to move out. That'd be nice. I think me and Noel deserve some peace and quiet. It'd be lovely to not *have* to mother every day. Zoe's practically moved out by now. Although not officially. She stays over with Emmet most nights of the week. He shares an inner-city apartment at the IFSC with a guy he works with. Most of her wardrobe is in that flat. So I guess she's almost gone.

I finally pluck the courage to press at the number on my phone, then tentatively hold it to my ear.

'You said you'd ring at quarter to... you're three minutes late!' she barks, answering before one tone had even rung out.

'I had to wait on my husband to go out,' I say. I hear the shake in my voice as I say that. I promised myself earlier that I'd be strong during this phone call. That didn't last long.

'Just get to it. What happened in that jury room today?

'Well... eh... what do you want to know exactly?' I ask.

'Tell me where the verdict is heading?'

I take a deep breath.

'Probably to a hung jury,' I say. I'm sure I hear a hint of a 'yes' through her exhale, but I just continue to fill her in. 'We had a verdict vote at the start of our deliberations and it came out eight guilty, four not guilty. It seemed to be pretty much the same by the end of the day, except one person who earlier said not guilty has changed his mind and I'm pretty sure one girl who said guilty is about to change her mind. She told me at the end of the day she was now undecided.'

'Okay… Tell me which jurors are not guilty.'

'Well, me—obviously.' I say. 'The red-headed girl.'

'Sinead Gormley.'

'Oh, you know the names?'

'Course I know the names,' she says.

I dip my brow, my mind whirring. Whoever this is must have hacked into every one of the jurors' phones, tried to get dirt on them all. Maybe I'm the only one they found dirt on. But the red head is arguing just as adamantly as I have been… I bet they have something on her too.

'And, eh… you know the big guy, the fat one with the grey hair?' I say.

'Gerry McDonagh,' she says.

'Eh yeah, him… and, ehm, the young girl with the braces.'

'Lisa Glennon.'

'Yeah, Lisa. Well, she is the one who told me she was now undecided.'

'Interesting,' the distorted voice says, then I hear her click her tongue off the top pallet of her mouth. 'You, Sinead, Gerry and Lisa. Not what I had in mind, but….' She pauses again. I think she's taking notes. 'How watertight do you think the four jurors are who are saying not guilty, then?'

'Well, Lisa is not watertight because she initially voted guilty, then the arguments started to change her mind. Especially because me and the red head were going on and on about there just not being enough evidence. I think me and the red head will hold out.'

'And Gerry... the fat guy?'

'I think he'll hold out too,' I say.

'That's all you need, Alice. Keep those two on your side and you will get out of this whole mess. Just make sure at least three of you hang on. The judge will end up accepting a ten:two vote, probably at some stage tomorrow. So make it your job to ensure those guys hang on. If you don't... you know what'll happen. That's a very compromising position you tried there with your daughter's boyfriend. Right from behind. A pounding, I would call it. Surely your husband would just throw up if he saw that video,' she says.

I hold my eyes closed, an attempt to simmer down the boiling of my blood.

'Who else are you playing this game with?' I hiss.

'Sorry?'

'Who else are you blackmailing? The red head?'

'You're the only one,' she replies.

I don't believe her.

'Really? The red head, surely. She's as adamant as I am that the twins are not guilty.'

'You're the only one, Alice. It's all up to you.'

'Why do I not believe you?'

She sniggers out a laugh.

'Alice, do you think most women go around sleeping with their daughter's boyfriends? Of course I don't have dirt on anybody else. You're the only slut sitting around that jury table.'

I hold my eyes closed again.

I really don't want to lose it with her. I just need to concentrate on how best I can keep this jury hung. Then this whole bullshit will be in the past. I can't fuckin' wait for it to be all over. Jesus. The Tiddle case. Feels like it's been in my life forever.

I lied to the judge. I'm certain I wasn't the only juror who did. Nobody could have let that story pass them by. Course I read about the Tiddles when they were all over the news. Everyone was talking about the strange double homicide in the Dublin mountains. The twins were only known as Child X and Y in the newspapers and on TV as they couldn't be named for legal reasons. But it's been more about them than it has been about Clive and Dorothy. They had initially been arrested for a few hours three days in to the investigation before being let out with an apology, but then they were re-arrested two days later. And it's been pretty much in the news relentlessly ever since. It took the guts of two years for the case to get to court.

Because Faith and Grace were only nine, early reports said they may never face a big trial—something to do with the Children's Act in 2001 or something. There was a lot of legal to-ing and fro-ing, which got even further complicated when Gerd Bracken took over the twins' case; no doubt driven by the mass exposure it would bring to his brand. He wasn't successful in keeping this trial from the courts though; eventually it was decided Faith and Grace would face a jury in Dublin's Criminal Courts—to be tried in much the same way an adult would under such circumstances. Faith and Grace remain only the third and fourth children respectively to ever be tried as adults in the history of the Irish court system. I know everything about the case. Because I read all about it as it was happening.

I was pretty chuffed when I was called for jury duty. I know most people think it's a pain in the ass to get that letter in the post. But I immediately felt it'd be a week away from organising a friend of a friend's fiftieth or sixtieth birthday snacks. I fancied the break from the norm. Though I had no idea I'd be on this bloody trial—one of the biggest in the history of the state. The whole country's been glued to this.

When Judge Delia McCormick looked us jurors square in the eyes at the beginning of this trial and asked us if we followed the Child X and Y case in the media over the past couple of years, I held her stare and shook my head.

'No, Your Honour. Nothing,' I said. And about half an hour later I was the second to be given a juror's chair. The days were long and the silences were plenty, but the trial itself was fascinating in so many ways… I was really enjoying it. Right up until this psycho bitch texted me yesterday.

'Listen,' I say. 'I'm going to do my best for you… I'll make sure both the red head and the fat guy keep their not guilty verdict. But please — I beg you — don't send that video to my husband… to my daughter. No matter what happens. They don't deserve this.'

'No, but perhaps you do,' she says. 'Now you listen to me, Alice. This isn't a fucking negotiation. You make sure it's a not guilty verdict, or Noel and Zoe get sent that video. Simple as that. You either win. Or you lose. And you stand to lose everything.'

I hold the phone away from my ear and reel my head backwards. Then I snap the phone back to my ear.

'I would benefit from knowing if the red head is part of the deal. Do you have dirt on her too? Is she with me on this?'

'She's not fuckin' part of any deal, Alice. Don't make me repeat myself. It's only you. It's only up to you.'

A tear falls from my eye, surprising me. I didn't know I was close to crying.

'Okay,' I say. 'I'll do my best. It's all I can do.'

'Maybe I can help you a bit. What arguments are you, Sinead and Gerry using to defend your not guilty verdicts?'

'Evidence, mainly. Or the lack of evidence. There is

nothing concrete about this at all… That's what we keep saying.'

'Good. Good,' she says. 'But you should also argue the money.'

'The money?'

'Yeah… the safe. It brings doubt into the equation and doubt gives a legitimate reason for a juror to hold out. The Tiddles had almost half a million euros in used notes in their bedroom, it shines a light on different possibilities. That brings doubt, enough reasonable doubt to acquit.'

'Does it really?' I say. I kinda dismissed the money argument as soon as it was brought up at trial. Admittedly I was nailed on finding the twins guilty by that point, but still… stealing money or saving money or whatever it was the Tiddles were doing with so many used notes wasn't strong enough evidence for me to change my mind. Faith and Grace did this. I've no doubt about that at all.

'Of course it does. Well… as much as doubt gets in this case.'

'Hold on… you think they're guilty, don't you?'

She laughs.

'It doesn't matter one jot what I think. I'm not on the jury. The truth of the matter is, if you press the money argument you stand the best chance of having a legitimate reasoning for holding on to your not guilty vote. Just keep pushing back on every jury who is demanding they are guilty. Keep pushing, pushing, pushing. Hold on… and at some point the judge will deem you hung.'

I nod my head, soaking in what she's saying.

'Okay,' I whisper down the line as another tear falls.

Then the dead tone sounds.

DAY THREE

Tunstead wanted Tusla to escort the twins to the police station, but I was insistent I would do it. I fancied a little time with the two of them before we officially sat them down; felt I owed it to them to treat them like children before we started to treat them like suspects.

'I'll take them in my car, you guys follow,' I said to Joe and Dinah as we were leaving the Tusla premises. They had to be present for the interview. Which suited me. Anything that could dilute the Tallaght detectives' influence on the twins.

Faith and Grace were offered legal assistance, but they suggested having Dinah and Joe was adequate enough for them. After all, I had promised them they were only being brought in for a routine interview.

I tried to make them feel as relaxed as possible as I drove them to Rathcoole Garda Station. I asked them about their dance lessons. About their favourite popstars. About what they watch on TV. They didn't have much to say. Not just because they were naturally quiet, not to mention in the thick of the grieving process, but because they didn't have answers. They didn't have a favourite popstar and they didn't have a preferred TV show. Because they didn't listen to music. Nor watch TV, except for the odd cartoon.

'What about Mickey Mouse, Minnie Mouse, that sort of thing? You like them?' I asked.

I stared in my rearview mirror, to gauge Grace's reaction. She stuck out her bottom lip and squinted.

'Disney?' she asked.

'Uh-huh, Mickey and Minnie are the king and queen of Disney,' I say. 'You eh… like Disney?'

'It's a dream. Our dream. Isn't it, Faith?' Grace nudged her sister, then nodded her head before she met my eyes in the rearview mirror.

'Did you know you were, eh…' I paused, uncertain how to phrase exactly what I wanted to ask, 'you were going on holiday to Disneyland?'

I stared at both of their reflections for their reaction. Grace looked up at Faith and I am certain I noticed her clench her jaw. They didn't reply. Not with words.

'Girls, did you know your mother and father had booked tickets for a holiday to Disneyland in Florida?'

No answer. Both of them looked away from each other and stared out of their respective windows. Then I noticed Grace brush a tear away from her eye with one finger.

So I indicated, slowed the car to a stop and turned to them.

'Faith. Grace. You are going to be asked questions in the police station. And you're going to need to be more vocal. You need to speak. It is the only way we will ever find out who did this to your mother and father. Please don't be silent when me and the other detectives speak with you. Be open. Honest. Do it for your mother and father. Tell us everything you know.'

They both looked towards me, but their faces were blank

of expression. No tears. No words. It was no wonder everybody found them odd. My heart went out to them.

'It will help you if you tell the detectives that you knew you were about to go on holiday; that you knew about the trip to Florida,' I said.

Grace stared at me.

'We did know,' she said. 'Daddy surprised us with that a few weeks ago. We were really excited about it.' Then she started to cry. Hysterically. She reached out a hand to grab at Faith's arm. And then Faith started crying too. I waved my hand side-to-side in apology and waited for them to calm down. When they eventually did, I turned the key in the ignition and we were back on our way.

I had insisted the questioning go on inside Fairweather's office, rather than one of the two tiny interview rooms in Rathcoole Station. Fairweather's office wasn't big by any means — about the size of a single bedroom, mostly taken up by a small oak desk parked in the middle of it — but it was the largest room in the whole station. It was so tight with us all huddled around that oak desk that all of our knees were practically touching.

I led the way—apologising once again for the twins' loss and letting them know that their welfare was of our highest priority. I tried to read from their body language whether or not they understood that they were suspects, but their body language seemed to say as much as their mouths did.

'It has been brought to our attention by experts that the incident in which your parents were murdered occurred sometime between ten-thirty and eleven o'clock on Saturday morning,' I said, pursing my lips at them. Grace stared back at me, stony faced. Faith just kept her gaze on the carved edges of Fairweather's desk. 'That means it is probable that your parents were murdered at a time when you were in your house. You say you didn't leave until ten forty-five to go to your dance lesson with Ms Claire. Correct?' Grace glanced at the two Tusla employees and then back at me before she nodded. 'But, eh... it couldn't be the case now, now could it, that your parents were dead before you left, because you say you kissed them goodbye before going to dance class...'

Grace nodded again.

'Faith?' Lowe asked, her voice delicate.

Faith took her stare up from the table towards Lowe and then gently nodded.

'Speak. Please.' Lowe softened her face and leaned herself closer to Faith.

'We kissed them goodbye,' Faith said, in a whisper.

I felt so sorry for her. I didn't want her — nor Grace — to be in this situation. I was pained for them. Genuinely. None of this felt right.

'Okay...' Tunstead said, trying to ease some of the tension that had become apparent as Lowe tried to coax something from Faith. 'You both kissed your parents goodbye, left your home at ten forty-five and then got to dance class which is a little less than a mile from where you live at approximately ten fifty-five. And when you got there and went through your lesson... ballet, I believe...'

Grace looked at Tunstead.

'We do ballet and tap,' she said.

Tunstead swallowed.

'It's just that your dance teacher Ms Claire, she tells us you, Faith, were particularly quiet in the lesson that day.'

'Faith is always quiet,' Grace replied.

'Yeah, she's always quiet,' I said. Tunstead and Lowe turned to glare at me, but I pretended not to notice and looked to Dinah and Joe instead. 'I've spent time with Faith these past few days and I've barely got a word out of her.'

Faith glanced up at me slowly and even though she didn't say anything, I could sense she wanted to meet my eye.

'Ms Claire knows you are usually quiet,' Tunstead said turning to Faith, 'but she said you were *particularly* quiet that day. Did you sense something was wrong at home, perhaps?'

That was a good question, in fairness to the prick. It gave the twins an opportunity to account for the "weirdness" everybody was suggesting they had adopted ever since the murders.

Grace shook her head. And then Faith mirrored her.

'Let's move on for a second then,' Tunstead said. 'I'm wondering if your parents had anything planned for the family that you are aware of.' Grace shrugged her shoulders. 'Any days out... holidays perhaps?'

Then Faith looked back up at me again, before turning to her sister.

'Florida,' she whispered.

'Huh?' Tunstead inched his ear closer to the twins.

'Florida,' Grace said. 'Mammy and Daddy had booked a holiday. We are going to Disneyland in Florida.'

Tunstead scratched the back of his neck, then stood up.

'Ye know what... Grace... we would like you to stay here with Detective Quayle and Joe. Dinah, if you wouldn't mind accompanying myself and Detective Lowe into another room with Faith, we can complete our line of questioning separately. Then we can get you two back to the Tusla premises as soon as possible.'

Faith and Grace both looked to me. As if I was going to plead with Tunstead that they shouldn't be separated. I wanted to speak up for them... but couldn't find much cause for complaint. It made sense that two suspects under any circumstance be questioned separately. So, instead, I nodded my head.

And then Tunstead, Lowe and Dinah stood up and waited until Grace nudged at Faith and Faith finally and reluctantly decided to leave with them.

'When will we get to go back to Tusla?' Grace asked me as soon as they had all left.

'Soon,' I said. 'I promise.' Then I turned to Joe and sucked on my lips. I wasn't sure what to ask next, where to take this.

'Grace, you know you may not be able to return to Tusla for too long, right? You know aunt Janet is on her way to Dublin soon.'

Grace's brow uncreased.

'Are we going to have to live with aunt Janet?' she asked.

'Well…' I paused to look at Joe. He offered nothing. Not because he didn't want to. But because he knew his job was to stay as neutral as possible.

'We'll see…' I eventually said.

A silence fell on the room. It was an awkward silence. I wasn't quite sure how Joe was feeling about all of this. Nor Dinah, for that matter. Tusla staff really were playing a blinder at keeping quiet. Their jobs, after all, were not to play judge and jury, but to maintain the welfare of these children as best they could.

'Why is nobody out there looking for the person who killed Mammy and Daddy?' Grace said, ending the silence

'Well…' I replied, 'there are people out looking for clues in and around where you live. Plenty of police officers. Dozens of them.'

'But you are the main detective. And these other two… Detective Lowe and Detective Tunstead… why are you all just in here, talking with me and Faith? Shouldn't you be doing… something else?'

I took in a deep breath.

'The issue seems to be, Grace,' I said, edging my face closer to her, 'that the team who study the scenes of crimes haven't found any trace of evidence that anybody else entered your kitchen during the morning of the murders. There was no DNA left at the scene.' Grace scrunched her mouth up again. 'DNA—it's evidence that suggests somebody was in the kitchen. There is some historic DNA, from you, Faith, your mother and father of course.'

'And Kelly?'

'Huh?'

'Kelly. Kelly is always in our kitchen. She comes in the back door, leaves by the back door.'

I leaned forward.

'Kelly McAllister? The young Scottish lady who helps run the church?'

Grace nodded her head. But before I could follow up with another question, the door to Fairweather's office swung open, and in stomped Tunstead.

'Grace Tiddle, we are placing you under arrest for the murder of your parents Clive and Dorothy Tiddle.'

✝

Grace was growing in frustration with her twin's inability to fetch an answer to her question.

'But can't you ask him one more time?' Grace pleaded.

She had been worried about killing that frog ever since it happened; genuinely frightened it might be a big enough sin to damn her to Hell for all of eternity.

'It doesn't work like that,' Faith said. 'He doesn't talk to me like that.'

The twins were still sat beside each other, perched on the edge of Faith's bed; Grace's face still sunken.

'Then how do you know he's talking to you if he doesn't talk to you?' she asked. Faith shrugged. 'Is it Jesus or God who talks to you?' Faith turned to face her sister. 'What's the difference actually?' Grace asked. 'Is Jesus God? Daddy has said that, hasn't he? But then... I thought... isn't Jesus God's son?'

Faith curled down her mouth and turned her bottom lip out.

'Oh yeah...' she said, nodding slowly.

'Is it a man's voice when he speaks to you?' Grace asked. Her seventh question in the space of ten seconds; all but one of them not answered.

✞

'I've told you... I don't hear his voice,' Faith said.

And then they both just sat there for ages, saying nothing while staring around their neat bedroom.

'But can you,' Grace broke the silence, *'ask him again... please? I just want to know if killing a frog means... means...'*

'You're not going to go to Hell,' Faith said. *'Cos you follow Jesus —and it says in the Bible that Jesus always forgives. What's the verse Daddy always says, "Be kind to one another..."'*

"'Be kind to one another, tenderhearted, forgiving one another, as God in Christ forgave you,"' Grace said.

'Yeah, 'sactly.'

'What, so... God will definitely forgive me for killing Grebit?'

'Yeah,' Faith said.

And then Grace got down on her knees and clasped her hands together.

'Lord Jesus Christ,' she said, squeezing her eyes shut. *'I am sorry for killing Grebit and thank you for forgiving me for doing it.'*

Then she opened her eyes and slapped Faith on the thigh.

'Right, let's play with our dolls. Which one do you want to play with?' she said.

The guilt of killing the frog dissipated somewhat for Grace after that little chat, but it darted to the forefront of her mind three years later when she was told she'd have to give a priest her first confession prior to making her Holy Communion.

'Dear Father,' she said to Fr. Michael—the local priest at Rathcoole Church, *'this is my first confession.'*

The priest pulled back the curtain inside his confession box and smiled at the tiny seven year-old sitting in front of him.

'I welcome you to the practice; it will cleanse your soul. And your name is...' he said, his country accent thick.

'Grace. Grace Tiddle, Father.'

'Ah yes... one of the Tiddle twins. You are a girl of strong faith, I believe.'

'Oh, that I am Father.'

'Well, what is it you wish to confess, my dear?'

'Eh....' She swung her legs back and forth under the wooden bench she was sat upon. 'I want to confess to lying to my mammy and daddy.'

'Hmm... mmm,' the priest murmured.

'I told them I was sick one time when I didn't want to go to dance class and I wasn't sick. I was just tired.' The priest cleared his throat. 'Is that bad, Father... that I lied?'

'Jesus will forgive you, my dear. You should say three Hail Marys in sorrow.'

The priest reached for the curtain.

'Eh... I have one more confession, Father,' Grace said, her legs swinging even quicker now.

'Yes, my dear?' Fr Michael said.

'I killed a frog.'

'A what?'

'A frog. I squashed it with my shoe?'

'You stamped a frog to death?'

Fr Michael's face contorted.

'And I know it says in the commandments... it says Thou Shall Not Kill. But... but... I, eh... I don't know why I did it. I was only four at the time. And it is just a frog though right, and doesn't Thou Shall Not Kill actually mean humans? I think it means just humans. Does it, Father? Does it just mean humans?'

'Well, er...' Fr Michael held a fist to his mouth, to disguise his twitching grin. 'Twenty Hail Marys.'

'Twenty?'

'Yes, twenty.'

'And Jesus will forgive me because my sister says that Jesus will forgive anything. Does he... does he forgive anything?'

The priest tweaked at the curtain again.

'Well, I'm afraid I must move this on, I have dozens of you Holy Communion boys and girls to see today.'

✝

Grace stood up, and was so small the priest could only see the tip of her bow through his window frame.

'Twenty three Hail Marys in total for me, Father, yes? And all is forgiven?'

The priest widened his grin.

'Yes my dear, twenty-three Hail Marys.'

It took Grace less than ten minutes to fire out the Hail Marys. It was a nothing punishment for her. She was made to do six times that by her dad while kneeling in front of their crucifix just after she'd killed the frog anyway. And now surely all was officially forgiven. Because that was an actual confession. To an actual priest. In an actual church.

The twins made their Holy Communion the Saturday following their first confessions. The problem with them being dressed as cute as pie practically every day of their lives was that when it came to their Holy Communion, they were dressed decidedly average in comparison to everybody else. They were still cute. As cute as any seven year old in a bride's dress can possibly look. But so was every one of their peers that day.

Though they still had a great time of it. And both collected over a thousand euros each. They just kept receiving card after card — mostly with pictures of angelic young girls on the front — and every time they opened one either a one-hundred euro note or a fifty euro note would fall out.

Poor aunt Janet was cringing when the girls were opening her and Eoin's card because they knew the blue notes they put inside were going to make them look cheap. Still, the twins looked up and thanked Janet and Eoin with as much authenticity and conviction as they thanked everybody else.

Their Holy Communion was only the fifth time they'd ever met their aunt Janet. She had long since moved to Monaghan — years before they were born – and yet they had never been to visit that county in all their seven and a half years. They only saw her on the odd occasion she would visit Dublin; perhaps for a family funeral, *or — on this occasion — a Holy Communion. The twins were confused about Janet; never quite realising why she wasn't part of their church family. Neither Clive nor Dorothy had ever brought up the reality that outside their 'family' there were people who didn't actually take what was written in the Bible quite so literally. Janet and Eoin, though, weren't all that different from those who attended The New St Benedict's Church. They were down and outs, and lonely too. Neither of them held down a job in Monaghan; preferring to live off benefits. They certainly weren't living their best lives; but they still didn't reach low enough to seek refuge in any church—let alone the Tiddle church. Janet resented Clive for becoming all holy because she never thought for one minute that he believed any of that stuff. She'd often try to strike up the argument with him, but he would douse it pretty quickly.*

The night of the twins' Holy Communion was the first time they'd ever spent in proper conversation with their aunt Janet and uncle Eoin. They were yawning by eight p.m. and so Dorothy suggested Janet and Eoin bring the twins back to the bungalow while she, Clive and Kelly cleaned up after the long day of celebrations.

'Did yis have a good day?' Janet asked as the four of them slowly walked back up the winding roads that led to the Tiddle bungalow.

'The best,' Grace said.

'And you... Faith?' Eoin asked.

Faith didn't move a muscle in her face. She just continued to walk, her eyes rolled back in her head.

'Oh, she's praying,' Grace said. 'She does that. Well, she's not really praying... she's listening.'

Eoin turned to stare at his wife and as he did so Janet stiffened her nose at him, disguising her laugh. Then she tried to change the subject to something that didn't give her the heebie jeebies.

Dorothy didn't erupt when she came home just gone midnight to see the twins still up talking to Janet and Eoin; she just stared at the clock, then raised an eyebrow at them before they jumped up. They raced each other to their bedroom, calling out a goodnight to Janet and Eoin, then they climbed out of their white dresses and in to their patterned pyjamas before they both knelt down to pray.

Dorothy had come home alone because Clive suggested he'd stay behind to do some editing on the sermon he was to offer his 'family' the following day. He was lying. He didn't do any paperwork. Instead, he spent the next hour and half fucking Kelly. Mostly from behind.

They were pretty much at it every week then; whenever Clive was in the humour and he could come up with an excuse to Dorothy that his needs lay elsewhere. Kelly had long since stopped enjoying the sex, but she sure was still loving the attention she was getting from the leader of her church. His predominance was still very much an attraction for her; as if she was getting fucked by the most popular guy at school. The fact that he was an awkwardly tall chap with a rotund belly and a bristle-like moustache with blotchy pink skin wasn't of much importance. What was important was that lots of people wanted his attention. And he was giving it to her.

Dorothy hadn't a clue. Not an iota of a clue. She trusted her husband too much. Trusted Kelly, too.

At this stage, Clive's responsibilities in the church involved the sermons and the counselling of 'family'. Dorothy's input, meanwhile, in to those two areas receded as the church evolved. She became more interested in the accounts; how much each sermon would cost; how much petrol they could put in the bus to bring members of the family to and from the community centre; how much they needed to pay the community centre for rental of the space. Though in truth she didn't have to worry about any of that—because the spend was so insignificant when compared to what was actually coming in. She had to tell Clive one day that they'd need to start hiding the cash somewhere, because so much of it was pouring in. They had always agreed they couldn't use a bank—they had absolutely no paperwork to back up having such large amounts of cash. So they had a large safe installed within the floorboards of their bedroom and began to pack it full of used notes. It took them four years to earn their first one-hundred thousand euro, but less than half that time to earn their second one-hundred thousand. And then the money just wouldn't stop.

Dorothy kept the sums well hidden, though Kelly would ask the odd question here and there about the collections, especially on occasions she would see Dorothy leafing through notes in the office. But she never stumped Dorothy so much as she did the day she suggested the Tiddles must have a huge safe in their house to hold all of those notes. She was genuinely trying to be humorous. It was a quick quip, not meant to cause any offence.

But Dorothy froze in disdain for a moment before she continued to leaf through the notes.

'Mind your own fucking business, Kelly,' she snapped. And that was the start of their falling out.

ALICE

'Morning.'

Obese Guy greets me with a wide smile as soon as I turn onto the corridor us jurors gather in every morning. I look up the line of them and realise I'm the last one to arrive. Again.

'Good night's sleep?' he asks.

'Eh… yeah,' I reply, nodding. Lying.

And then it goes silent between us for way too long. Because all we really want to talk about — all we have in common — is the case. But we can't. Because the twelve of us can only discuss it when we're all together.

When I look down the line of jurors again I notice everybody is in the same boat; afraid to talk to one another. All eleven of them are resting their backs against the wall, until I notice the front few lean off and it causes a domino effect down the line. The young woman dressed all in black must have just opened the door.

We file in one by one, the shuffling of our feet off the blue carpet the only sound that can be heard until Red Head sees me heading for my usual seat next to her and greets me with an overly-familiar welcome, hugging me with one arm.

'How are ya?' she says. 'Sleep well?'

Everyone seems obsessed with how I slept? Maybe I look like shit.

I offer her a thin smile.

'Not really,' I say. Being honest.

I did sleep for a few hours, but on and off. I kept tossing and turning, playing the arguments on repeat over and over in my head, playing the responses I would give to jurors who were demanding the twins were guilty, playing Noel's face on repeat as he watched the video of me and Emmet fucking. Like proper full on fucking. Me being drilled from behind like a slut.

'Me neither,' she says. And then she sits down. And I do the same. Just in time for Scarhead to bark his first order of the day.

'I am just going to open by saying that when I reflected on my performance as Head Juror yesterday I was disappointed. I feel I can do a better job. But that means I need to have more of a rein on proceedings.' Red Head looks back at me, sucking her lips and raising her eyebrows. I really wanna know what her game is. 'Now, I know we have an idea of how everybody was thinking when we left this room yesterday. So I don't propose we do a verdict vote right now... not until we have discussed the case in more detail. We've a long day ahead of us. And I suggest we really kick into the arguments. There are vital parts of this case that we didn't even discuss yesterday.' A few heads nod around the table. 'The safe,' he continues. 'Most of the witnesses. The confession.'

Red Head puffs out a snigger.

'The safe is interesting,' I say. Because that is the argument I rehearsed the most while I was tossing and turning.

The bitch on the phone said the money offers reason for doubt.

'I agree,' Scarhead says, placing his forearms on to the table and leaning forward. 'I'm up for opening our deliberations about what was found in the Tiddle's bedroom safe. Is that a fair place to start day two of our deliberations? Anyone have any objections to that?' He looks down at his notes as mumbles of 'yeses' float around the table. 'The contents of the safe was one of the early points raised by the defendants, but did it *really* tell us much?' Scarhead asks.

Two jurors try to talk over each other—Red Head, who seems awfully keen to race out of the traps, and the old woman with the oversized bust.

'Actually, hold on,' Scarhead shouts over them, waving his hand in the air. 'I said I was going to be a better Head Juror, so rather than just throw questions out there, I want to aim them at individuals, so we all get a chance to talk. Eh... Sinead,' he says, turning to the red head. 'Please... you first. You were quite vocal in your support for a not guilty verdict yesterday, does the money found in the safe play a huge part in that?'

'Not just the money. But the tickets.'

'Really?' Thick-rimmed Glasses says, poking in his first oar of the day.

'Yeah—why would two nine-year-old girls kill their parents on the eve of going on their dream holiday?'

'It was hardly the eve of the holiday,' Scarhead bats straight back at her.

'The holiday was seven weeks away. That is the ultimate time of buzz for a kid going on holiday. The countdown to the holiday itself. Especially this kind of holiday. They'd never been anywhere else like it before. They only ever holidayed in Ireland. Their excitement would have been huge.'

'But do we believe they even knew about the holiday?' Thick-rimmed Glasses asks.

'Yeah… well, they said they did.'

'*They* said they did?' Scarhead raises his eyebrows to a ridiculously high level.

'Hold on. The question was put to them — we all heard the tape of the interview — by Detective…. what was his name, the handsome one?'

'Detective Tunstead,' I say. My first words of the day.

Red Head looks at me, smiles and then stares back at Scarhead.

'Yeah… Tunstead. When he asked her about a holiday, Grace mentioned Disneyland. She knew about this holiday. The twins knew. Why would they kill their par—'

'Hang on,' Scarhead says. 'I don't think it mattered one jot whether these two knew about the holiday or not. They killed their parents. I can't believe we have people in this room who listened to that entire trial and heard everything every witness had to say, and despite that they are *still* saying not guilty.'

'The holiday is absolutely worth arguing about,' Red Head snaps back.

'I agree,' I say, sitting forward, cutting through the tension that was threatening to flare so early into the morning. We're only about four minutes in. It seems to me everybody prepared their arsenals over night, and they're all ready to fire. '*Everything* found in that safe is of huge importance.' Then I cough. Giving myself a vital second to locate the monologue I tried to store to memory last night. 'From a legal point of view, if we here in this room are to find Faith and Grace guilty of this charge, then we must do so without any reasonable doubt, okay?' Heads nod back at me. 'Well, the money drops us all in the reasonable doubt camp.' I shake my hand to the middle of the table waving away anyone who was even thinking of responding so swiftly to that—all part of my rehearsal. 'Because the money opens up the possibility of a motive lying elsewhere. And whilst it is not our job to determine *who* or *what* that motive is or even *how* it came about, we do have to consider the contents of the safe as part of our evidence. And the money found in that safe informs all of us that we don't know the full story of the Tiddle family; especially what Clive and Dorothy were up to.'

'Ah… for crying out loud, they were just Jesus freaks,' Scarhead says. 'They were collecting money every week. That's where all the cash came from.'

'Five hundred grand?' Red Head says, all high-pitched.

'Hold on. Hold on. Hold on,' I say, waving my hand again. 'I wasn't finished yet. I just want to say that once there is doubt about a particular piece of the jig saw, then all the playing pieces must come down.'

Scarhead scrunches up his face.

'That doesn't even make sense,' he says. That's not exactly the reaction I thought I was going to get at the end of my prepared speech. When I rehearsed it last night, I imagined the whole of the jury table nodding back at me and turning their lips downwards. Impressed.

'Jigsaw pieces falling down? Jigsaws don't fall down,' Scarhead says.

'Huh?' I offer back to him. And then I think through what he's saying. And I feel like a fucking idiot. How the hell did I get that muddled up? I must have rehearsed that phrase twenty times over and over to myself last night—and genuinely thought it was impressive every time.

A spark of debate ignites again. But Scarhead silences it by leaning himself across the table and yelling.

'I don't think the safe holds anything of significance,' Oversized Bust says, ending the silence Scarhead's yell created. 'I mean... it's interesting. But didn't we all know the

Tiddle family were a little bit...' she wires her index finger around her temple. 'Everyone who testified in the trial said they were an odd family. Clive's sister Janet says they were strange. Claire Barry the dance teacher. The neighbours. Even their best friend Kelly McAllister admitted to them being different...'

'So?' Red Head says.

'Well, doesn't them having all the church money inside a safe in their house only reaffirm that? That they are different to all of us. They run a church. Money comes through that church. They take it all in... They don't use banks. It's not a traditional—'

'It offers up another motive, that's all we have to understand,' I say interrupting her, trying to reaffirm my point, even though I totally agree with everything she is saying. No matter what angle you look at this trial from, one thing's for certain—the Tiddles are one hell of a strange bunch. 'And if we can agree that it does open the door of even the smallest possibility of another motive, then it gives us legitimate reason to acquit Faith and Grace.'

'You don't really believe they're not guilty, do you?' Thick-rimmed Glasses leans forward to look towards me. He's actually looking at me as if he's disgusted. 'You are just looking to get them off on some technicality, aren't you?'

'I'm trying to do my job properly,' I reply. 'If we are to find Faith and Grace guilty of this crime, then we must be able to swear to do so beyond all reasonable doubt. The Tiddles having that much money in their house offers reasonable doubt.'

'But it doesn't,' Scarhead says. 'It only tells us that Clive and Dorothy were running a church. And pocketing the money. Tell ya what... let me put it to the table by show of hands. Does the contents of what was found in the safe change anybody's mind in terms of what you were thinking yesterday?'

I hold my breath in anticipation of anybody changing their mind over this. Because I worked bloody hard on that argument...

But everybody stays still. Every fucking one. I convinced nobody.

'Okay... well then perhaps we can—'

'The argument about the safe hasn't changed my mind,' Braces interrupts Scarhead. 'But I should say, seeing as you asked, that my mind was changed overnight.' I begin to fidget with my fingers. I spent part of my night wondering about Braces. 'I know I voted guilty yesterday and by the end of the day I said I was undecided... well, I had a good think last night and I wanna say...' She holds a silence for way too long. As if she's revealing the winner of The fucking X Factor. 'I am going back to my original verdict. I think they are definitely guilty.'

Bollocks!

Red Head looks back at me. Then leans in and whispers, 'You argued that well...' I smile back at her. But I feel gutted. I thought I was going to nail it with that little speech, but instead of gaining people to our side, we lost one to the guilty camp. My head begins to spin again. And my hands are getting moist. It's only me, Red Head and Obese Guy now. Jesus. This is close. We've got to hold on. We have to be strong.

'Okay, well, eh... thanks for letting us know you had a good think about it last night and finally came to a settled decision,' Scarhead says, offering Braces a grin.

'Another thing,' he says, before puffing out a pretentious laugh, 'that we didn't really mention yesterday was Faith's confession. Now... Detectives Tunstead and Lowe are on record, in more ways than one, of saying Faith confessed to these murders.'

Red Head laughs. Out loud.

'The confession is a crazy argument,' she says. 'Faith didn't confess to jack shit.'

DAY FOUR

I was furious. Fuming.

I spent most of that night in a stand-off with Tunstead and Lowe—one I didn't win. It was an outrage. A fucking "confession" they called it. We rang Ashe and argued it out over the phone. He decided the twins should spend the night in two separate holding cells with a lawyer called to meet with them the next morning. He said he would reassess as soon as he could get Riordan to view the tape of Tunstead and Lowe's four-minute interview with Faith. I was slapping my hands against the walls of Fairweather's office, snapping at both Tunstead and Lowe. I'd never acted like that before; had never had reason to. The fury was overwhelming. I only managed to calm down when I got home and listened to my wife's light snore as I lay next to her in bed.

Tunstead arrested them on silence. *Silence*—that was his feckin' reasoning. Him and Lowe claimed Faith nodded her head when she was asked outright if she had anything to do with their parents' murders. I watched the tape of their interview, over and over that night. Close to a hundred times. Faith stayed absolutely silent when Tunstead asked her that question, then her forehead slightly tipped forward. It was scandalous.

The footage was grainy and black and white — that's how outdated Rathcoole Station's security system was — but you could clearly see Tunstead get a little over excited as soon as Faith's head took the slightest dip. 'For the record, Faith just nodded her head,' he said, excitedly. And then he repeated the question twice to her. He got no further response, so decided to arrest her there and then. And without further hesitation, he stormed out of that room and into my interview room to arrest Grace.

'I promise you she nodded her head,' Tunstead argued with me. 'The footage doesn't do it justice, but you can see... you can see the nod.'

Lowe agreed with him. Dinah — who was also in the room when they were interviewing Faith — said she wasn't looking at the twin when she made the apparent gesture.

I sat up in the bed that night and replayed the footage in my head again and again until I eventually fell asleep.

It was a heavy sleep my alarm woke me from at seven a.m the next morning but I darted out of bed, my mind immediately alert. I headed straight for the station; in the same clothes as the day before and without a breakfast. Again.

Johnny was there, waiting on me so he could finish his shift. He, along with twenty-four other uniforms — and some volunteers — had spent much of the night combing the areas within a two mile radius of the Tiddle bungalow. After I got an update from Johnny, I popped in to the holding cells to speak with the twins. I kept apologising and let them know I was doing my best to get them back... back to wherever it was they were supposed to go back to. I'd often wondered where they'd end up. They could hardly live in Tusla forever. Though their alternative options didn't sound particularly appealing. Clive's sister Janet, who was taking her time reacting to her brother and sister-in-law's tragic murder, didn't exactly seem like the nurturing type. I'd checked their records in the system. They'd both been arrested for petty crimes over the years. Nothing major. Shoplifting. Minor fraud, where Eoin scammed three hundred euros from door-to-door collections using a fake charity laminate. He never spent time behind bars; just community service—painting fences for two weeks. Kelly had had one arrest to her name. A drunk and disorderly. In and out of the cell in one night, she was. All in all, it hardly seemed like the ideal environment for two grieving girls to be living amongst.

I did wonder if those connected to the church would take Faith and Grace on. I thought initially Kelly McAllister might end up with them. From everybody I questioned during the investigation, it seemed she was the closest to the family; certainly closer than Janet and Eoin. The Tiddles ran quite the church—between four and five hundred devoted followers attending every Sunday sermon. It was a hell of an operation. And Kelly McAllister was at the top of that organisation. She was the Tiddle's left-hand woman. Her and Clive and Dorothy spent day-in and day-out with each other. Though when Quayle had spoken to Kelly, he got the distinct impression she wasn't exactly enamoured by the twins. She asked how they were, constantly. But she didn't go to Tusla to meet them; certainly didn't suggest she would take care of them.

As soon as I heard Fairweather's familiar footsteps at the door of the station I raced out to meet her.

'Have you seen this tape?' I snapped.

'Ashe sent it to me last night,' she replied.

I shrugged my shoulders at her. She knew what I meant; knew I was furious she didn't return any my calls.

'Quayle... you and I go back twenty-five years together. I

adore you. You are like family to me.' She looked down. 'Everyone is saying they did it. Nobody knows what psychological condition these girls have, but we need to get tests done on them. They could be psychotic in some capacity. Clive and Dorothy... they were killed with knife wounds consistent to those delivered by somebody of the twins' height and strength and—'

'Uuuuugh,' I grunted, interrupting her.

My blood was about to boil over. I thought if I was going to get support from anyone it would be her.

'Look, Quayle,' she said. 'Everybody wants to get this case right. Ashe is absolutely certain that the arrest is fully warranted and I've been led to believe Riordan is going to agree with him this morning, officially. I've heard he has viewed the tape and feels we must do our job and take these girls in. He is due to ring me first thing this morning to confirm. It's why I'm in so early.'

I held my hand to my forehead and just stared back at my boss. Then she shrugged *her* shoulder.

'The girls have been appointed council. A Mr. Phelim O'Brien. It was all arranged last night.'

O'Brien wasn't a run-of-the-mill defence council lawyer. He was from a decent firm—Costello and Lynam. The best man in Dublin Tusla could organise for the twins at such short notice. He ended up coming to their rescue that morning; proving to be more than a match for Riordan in a phone conversation we were all in on. Ashe, Tunstead and Lowe as well as me and Fairweather were standing around a speakerphone inside Fairweather's pokey office, my toes constantly tapping in frustration.

'It is a nod of the head,' O'Brien said, 'no doubt. But a nod of the head is not an affirmative answer to Detective Tunstead's question. Faith is a child lacking a huge amount of confidence. She repeatedly looks downwards when asked a question. And I know that having only spent ten minutes with her before this phone call. You know and I know there will be a diagnosis for this child. Perhaps both children.'

And that was that. The twins were out of their holding cells within half an hour. And I was feeling pretty smug.

I thought O'Brien was great. I've often wondered how differently he would have handled Faith and Grace's trial had Gerd Bracken not jumped on it for the exposure.

Johnny and Sully contacted me soon after the twins were released and told me aunt Janet was due in Dublin later that afternoon.

I met her for the first time at Tusla. She had been asked to visit the children as soon as she arrived from Monaghan. She was dressed in a tracksuit and her hair was matted to her head; unlikely washed in quite a few days. Maybe weeks. And her eyes looked heavy; worn from what looked like a tough life.

She was a strange sort; but in a different way. She looked like she didn't have any direction in life. Perhaps she needed to belong to Clive and Dorothy's church, but when I asked her if she too was a woman of faith while we were alone in Tusla, she produced a sarcastic snort.

It wasn't a surprise that she was odd. Isn't that what they say about all the Tiddles—that they're odd. Though her name wasn't Tiddle anymore. It was Petersen. She'd married a Monaghan man twenty years prior after meeting him at a former friend's hen party. They lived in a tiny flat on the edge of a town that reached pretty much to the Northern Irish border. She told me that she barely saw nor heard from Clive practically her whole life. They might meet up at the odd Christmas and almost certainly at a family funeral. She insisted it wasn't Clive's dedication to the church that drove them apart; it was that she always felt him to be different to her.

'We never felt like brother and sister,' she said before she curled a stick of gum into her mouth. 'Not even when we were kids. And I think when he went to the church, that was kinda the feather that broke the camel's back for us. Because he was looking for a new family, and I guess I was kinda happy to let him find a new family. I feel sorry for him. And Dorothy. I do. I never hated them. I just didn't love them. That's all. That's not a crime.'

She slowly counted in her head when I asked her how many times she had met the twins. 'About eight or nine,' was the answer she came up with. Pretty much once a year.

'When's the last time you saw the twins?'

'I think it was their Holy Communion a couple of years ago.'

'And you haven't spoken with them since?'

'A few phone calls. They liked to call me. But not that many.'

'What's your impression of the twins?'

She sat back in her chair.

'Bit odd, aren't they? I mean... why wouldn't they be? Being raised inside a church. No chance of being normal, had they?'

I pursed my lips at her and nodded my head.

'I believe you were in Dublin two days prior to the murders. You didn't see your family then?'

She shook her head.

'Very rarely popped by to see Clive when I'm in Dublin. I'd see some friends, do some shopping on Henry Street... that's about it.'

'Well, I have to inform you, Janet. You are Faith and Grace's next of kin,' I said.

She didn't react. She just sat there; almost non-plussed, twisting at her hooped earrings

'Of course. They can move in with me and Eoin,' she said '...if they've nowhere else to go.'

The twins weren't hesitant to leave Tusla with her. But they didn't exactly seem in a rush to get out of there either. Though, as Johnny repeatedly said to me, they never seemed to feel any way about anything.

I waved at the twins as they were driven away. Only Grace noticed me—she wiggled a goodbye with her baby finger.

I'd watched Tunstead and Lowe's interview with Faith so many times, I had almost forgot about my own interview with Grace. So I turned on my heels, settled in to the monitor room at Rathcoole Garda Station and pressed play on the tape of my short interview.

From the high angle of the recording, Grace looked even smaller than she really was, sat back into one of Fairweather's oversized office chairs.

'Kelly,' she said. And my nose inched closer to the monitor.

'Huh?' I replied to her on the tape.

'Kelly. Kelly is always in our kitchen. She comes in the back door, leaves by the back door.'

I stopped the recording, sat there in silence for a while, then snatched at my blazer and headed for the door.

'Where you off to, Quayle?' Fairweather called out as I passed her.

I didn't answer. I sprint-walked to my car, hopped inside and drove straight to the community centre.

ALICE

We watched the footage on loop. Probably twenty to twenty-five times—Tunstead asking the question, Faith's head slightly dipping as an answer.

When this was shown in court for the first time I was adamant she was admitting to everything; she literally tilted her forehead forward to answer 'yes' to a direct question.

'She's just looking down. That's no confession,' I say.

'It isn't so much that it's a confession,' Thick-rimmed Glasses says, 'it's her natural reaction to being asked the question. Her and Grace had obviously sworn each other to secrecy over this; that they wouldn't admit anything to anyone. And my God are they good at it... even to today they are denying everything. But here...' he says, standing up and jamming his finger onto the screen hanging on the wall of the jury room, 'she let her guard slip.'

'So you are saying she let her guard slip for one millisecond of this whole debacle ... yet for the past two years, she managed to keep her guard up? What you're saying doesn't make sense. This is not a confession.'

I look around the table and shake my head.

'C'mon, Alice, she nodded,' Scarhead says.

'She dipped her head, afraid to answer the question, just like she's afraid to answer any question. If you asked Faith Tiddle what her favourite colour was, she'd dip her head. She is not a communicator. There should have been a bloody investigation into why these guards thought it was okay to interview the twins separately without any legal representation.'

'They had the Tusla reps with them. It was legitimate.'

'That's not legal representation!'

I was handling this as well as I could. Faith slipped up for a second, almost fell out of character. She nodded when Tunstead asked her if she had anything to do with the murders as a natural reaction. Then she froze. I'm certain of it.

'Listen,' Red Head says, cutting through the tension that's threatening to flare. 'Regardless of what you think happened or didn't happen in that interview with Faith, the fact of the matter is we can not convict based on that nod of her head. It's not evidence. It is not a smoking gun. It is a frightened nine-year-old girl who had just lost her parents, and just been separated from her twin sister — her other half — for the first time since they'd lost her parents. For the first time ever, probably. She was frightened and confused. I — like Alice here — think it's an absolute disgrace that the cops were allowed to interview in this manner. I urge you all to not consider this... this *confession* as you all call it as reason enough to find these girls guilty. In no way is this a confession. As I said earlier, it really is jack shit.'

'But the judge allowed this tape in court, Sinead... he wants us to deliberate it. He wants us to consider it as part of the evidence,' Thick-rimmed Glasses says.

'I think I'd even be shy being interviewed by Detective

Tunstead, right? What is he... six foot four, handsome like a movie star,' I say.

'What's what he looks like got to do with it?' Scarhead replies.

'Well... because to a shy girl of nine years of age who has only ever been in communication with her mam and dad and twin sister her whole life, she must have felt all kinds of intimidation sat opposite him. I mean... I know I would and I'm a grown woman.'

'Ah come on. Faith had experience of being at church gatherings every week... she didn't just deal with her direct family. She had new people to meet all the time. Hundreds of them. You're just making excuses for her now—'

'Hold on... hold on,' the woman with the big bust says. 'I'm with you.' She points at Scarhead. 'But this lady has a point too.' She curls her finger to me. 'There is no question, as Gerd Bracken argued during the trial, that Faith suffers with levels of anxiety... what was it he called it?'

'Social anxiety disorder,' Red Head says.

'Yes. Well... we can all agree from seeing her at the trial that she is not a girl who likes to communicate. I don't even remember seeing her talk to Grace, just a nod of the head and the odd whisper in the entire two weeks. Have to say... I am certain these girls are guilty of this crime and I won't be changing my verdict. But I think we should, in this instance, agree that Faith suffers with some kind of disorder and to argue that the twins *definitely* did this because Faith slightly nodded her head is being unfair to justice. We have now watched that tape I don't know how many times... we have gone around in circles arguing what is on that footage and we are getting nowhere.'

The room falls silent. It's always awkward when it falls silent, even though it falls silent quite a lot. It's just a case of jurors allowing a realisation to seep in.

'You're right,' Acne Girl replies to Big Bust. 'Perhaps we shouldn't fixate on the actual video footage of the interview... what about this Detective... what's his name again... the tall handsome one?'

'Tunstead,' I said.

'Yeah... Tunstead, perhaps we'd serve our time better discussing his testimony rather than obsessing about this tape. He did say a few interesting things on the stand. He came across a hell of a lot better than that Quayle guy.'

'That's not fair,' Red Head says. 'Why is everyone so keen to belittle Detective Quayle? As far as I make out, he was the most caring person involved in this case; he had everybody's best interests at heart right from the beginning.'

'Not this again,' Scarhead says. 'We've argued about Quayle. We've argued how he investigated this. We've argued his testimony. Lets move on. Otherwise we're going to get nowhere. We're going around in circles. I agree with this gentleman. Let's discuss Detective Tunstead... an interesting man, I found.'

'I trust him,' Braces says. And immediately after she does so, I tut. I feel like I've totally lost her now. She swayed yesterday. But today she's right back in the guilty camp. Firmly back in it. 'He just came across as very precise. As if he was in total control. He believes the girls did it. Is adamant.'

'I, personally, thought he was a little bit sleazy,' Obese Guy says.

'Me too,' I say. Even though I didn't think that at all. Tunstead *is* like a movie star; he has real presence—is very fanciable. I believed every word that came out of his mouth. 'He came across as someone who has way too high an opinion of himself. You can't trust people like that.'

'Jesus Christ. We can't even agree on the personality of a bloody witness,' Thick-rimmed Glasses says. 'As a twelve, we don't agree on anything, do we? We all have different opinions on every bleedin' aspect of this trial. Not just whether the twins are guilty or not, but whether Quayle is a good detective, whether Tunstead is a good detective. I'm just getting sick to the back teeth of this back and forth, arguing about stuff that isn't even relevant. Did the fuckin' twins kill their parents or not... that is all we have to answer to. Not whether Tunstead was handsome or sleazy. Christ!' He covers his face with his hands, pushing his glasses upwards. Probably because he was aware he was turning beetroot red. I totally get his frustration. We have been spending way too much time going off on tangents we really don't need to be going off on. Though the tangents are suiting me. Holding out is key.

'I'm sorry,' I say. 'But our job is to argue all aspects of this case. We're not going to deliberate such a long trial in such a short amount of time.'

'Please can we just end this today?' Thick-rimmed Glasses pleads, taking off his glasses and rubbing at his eyes. 'The last thing we need is us all coming back here next week.'

He isn't the only juror hoping we can end this before the weekend started. A few others nod their heads and mumble in agreement with him.

The fact that it is a Friday is playing on their minds. It has been playing on mine too. If we don't conclude our verdict today, there is a really big chance we will all be back here next Monday morning, sitting around this table again, arguing nonsensical aspects of the trial. My mind is focusing, however, on something that I am hoping may come to fruition.

'Perhaps the judge won't have us back next week,' I say. 'If we don't come to an agreed verdict by the end of the day, maybe she'll declare a hung jury.'

'Ye think so?' Quiff asks me.

'It's possible. We'll have been arguing for practically two whole days…Judge McCormick might feel that's enough.'

'But sure, she hasn't even come back to us yet to say she'd take less than a unanimous verdict. I don't think she's close to putting an end to these deliberations as you may hope, Alice,' Scarhead says.

'Listen,' Big Bust intervenes. 'Why don't we all see where we're at right this minute? Things may have changed for jurors over the course of this morning's deliberations. I know a couple of jurors were swaying in their verdicts yesterday afternoon. Do you think we should have another vote?'

'I guess that makes sense,' Scarhead says. 'Perhaps we're closer to a verdict than we realise.'

'I don't think so,' I say. And then a huff of groans sound out from different seats. They all hate me. Me and Red Head and Obese Guy. Because we're the ones stopping them from returning to normality.

'Right, let's have a vote,' Scarhead says. 'By a show of hands.' I rub my sweating palms up and down my thighs as he speaks. 'Those whose verdict is not guilty, can you raise your hand?'

My hand and Red Head's hand shoot up. Then we both slightly lean forward to look down the line of heads on our side of the table and notice Obese Guy raise his hand. I glance to my left. Towards Quiff and Braces. But they remain still. It's not really a surprise.

'And those whose verdict is Guilty, can you please raise your hands?'

All of the remaining jurors hold their hands aloft. Except for Quiff. He's still motionless.

'Sorry young man,' Scarhead says to him. 'You, eh…'

'I'm undecided,' Quiff says.

Thick-rimmed glasses audibly puffs out his cheeks,

making a loud fart-like sound. But he's not the only one who has shown a touch of exhaustion at what Quiff has just said, others reel themselves back in their chair and wash their hands over their faces.

They're all beginning to think what I've been thinking.

We're gonna be a hung jury.

DAY FOUR

A déjá vu hit me as soon as I pushed open the double doors to the church. All heads turned to face me—just as they had done when I'd pushed those doors open two days prior.

I took two steps into the awkward silence, then paused and clasped my hands.

Ever so slowly, Kelly eventually stepped down from the makeshift altar and click-clacked her way up the long aisle to approach me. She moved so slowly that it was genuinely creepy; like something from a horror movie—her stumpy high-heels slapping off the floorboards of the basketball court.

'G'd afternoon, Detective Quayle,' she said in her sweet Glaswegian purr. 'Have ya more news fo' us?'

I took a step and leaned my cheek towards her ear.

'I, eh… I was hoping to talk to you… alone,' I whispered. I leaned back to observe her face. She just turned her lips downwards and nodded her head.

'Well... am in the middle of a mass dedicated to the

memories of our leaders, Can you wait till am finished?' she said.

I looked up at the multiple rows of faces still staring back at me.

'Sure.'

Kelly touched me on my shoulder, then turned on her heels and walked slowly — *painfully* slowly — back to the stage. When everybody's eyes followed the click-clacking of her shoes, I snuck myself on to a chair in the back row and then listened as Kelly bullshitted her congregation in the sweetest of Scottish lilts.

The gist of her nonsense was about how God had a plan for Clive and Dorothy and that they were taken from this earth, in this way, for a purpose.

It unnerved me a little that the praying all focused on the two dead Tiddles; not necessarily the two who were still alive. But it didn't shock me. It's hard to be shocked by anything these staunch believers say anyway. So much of their beliefs are contradictory. If they truly believed God had a plan and that Clive and Dorothy were in a happier place... why the hell were they all dabbing at their eyes with tissues?

'Why, eh... why no mention of Faith and Grace?' I asked Kelly as soon as she led me into the back office, behind the stage, once her eulogy was over. It was the first question I nailed her with—she had barely closed the door behind us when I asked it.

She stared at me, then fidgeted with her fingers.

'I did mention Faith and Grace, Detective,' she said.

'Barely. You said you were praying for them, that you know God has a plan for them... actually... lemme ask you this, what do you mean by that exactly?'

She sat down, then motioned her hand to the chair opposite hers, across from a desk strewn with paperwork.

I took the seat, then leaned forward... letting her know I was still awaiting an answer to the question I'd posed.

'Do you want me explain to you how we here in this church believe the world works, Detective, s'that what yer askin'?' she says.

'I'm asking a simpler question than that, Kelly. You said you knew God had plan for Faith and Grace…. what is this plan?'

She leaned forward, mirroring my two elbows on the desk and smiled.

'God has a plan fo' us all, Detective.'

I pinched the bridge of my nose and silently sighed.

'I don't need a sermon, with all due respect, Kelly, on your beliefs. I just need you to let me know what you think God has planned for the twins.'

She sat back and clasped her hands.

'I don't know,' she said.

'But you just told everyone out there you knew God had a plan.'

'Yes, but what that plan is I don't know. We are not privy to God's—'

I held my hand up to stop her going on and on about absolutely nothing.

'Did you or did you not reluctantly mention Faith and Grace in your sermon because you believe they had something to do with Clive and Dorothy's murders?' I asked. Getting to the point. She fidgeted again, looking down at her clasped fingers. 'They are not the only suspects,' I said. She shot a look up at me.

'But they've been arrested for the murders, right? It's been all over the newspapers, Detective. We all... all of us here... we all know who Child X and Y are.'

'I'm sorry to inform you that that was a miscommunication between one of our detectives and one of the twins.'

Her face contorted.

'Huh? So... they've bin let out?' Her Scottish lilt went even more high pitched.

'Yes.' They have been brought to the home of Janet Petersen—Clive's sister.' Kelly looked to her hands again. 'Do, eh... do you know Janet?' I asked.

'Yes, well.... I've met her a few times.' She sat back upright. 'Who, eh... who else are your suspects, Detective?'

I tilted my head

'I'm sorry, Kelly. I can't divulge that information.'

'It was the twins!' she said, her face still, her eyes wide. She was glaring at me as if she was willing herself to not blink.

'Kelly, with all due respect—'

'It said in the papers the stab wounds were by the hands of children.'

'Don't believe all you read in the papers, Kelly,' I said. 'The stab wounds may not necessarily have come from children. They came from somebody short.'

She creased her face at me again.

'They are short, Detective. Of course it was them. Who else could it be?'

I fell silent; not because I didn't want to answer her, but because I wanted to study how straight she was being with me. I wanted her to know that when I said the word 'short' that I was staring straight at her petite little features. She didn't baulk though, nor give anything away.

'How much do you know about the running of this place, from a business point of view?' I asked.

'Detective... it was the twins. There is no conspiracy to be had here.'

'What if I told you,' I said, tilting forward, 'that half a million euros in used notes were found in Clive and Dorothy's bedroom?'

She looked down at the table first, then her mouth slightly parted. I knew right then and there she was about to lie to me.

'I don't know anythin' about no money,' she said.

'Really?'

'Really,' she said.

'Why are you so certain the twins did this?' I asked.

'Well… given everythin' we've heard. It's not just the newspapers. Some of your uniformed officers have been very good to us… calling in here each day to keep us up to date with the case.'

'No. No. Hold on,' I said, shaking my finger at her. 'I don't want to know what the newspapers told you or what police officers have told you. I want to know why *you* are saying the twins did it.'

Kelly held her eyes closed for a brief moment. And when she opened them, they were glistened with forming tears.

'Because Faith and Grace… well… eh… well, they're just… they've always been really strange. Creepy,' she says.

'That's tough judgement,' I said to her, 'coming from a Christian.'

'Och… It's just that I know the twins. *We* know the twins,' she said nodding over my shoulder, back out to her 'family' in the church.

'And?' I said.

'And… like I said, we'd all agree that the twins have just always been a bit odd.'

'Odd as in serial killer odd?' I asked.

She grimaced and shook her head at the same time.

'That's not what I'm saying.'

'What about the money, Kelly? Why don't you leave the detective work of trying to determine who the killer is and help the enquiries by answering straightforward questions?

Clive and Dorothy Tiddle had half a million euros in used notes inside a safe in their bedroom. Why?'

'I... I.... I don't know,' she said. 'I am...' she paused.

'Surprised?' I said. I was beginning to enjoy this. It was so rare I ever got to lead the questioning on a suspect in a case like this. I was convinced I was doing great at getting under Kelly's skin. Then again, perhaps a five-foot, high-pitched Scottish lass isn't exactly difficult opposition.

'Surprised? At the amount, yes. That they had money... no.'

'So you knew they had big money?'

'I knew nothing.... that's the truth,' she said. 'I just suspected that they 'ad money. They were very generous. I got so many gifts from them... lots of us did.'

'Where do you suspect their money came from?' I asked.

'Well... here,' she said.

'Half a million?'

She thinned her lips.

'Like I said, I'm surprised with the amount...'

'Me too,' I said.

'You knew the business of the church inside out, did you not, Ms McAllister?'

'I.... I... I think I'm going to need to speak with my lawyer,' she said.

Bingo!

'Ms McAllister, you are not under caution in any way. I am here, asking you questions as a witness. You knew the family better than most.... better than anyone, given what I understand. I am simply trying to solve the case of—'

'I am no longer gonnae answer any of ya questions, Detective. If you wish to continue to interview me, I will insist on the presence of legal representation.'

I held my hands up and dipped my head.

'Kelly, I will leave you in peace,' I said, 'if you will just do me and the investigation a good turn by answering one more question.'

She flicked her eyes up to meet mine, but didn't say anything.

'Where were you between half past ten and midday last Saturday the fifteenth of August?'

She huffed a tiny laugh at me.

'You think I'm a suspect?' she asked.

'It's a simple question, Ms McAllister.'

She looked all around herself, down at her clasped hands, then left, then right.

'Saturdays are my days off. The only day off I have each week. I was… where I normally am on a Saturday afternoon. Home for the morning before I went to the, eh… I was in The Velvet Inn. Watching the horse racin'.'

'You were in the pub that early in the day?' I asked.

'You said one more question, Detective.'

I grinned.

'Like I say… I'm sorry for your losses, Ms McAllister. I'll leave you to it.

I stood up, nodded my head at her and walked out of her office, past the stage and down the aisle; my head down so as not to make eye contact with any of the congregation who all seemed eager to talk to me. I paced as swiftly as I could without coming across as rude, my mind whirring. Something wasn't adding up. Kelly seemed very defensive; hesitant to answer some of my questions. Though it wasn't my questions that seemed to be irking me. It was one of her answers.

The Velvet Inn. That's where Tommo Nevin drinks.

✝

Clive sharply stood up — his matted-with-sweat hairy belly hanging over his y-fronts — and rested both of his hands on his hips.

'What are you talking about?' he hissed, his tone curt, sharp.

They were both standing either side of a double bed in one of the city-centre's Ibis Hotel rooms. Even though The New St Benedict's Church was bringing in over ten thousand euro a week in collections, Clive never got out of the habit of using cheap hotels for his rendezvous with Kelly.

She puffed out her cheeks and looked down at her toes.

'I'm talkin' bout us... being more together. Committin' to each other.'

Clive squinted at her, his bottom jaw hanging open in shock.

'You want me to... you want to...'

'Leave Dorothy!'

Clive's mouth popped as it snapped shut. Then he sat on the edge of the bed with his back to Kelly and washed a hand over his face.

'Don't be a silly woman!' he said.

'Clive—'

'Don't be a silly woman, Kelly!' he snapped, turning around. He got on to his knees on the bed and gripped both of her biceps. 'Why would you ask such a thing you silly, silly woman. You need to... you need to repent for asking such things—'

'You've been having sex with me for o'er fifteen years, Clive. Dorothy is... Look, Dorothy is old. She's getting cranky in her old age. You guys barely speak. She doesn't speak with me anymore. She sits in the office all day countin' money and you... well, you're either meetin' members of the family or saying a mass. And when you're not doing either of those things you're having sex with me. Your marriage is nothin' anymore. Leave her. I need someone to wake up with in the mornings... I'm forty-two now...'

Clive's grip squeezed tight around her biceps. Then he began to shake her.

'You will repent for what you have just said. You seek the forgiveness of not only our Lord Jesus, but me also—your man. "I do not permit a woman to teach or to exercise authority over a man; rather, she is to remain silent."' Clive heavy-breathed as he spat the Bible verse at her. 'Never let this thought cross your mind again, Kelly. Listen to me carefully... if this does cross your mind, you will need to find another family.'

Kelly's eyes had already been filling with tears, but as she nodded her head in response — Clive's fingers still tight around her biceps — one finally fell.

'Okay,' she said, slapping the streaming tear away with her palm.

And then she quietly slipped on the clothes she had worn to the hotel the night before and left the room, closing the door carefully behind herself.

Kelly wasn't entirely sure why she made that proposal to Clive that morning. She was feeling isolated, frustrated. And that led to her eventually snapping at him by asking him to leave his wife... even though that wasn't exactly what she wanted herself. Her relationship with Dorothy had soured after she was sworn at. And soon after that Kelly's role within the church was diluted; she was certainly never allowed in the office where the money was being counted again. And other 'family' members were beginning to get picked over her for some routine duties that she had been responsible for over many years. The only time she really spent with the Tiddles was on Sundays, at the sermon. Just like everybody else.

She turned back to the drink for comfort. And the gambling. She was actually drunk the day Tommo Nevin cornered Clive outside the community centre one Friday evening. Though the confrontation — as soon as it got heated — sobered her up somewhat.

'We don't want none of those kind around here, no more,' Nevin shouted.

'What do you mean those kind?' Clive replied, as calmly as he could; trying to ease the tension that had already become apparent.

'This is Ireland, Tiddle. A beautiful part of the country. Let's keep it Irish.'

Nevin took an intimidating step towards Clive after saying that. But Clive held his ground and smiled through the bristles of his thick moustache.

'You're correct. It is Ireland,' he said.

'Well then, stop bringing them darkies up this neck of the woods. They're everywhere. They're in the bloody Spar doing groceries, hanging around the cafes. I even saw two of them in the pub the other day. The neighbours didn't mind them going to your church, Tiddle, but they're all drawing a line now. Nobody wants them hanging around the mountains.'

Clive interlinked his fingers and placed them on his bulging belly.

'Darkies? Are you referring to their skin; for I see dark skin as not a problem at all. Dark souls... ah now, that is a different matter altogether. And I fear it is a dark soul you may possess, my dear neighbour. Fancy a talk up in my office? We do cups of tea and Jammy Dodg—'

'Don't you fucking dare try to preach to me, you deluded gombeen,' Nevin said, taking one more step towards Clive in an attempt to match him for stature. But his chest only reached to Clive's navel and a moment of awkwardness grew over them both. Kelly, who had been standing watching the confrontation in silence, noticed Nevin curl his fists into a ball and then ran towards them.

'Stop it, stop it, you two,' she said, getting between them and stretching her arms out wide.

Nevin eventually backed away, smirking out of the side of his mouth, and left to walk back down the winding roads that led to the tiny terraced estate he lived in at the bottom of the mountains. Clive didn't even take the time to consider thanking Kelly for her input, and instead huffed and puffed his way back inside the community centre all hot and bothered because somebody had the audacity to talk to him that way. It gave him flashbacks to school; flashbacks he hadn't had in decades.

Kelly had actually known Tommo Nevin's face. He drank in the same pub she had been frequenting since she'd turned back to the booze. She was aware of his first name and the fact that he seemed like an old-school Jack the Lad, though she barely took much notice of him, nor his mates as they'd sit at the bar and rip the piss out of each other. She was too consumed with the horse racing on the screen in front of her every time she went in to The Velvet Inn. Though she did begin to take a bit more notice of Tommo after his confrontation with Clive. She'd often peer over her glass of vodka and coke to stare at him in between races. He was old — almost seventy — but she began to imagine him fucking her; gripping her hair with his tattooed fist and yanking it as hard as he could while he thrusted in and out of her. It was the power of a man that turned Kelly on. Clive had practically convinced her of that. The confrontation Nevin had with Clive that day in the community centre car park had actually made her hot under the collar because somebody was questioning a man she had never seen questioned before.

She would never fuck him. Of course not. He'd probably die of a heart attack if he was to fuck Kelly how she was imagining it in her daydreams. But she liked to fantasise about it. And did so often.

The twins had heard rumours of the confrontation, but as was usually the case, they bit their tongues and didn't ask any questions.

They were too busy doing their own thing anyway, and by this stage and age were much preferring their own company than any congregating with their 'family'. Not that they'd lost their passion for all things Jesus; it was just that they could be themselves when they were in their own company and preferred it that way. The novelty of seeing their daddy speak to a large room full of people had long since worn off. But then again, so too had the novelty of the twins themselves. They just weren't as much of a draw as they used to be, given that a lot of their cuteness had been lost as their bodies stretched. So their staying inside their bedroom most of the time kind of suited everybody. Not that they'd ever miss the Sunday sermon. No chance. They just stopped hanging around the community centre after school to watch 'family' members come and go without so much as holding a polite conversation with them. Staying home was much more enjoyable; much more pleasurable for them.

'What you doing?' Grace asked Faith when she saw her stretching to her tippy toes to turn at the tap.

'Just watering the plants for Daddy.'

'You? Why?'

'Jesus told me to.'

'Oh...' Grace said.

'I saw a picture of flowers being watered in a magazine and I know it was Jesus telling me that the flowers must be thirsty... and look.' Faith walked out of the bathroom carefully carrying a heavy can of water with both hands, and led Grace to the flowerbed at the front of the house. 'They're all dry. Daddy never lets them get this

dry. And then I find a magazine at the bottom of our garden about watering plants and... so...'

Grace tilted her head back.

'So that's how he contacts you, that's how he talks to you? Pictures in a magazine?'

Faith shrugged.

'He just talks to me how he talks to me; different ways for different things.'

'So, not through magazine pictures then?'

Faith shook her head.

'No. That's the first time he's done it through a magazine.'

Grace held a knuckle to her left temple and rolled it around. She was massaging herself; had got a little excited thinking Faith had finally revealed the code. But now she was back to being confused about how Faith and Jesus communicated as she had ever been.

Grace was never jealous that Faith had a direct line to Jesus. She felt if Faith had it, then so did she. Because they came as a pair. It would just go through Faith first and then eventually to her.

She would often look for signs herself, Grace. But it never worked for her. Her lateral thinking was much more advanced than her sister's. What wasn't advanced was her understanding that her sister wasn't as clever as she was.

Grace would take long baths, close her eyes tight and pray to Jesus to drop something inside her head. But it never worked. Or she would kneel down and pray for over an hour at times in the community centre, her eyes fixed on a burning candle wick, begging Jesus to blow it out, just to let her knew he was listening. Or she would stare out her bedroom window, into the long fields that stretched beyond the back of the bungalow, hoping the stars in the night sky would spell out a sign to her. She was actually doing just that at the unusual time of two a.m. one morning when she saw Clive dragging a heavy-looking black plastic bag across the *field. He left it at the foot of the oak tree and then walked back to help Dorothy carry a small step-ladder to the same location.*

Grace rubbed her eyes.

Then she watched as Clive climbed the ladder and fidgeted with a thick branch until a large hole opened up in the trunk. The branch just seemed to spring open, like a special effect in a movie. Then he dropped the bag inside the hole, crunched the branch closed and climbed back down the ladder.

DAY FOUR

The sun had almost disappeared by the time I was strolling up his tiny garden path.

I rattled on the door as hard as I could, not stopping until, through the frosted glass, I could see his blurry figure making his way towards me.

He fake-laughed when he opened the door.

'What are ye accusing me of today, Detective? The disappearance of Betsy Blake?'

Then he produced that horrible side-mouthed grin.

'Mr Nevin, may I?' I motioned over his shoulder and, after a pause, he stepped aside.

'I'm in the middle of me tea,' he said.

When I walked into his living room a plate of unfinished lasagna was sitting on the sofa; an episode of Eastenders paused on the television.

'Wouldn't have put you down as a soap fan, Nevin,' I said.

He shrugged his shoulders.

'Your problem seems to be that you judge books by their covers, Quayle,' he said.

Then he motioned his hand to the worn leather armchair adjacent to where he was eating and nodded.

I took out my notepad before I sat.

'Mr Nevin, when I spoke to you two days ago you discussed, briefly, with me the issue you had with Clive and Dorothy Tiddle bringing immigrants to this neck of the woods for sermons; can you give me more detail on the specific issue you had?'

He shook his head.

'I don't have an issue with them coming to their sermons or to pray or do whatever nonsense it is they do in that community centre. If they wanna come to the community centre and get down on bended knee and talk to the stars... fine by me. That's not the problem I had with Tiddle.' He shivered. Like a bad actor. 'I actually can't believe they're dead. It's eh…. It's…'

'If you can stay on track, Mr Nevin.' I said.

'My problem isn't them coming to do what they wanted to do; my problem is that they don't just go the their church and go home. They stay around the area... shopping, going to the pubs, talking to the neighbours…'

'You have a problem with them talking to other people?'

'Ah, but they don't talk normal, do they? It's preaching. Going around telling folk that God is in their hearts... fuck right off, ye get me?'

'So you *do* have a problem with their religion... I thought your problem was the colour of people's skin?'

He scratched at the back of his head, then picked up his plate and began forking lasagna into his mouth.

'It's not a racist thing, it's just…' he said, chewing, 'it's the silly accents, the differences in people. We don't need that around here.'

'And you think not wanting people here because they have funny accents is *not* racist?'

'Listen, call it what you want, Detective. This is a quiet little town filled with Irish people — Irish people for centuries — and we want to keep it that way.'

'We?'

He swallowed. Picked up another forkful.

'Well... me and whoever else... I know there are other people around here who feel the same as I do. They'd just never say it out loud. I was the only one to confront Tiddle. And that's why you're here, isn't it? Because I was the only one who had the balls to tell him we didn't want that kind round here. But that's as far as I went... I had words with him. I didn't — for Christ sake! — have anything to do with him being killed.' His voice tensed. 'Anyway, I thought you had the killers locked up... their kids did it, right? Probably sick of their parents going on and on about religion. What were they... nine, the papers said? Yeah, probably just grown up enough to realise their parents had them locked inside a cult.'

'The kids didn't do it,' I said.

He looked up at me, and one of his eyebrows raised.

'What, so the newspapers have it all wrong—this Child X and Y thing is a load of bollocks, is it?'

'It was a misunderstanding. Child X and Y were brought in for routine questioning... they were not arrested.'

'Every newspaper reported they were arrested, Quayle. Is this how much you've fucked up this investigation already?' He sniggered out of the side of his mouth again. 'You're arresting their children one minute, coming to me the next.'

I wasn't put out by him laughing at me. I knew I was about to put him up against the ropes. I still had big punches to hit him with.

'Do you think the Tiddle family were worth much money?' I asked him.

He scoffed.

'Probably. Aren't all these religious freaks collecting big dosh? It's the only reason they're in it, right? See those big players in America with their super churches... rolling around in money they are. And they don't pay tax... did ye know that? Not a penny.'

'So you *are* aware the Tiddle family may have had some money?'

'Listen. I don't know nothin' about the Tiddle family, other than they run the church and bring foreigners to this neck of the woods. Yes, I had a row with Clive Tiddle—but don't even think about treating me as a suspect in this murder. You'll be barking up the wrong tree.'

'It's my job to bark up all the trees, Mr Nevin. I've spoken to many people around the mountain side, and those who visit the church. Do you know the only person who ever had a problem with the Tiddles seems to be you?'

'Obviously not, Quayle. Somebody else must have had more of a problem with them than I did, huh?'

'Well, let me put it to you this way, Mr Nevin,' I said. 'You had a problem with the Tiddle family bringing immigrants to the church. You unloaded a racist tirade at Clive Tiddle on the twelfth of June this year. And you have just admitted that you felt the Tiddle family had money.'

He did that stupid snigger thing again.

'You're just making this up as you're going along, Quayle, aren't ya? You don't know what you're doing.'

'You've already fucked up, Mr Nevin—and you are totally unaware of it.'

He dipped his chin into his chest and stared at me.

'Are you gonna tell me how I fucked up?' he asked before burping.

'When I was here two days ago, Mr Nevin, you told me you never heard of Kelly McAllister.'

He made a funny face at me, as if he was squelching up his nose. More proof of his bad acting.

My phone buzzed in my pocket, but I didn't want to take my gaze away from Nevin's scrunched up face.

'Is she the little Scottish lady—'

'Ah... you do know her? So you lied to me the first time I asked you that question...'

My phone buzzed again. It was a text. From Fairweather.

Ring me now!

I held a finger up to Nevin.

'Gimme one sec.'

I pushed at the green button and strolled into Nevin's square hallway.

'Ever hear of Gerd Bracken?' Fairweather said as soon as I held the phone to my ear.

'Course,' I said. And in the silence between me saying that and Fairweather speaking, I knew what she was getting at. The hungry bastard of a lawyer was attaching himself to the twins. Sleazy fecker. The biggest defence lawyer in Dublin— a man as desperate for attention as he is for money.

'You're joking me,' I said.

'Nope. He's out in Janet Petersen's house right now, talking to the twins. He's asked to speak with you as a matter of urgency.'

I peeked back inside at Nevin who was slouching on his sofa, the plate of lasagna now resting on his belly.

'Okay—I'll get myself out there asap,' I said. Then I hung up and called out.

'I'll be back, Nevin.'

He fake laughed loudly as I stormed out of his house, slamming the door shut behind me.

Bracken looked just as slimy and tanned in real life as he

did on TV. I almost baulked backwards when he stretched his hand towards me to introduce himself, his tan was that orange.

'Grace and Faith tell me you have been the only officer they feel they can trust,' Bracken said when we all sat down around the Petersen's round kitchen table. There was me, Janet and her husband Eoin, as well as Bracken's assistant lawyer—a quiet girl called Imogen. She just stared down at the papers in front of her the whole time, taking notes while Bracken threw questions at me. The twins sat in the living room on their own watching cartoon after cartoon.

'Regardless of whether or not Faith and Grace say you have been great with them, ultimately — as lead detective on this case, Detective Quayle — it is your responsibility that they were wrongfully arrested last night. As soon as I heard about their arrest — and the reason for it — I picked up my phone and made sure I was attached to this case. I've taken over from Phelim O'Brien—and now you must answer to me.'

I felt instantly intimidated, though I was well aware Detective/Defence Lawyer relationships were suppose to work the other way around. But he just seemed to ooze control. Somehow.

'Hold on one second,' I said. But I was immediately interrupted by the louder voice.

'No, you hold on, Detective. I have watched the footage of Faith's interview with Detectives Tunstead and Lowe. How could you allow this to happen? How could you allow two innocent girls to be questioned in a police station without appropriate legal council?'

'They had members of Tusla with them... they were offered legal council, they said they were fine with Dinah and Joe.'

He tutted at me, then flicked over his paperwork.

'Have you any idea, Detective Quayle, how much damage arresting two innocent nine-year-old girls could have on their mindsets for the rest of their lives? They have just found their mother's and father's bodies in pools of blood inside their own home, they are right in the middle of the grieving process and then you go and arrest them and keep them locked up in a holding cell overnight...'

'I didn't arrest them!' I said.

'You are the lead detective are you not? This is your case is it not?'

I looked around at the faces staring at me; Janet's face was long and jaded looking. Eoin didn't show much emotion at all, he just sat there with his arms folded. There was no noise from Imogen, except for the sweeping of her pen on paper. When I looked up at Bracken again, his eyebrow was raised —he was still waiting on an answer to his question.

'Listen,' I said holding my palms outwards. 'I *am* in control of this investigation. In fact, when I got the call to come here to meet you I was in the midst of interviewing a suspect who had had issues with the Tiddle family.'

Bracken leaned back in his chair.

'Ah...' he said, turning his bottom lip downwards. 'So you *are* doing other work on this case...'

'I obviously can not divulge any information to you, Mr Bracken.'

'I don't need any more information than you've already given me, Detective Quayle... except perhaps for an answer to one more question.' He leaned forward. 'Sir,' he said, 'do you believe my clients are guilty of this crime?'

'No,' I said, holding his stare. 'You can take it from me, Mr Bracken—the twins didn't have anything to do with this.'

ALICE

I kept eyeballing Quiff across the table, hoping he'd meet my stare—give me some indication that he was going to sway back over to our not guilty camp.

The poor youngfella looked confused. Pained almost. He didn't know what to do; was being dragged by his mind from pillar to post. Yesterday morning he voted not guilty, then changed to guilty by the end of the day. This morning he's being swayed back again; is now undecided. That's great. The more confused he is, the longer he's likely to hold out. And that's what this is all about. Holding out; holding out until the judge's patience wears thin.

I try to put an age on Quiff; he's older than my Zoe but probably only by about four or five years. I'd imagine he's somewhere in his late twenties. I look down the line of heads on my side of the table as deliberations continue around me, and stare at Obese Guy. He wasn't particularly quick to raise his hand to acknowledge his not guilty verdict in the last vote. I hope he's not being swayed. Though I don't think he will be. He seemed adamant the twins were not guilty—even told me so before deliberations began. Red Head won't be swayed either. She seems really intelligent. Her mind is made up. Besides, I've a feeling she might be getting blackmailed too. I'm feeling positive the three of us will hold out.

Then, when this trial is over and done with and the judge declares us a hung jury, I'm going to tell Emmet I can't see him anymore; that our affair has to stop. I'll miss it, of course. The orgasms are just so bloody divine... but they can't be worth it. I'll just have to remember them... play with myself a bit more as I think about Emmet to rid myself of the addiction. I just can't risk Noel and Zoe ever finding out. I was stupid and naïve to even start the affair in the first place. The more I think of it, the more I feel this bitch — whoever she is; the one blackmailing me — has actually done me the world of good. I needed this scare; needed a good reason to finish things with Emmet.

'Right-ee-o,' Scarhead says. 'It seems as if we're at a bit of stalemate.'

'We're going to be a hung jury,' I say, probably a little too exuberantly.

'Calm down, Alice,' Thick-rimmed Glasses says. I hate that everybody in here knows my name. It feels wrong. Creepy. I wish they'd all done what I'd done; not even bother to remember anyone's name. 'We're only half-way trough our second day of deliberation. The judge will be expecting us to argue for a lot longer than this.'

'Oh, I don't know. Alice might be right.' Scarhead says, agreeing with me for the very first time. 'Juries don't deliberate for too long. Maybe two days, perhaps three at most. But given that this is a Friday, I wouldn't be surprised if the judge declared us hung by the end of the day, rather than take everybody back to court on Monday. Unless, of course, we can convince you three... and you of course, Cal,' he says, looking at Quiff, 'that this case *has* been proven beyond doubt.'

'I don't think so,' I say.

He purses his lips at me.

'Are you sure, Alice… there is no way you can be convinced of the twins' guilt?' I, ever so slowly, shake my head back at him whilst holding his stare. Then he turns to Red Head. 'What about you Sinead?'

She lets out a small moan; a pained moan.

'It's just. It's so wrong to have two children who look so vulnerable be in court like this. It doesn't sit right with me. But aside from that, I have to agree with Alice. I'm not sure this trial proved beyond all doubt that Faith and Grace did this. And we owe it to the twins, we owe it to Clive and Dorothy. And the church. And all their friends. The detectives. We owe it to *everybody* involved in this case to argue it out as much as we can.'

Scarhead looks disappointed in that answer. Perhaps he doesn't like the idea of more arguing. So he turns to Obese Guy.

'And you, Gerry?'

Gerry sucks his lips.

'The case hasn't been proven.'

'Jeez, well, who else do you think killed them, then?' Thick-rimmed Glasses says. He seems to be the one whose patience is stretched the furthest. 'Well… anybody got any other theory?'

'Out job isn't to decide who killed Clive and Dorothy—it's to deliberate whether or not Faith and Grace did it,' Red Head says.

'What about that little Scottish lady?' Obese Guy offers up.

'Huh?' Scarhead replies.

'Kelly, isn't it? The pretty-ish one who runs the church.'

'What—you think she killed the Tiddles? You playing detective now, Gerry?'

Gerry wobbles his chins.

'No... no... I'm just saying that the trial we just witnessed over the past weeks ended with two arguments, didn't it? Either Faith and Grace did it, or a professional hit man — someone clever enough to not leave a trace of themselves — did it.'

Scarhead shrugs his shoulders.

'You mean the Hollywood movie contract killer theory?' he says.

'Well... I guess if you are to buy into the theory of a contract killer doing it, then we'd have to assess who would have hired a contract killer.'

'And you think Kelly McAllister hired a contract killer?'

Scarhead laughs and Obese Guy looks up the line of faces to meet my stare. I just glance down to my lap.

'Eh... I guess she stood to benefit from Clive and Dorothy being out of the picture?' he says, shrugging.

'What the fuck?' Thick-rimmed Glasses says, rubbing at his face again.

'She took over the church, right?' Obese Guy says. 'Runs it all on her own now. She even testified to that when she was on the stand as a character witness. She also seemed dismissive of Faith and Grace, especially for somebody who is a woman of God. She was quite accusatory for someone who had known them their whole life.'

'Exactly,' Scarhead says.

'Exactly what?

'Well, she knows them as well as anybody, and even *she* is convinced they did it.'

'Well, she probably would say that, wouldn't she... especially if she has something to hide?'

Thick-rimmed Glasses slaps both of his hands to the table and heaves himself to his feet.

'This is getting outrageous now,' he says. 'You are going

off into the woods with your theories here. Are we really all going to sit around this table and let these two little murderers get away with this, just because you are more keen to play detective than to do the job you have actually been asked to do? I suggest we get back to talking about—'

He's silenced by a rattle of knuckles on the door, then plops himself back on to his chair as Red Head goes to answer it.

'Lunch time,' she says, looking over her shoulder at the rest of us. A collective sigh sounds from all corners of the table. Literally relief all around.

We all file out of the jury room like obedient students though, as if most of us hadn't, just seconds ago, had our fists balled up in frustration; our blood pumping.

'Psst... toilet break?' I whisper out of the side of my mouth to Red Head as we begin to stroll down the corridor.

She stares at me for a little too long without answering, then whispers, 'Sure.'

We excuse ourselves before heading into the dining-room, the young woman dressed in all black nodding at our request to visit the toilet.

I blow a raspberry out through my lips and place my hands on my hips as soon as the door swings closed behind us.

'You okay, Alice?' Red Head asks.

'We've got to hold on.'

'Calm down, Alice. You just need to stay strong with your beliefs. Just don't get bullied. Don't let them rile you up.'

'I won't. I won't,' I say, my hands still on my hips. 'I'm so worried.'

She holds a hand to my elbow and grips it.

'You really haven't handled the pressure of this trial well, have you? Do you normally suffer with levels of anxiety?'

I shake my head. And almost sob out a cry as I do so. I

want to ask her if she's being blackmailed too. It would make such a difference to know the two of us are in this together. If we are, then it's only a matter of convincing Obese Guy and all will be okay. I dab at my eye, to stop the tear from falling and then swallow.

'Anything going on outside the court that has caused you any… any other pressure this week?' I ask.

She stares away from me for a second, glancing at the door of one of the cubicles, then her eyes dart back to mine.

'No. Why?'

'Oh… don't mind me. You seem, like me, to be quite stressed by this too.' That's a lie. She doesn't seem fazed or stressed by this at all. In fact, she has taken this in her stride better than anybody else around that table. 'It's just… I've just got this other thing going on as well… and it seems like double the pressure and… agggh,' I say, shaking my head and laughing out loud. In the echo of the tiled bathroom it actually sounds as if I'm at the start of a bloody mental breakdown. 'No, it's just…' I compose myself. 'I wondered if you are feeling as stressed as I am.'

She shakes her head.

'I'm not saying this trial hasn't been stressful, or bloody frustrating more than anything else, but other than that….'

She leaves her sentence hanging there, perhaps hoping I'll just pick it up. Or maybe hoping I'll just shut the hell up and lead us to the dining room. After all, neither of us have actually used the loo since we came in here. I just rattled off question after question to her as soon as the door was closed. Yet I haven't actually asked her what I want to ask her. How am I even supposed to approach the subject of blackmail without giving the game away?

'I hope you stay strong in the jury room, I know I will,' is all I can muster. But then again, I guess that's all I really want to know; that's all this boils down to.

'I will be strong. To my convictions.'

'Those poor twins,' I say. Her eyes dart to the cubicle door again. 'You do believe the twins, right? You don't actually think they could have done this?'

She shifts her heels, steadying herself on the tiles.

'You really wanna know what I believe?' she asks, meeting my eye again. 'I know we weren't supposed to follow the case in the media in order to get on this jury, but I... I mean you couldn't miss the magnitude of this case. Who could?' she says.

'Yeah... course, me too.'

'I never believed as this case was being dragged through the system that these children should have been tried here. This case should have gone straight to the Children's Court in Smithfield. Instead both sides argued and argued and delayed and delayed this case until they finally ended up here... somehow. It's been a mess. We shouldn't be judging kids this way... at Dublin's Criminal Courts—as if they're adults. It's scandalous. This whole case has been handled terribly from the start. And if we find Faith and Grace guilty, they could end up in prison their whole life.'

'They won't though, surely?' I say.

'No. Well... we don't know what sentence they'd serve. But life in prison is a possibility. And that is why this case should never have been allowed to get this far. To these courts. The state pushed way too far on this. *Way* too far.'

'Wait,' I say, holding my hand up to her again, a penny dropping inside my head. 'You think they did it, don't you?'

The bathroom door sweeps open.

'Ladies, the jurors have something they wish to share with you,' the young woman dressed in all black says to us. We all look at each other awkwardly, and then she leads us back to the dining room where we sit down beside each other in the last two remaining seats at the far end of the table.

'We've been waiting for you two,' Scarhead says, twiddling an envelope with his fingers. 'We didn't want to open it until we were all seated together.'

'It's from the judge,' Big Bust says.

Scarhead rips at the top of the envelope, then scans the contents himself quickly before reading it aloud.

"'Ladies and gentlemen of the jury,'" he says. "'I write to you not to add pressure, but to perhaps relieve some. It has been a testing time for all involved in this trial. And while I understand you cannot take the huge decision that lies in your hands lightly, you have now been deliberating for ten full hours; six yesterday and four this morning. I am therefore — taking into consideration the length of your deliberations — now willing to accept a verdict agreed upon by ten jurors, and not a full unanimous decision. Regards, Judge Delia McCormick.'"

Braces, sitting directly across from me, whistles quietly.

'Y'know what?' Thick-rimmed Glasses says. 'You, Cal...' he points his finger at Quiff. 'You've been guilty, not guilty, undecided... may I ask you just for my own peace of mind and in light of the letter the judge just sent us... where do you stand now?'

Quiff sits more upright in his chair.

'I, eh... I always felt they did it. I think they're guilty, it's just...'

'Well, that's that sorted then. You think they're guilty!' Thick-rimmed Glasses waves his hand in the air, like a pretentious snob; except he has thick-rimmed glasses. Pretentiousness looks awkward coming from someone wearing thick-rimmed glasses.

'No... that's not what I'm saying,' Quiff says, readjusting his seating position again. He is literally uncomfortable.

'Hold on, didn't we say we wouldn't discuss the trial over lunch?' Red Head says, coming to Quiff's rescue.

'We won't discuss it. I just want to know where he stands, because then we'll know where everybody stands. And I think, given what the Judge has just sent us, it's about time we started making our minds up.'

Quiff coughs.

'I think they're guilty,' he says, his voice almost breaking. 'I guess I was just trying to give them the benefit of the doubt as we argued everything in the jury room, but even though I wanted somebody to give me a good reason to say not guilty, nobody really has. I'm, eh... no. I won't be changing my mind again. It's made up. I wish Faith and Grace all the best of health no matter what happens. And I hope they don't have to spend all their lives behind bars. But, eh... I find them guilty—guilty as charged.'

I groan silently in the back of my throat, then look to my right to meet the Red Head's eyes.

'Okay then,' Scarhead says. 'We are now nine guilty to three not guilty. The judge will accept a ten:two verdict. Seems as if we're getting very close.'

DAY FOUR

I was relieved to leave the Petersen house that night.

Bracken is quite intimidating. I guess that what makes him so successful at what he does. I'd seen him on TV and in the newspapers lots of times; he's probably the only celebrity lawyer in the country—hasn't lost a case in years. He held my stare as he lashed out at me over the twins' arrest the night before. And I just held my hands up in apology and told him I was doing all I could to get this investigation back on track.

I went in to the living room before I left to give them both a big hug. Grace muttered a soft "thank you" in to my ear; Faith was too busy staring at the cartoons over my shoulder to even realise I was hugging her.

I took a look at the clock on my dashboard as soon as I got back in the car. It had just gone ten p.m.—the pubs would still be open. As I drove, I counted up the hours I had left to convince Riordan and Ashe that I was on to something—or face being thrown off the case. Fourteen. Not a lot of hours. But I was starting to grow in belief I wouldn't need them all. Kelly and Nevin had already fucked up. I was convinced they were in this together. And I was going to prove it before Riordan's stopwatch reached zero.

'A non-alcoholic beer,' I called out.

When the barman nonchalantly placed a bottle in front of me, I flashed my badge.

'Detective Denis Quayle,' I said.

He looked taken aback at first, then he leaned his forearms on to the bar and bent towards me.

'This about the, eh... Tiddle murders?' he said.

I squinted at him.

'What do you know about the Tiddle murders?'

'As much as everyone else does,' he says leaning back up off the bar and flicking his head at another customer. The customer ordered a Guinness and then the barman stepped away from me to pull the pint. He left the Guinness to settle and came back, leaning onto the bar again.

'Who would have thought it... around here?' he says. 'And it's their own kids everyone is saying... that's who Child X and Y are—'

'It wasn't the kids,' I said, slapping my hand on the bar. Then I sighed. And the man waiting on his Guinness stared at me wide-eyed.

'What... so Child X and Y aren't actually *their* kids?' the bar man asked, scratching at his hair.

'No... no...' The two of them were glaring at me now. 'It's... listen... I can't divulge anything about the case. I am not here to answer questions. I'm here to ask them. Please...' I motioned to the settling Guinness. Then the bar man topped the pint's head and plonked it in front of the customer who handed over the exact change and left us to it.

'What questions would you like to ask, Detective?'

I looked around myself. The bar was busy with chatter; no more prying ears.

'Does a Tommo Nevin frequent this place?' I asked.

'Tommo? You think Tommo killed the Tiddles,' he laughed. 'Because he had that row with the husband that time? Tommo is a fucking looper... or a character is the best way to describe him. But a killer... no—that's crazy talk, Detective.'

'I just asked you a simple question, eh….what's your name?'

'Paul.'

'Well, Paul,' I said. 'I wasn't accusing anybody of anything... I just asked you a very simple question…. does Tommo Nevin frequent this bar?'

'Eh, yeah. Tommo's in here three or four times a week, I guess. Loves himself a pint of Heineken.'

'Thank you, Paul,' I said. 'And let me ask you this… does a Kelly McAllister frequent this pub?'

'Kelly… Kelly? Is that the little Scottish one? Pretty she is. But a bit...'

He left his sentence hanging there.

'Yes. Scottish lady. About five foot nothing.'

'She's in here every Saturday, I believe. Is big into the horse racing. Puts on a few bets, sips on vodka and cokes in that corner over there. Wait...' he said, shaking his head a little, 'why you asking about Kelly and Tommo?'

'I need you to tell me if they know each other, Paul.'

'Pffft… no. I mean not that I know of. Tommo sits here,' he says pointing at the bar stools next to where I'm sitting, 'she's always back there, right next to the tele.'

'Have you ever seen them in conversation?' I asked.

Paul shrugged his shoulders.

'Everybody knows everybody in this pub. But... Kelly seems to keep herself to herself as far as I know. I've heard stories of one or two of the lads messing with her, trying it on with her... but that nonsense didn't last long. Lesbian, she is. Did ye know that? That's what she told one of the lads.'

I tilted my head, trying not to act surprised by that.

'But they know of each other, Kelly and Tommo, right?' I said.

Paul folded his arms.

'To be honest, I don't really know. I don't usually work Saturdays. That's the only time that Scottish woman comes in. So I'm not really aware how she mingles with the other punters. Far as I know she just keeps herself to herself.'

'So you weren't here for opening hours last Saturday?' He shook his head. 'Were any of these bar staff?' I asked.

He looked around at the guy and girl pulling pints down the other end of the bar.

'None of us... it's the other shift pattern. Mike, Jamie and Nina would have been in first thing on Saturday.'

I put my Detective badge back in the inside pocket of my blazer.

'Well in that case I'm gonna need to see your CCTV footage from that day,' I said. 'Can I view it on site?'

Paul hadn't a clue how the CCTV worked, but luckily Tracey — his colleague — did. She led me to a small office-cum-stock room at the back of the pub that had a tiny grey — and grainy — monitor in it, sitting on top of three old-school phonebooks. She slipped in a tape labelled with last Saturday's date and I watched the footage play from the time stamped 10:30 a.m. I was certain I was going to find a flaw in Kelly and Tommo's alibis.

The shutters of the pub had barely gone up when Tommo arrived with two other men. It was 10:33 p.m.

'Who are they?' I asked Tracey.

'Tommo in the middle, Matty on the right and that's Chaz —his real name is Dave but they call him Chaz... because of Chaz 'n' Dave...'

I stared over my shoulder at her and her face dropped from smiling to stifling.

Sure enough, Tommo and his mates sat on the stools at the bar Paul had told me they always sit in.

Three more men came in, and after ordering their pints they sat on the far side of the pub. Then another four arrived, followed by a young-enough couple. I bit my lips as I stared at the blinking footage of the front entrance. I wasn't sure if I wanted to see Kelly arrive or not. If she didn't arrive, then her alibi of being at the pub during the murders was blown and I had made a major breakthrough in the case. But if she did arrive, I was desperate to see if her eyes met Tommo Nevin's; certain that if they did then they must have known what was happening in the Tiddle bungalow at this exact time.

It didn't take long. It was exactly 10:48 when her miniature frame strolled through the door. She sidled straight up to the bar and spoke briefly to a bald bar man. I leaned forward, my nose close to the screen and stared at her; waiting to see if she looked to her right; made any inkling of an acknowledgement towards Nevin. I was growing in certainty that they were up to something and that they must have been consciously using The Velvet Inn's CCTV as their alibi.

When Kelly grabbed at her drink and made her way to sit down at the back of the pub, right beside the big screen, I was gutted. The footage I was watching was grainy and blinking, but it certainly didn't show any acknowledgement between the two of them.

'Fuck it!' I hissed.

'You okay, Detective?' Tracey asked me.

'Can I, eh… can I take that tape back to the station with me?' I asked her. 'I need to pour over it in more detail…'

She turned her lips downwards and nodded her head.

'I guess so,' she said.

I called Sheila when I was back in the car; told her I'd be

home late again. I didn't like her having to go to bed alone for the fourth night in a row, but she wasn't complaining. She never complains. Ever. Sheila doesn't have it in her nature to moan.

I thought I'd be pretty much left alone in the police station; just me with the TV monitors for company. But I knew that wouldn't be the case as soon as I got to the front door. I could hear voices. Mumbled voices coming from Fairweather's office.

I walked in to see Fairweather, Ashe, Tunstead and Riordan all seated around the desk in deep conversation. I knew instantly they were talking about me, because the chatter dropped as soon as I walked in.

Riordan stood up and took a couple steps towards me.

'Detective Quayle, David Riordan.'

'I know who you are, sir. I've seen you speak at the Garda Ceremony a couple of times.'

He smiled.

'Well, we were just talking about you,' he said.

'No shit!'

He puffed out a rather feminine giggle for such a rough looking man and then pointed his hand to Fairweather's desk; motioning for me to join them.

'Before you start,' I said. 'I'm on to something. I have suspects. I have motive. I have opportunity.' Tunstead tutted. The prick. Everybody else just stared at me. 'Clive Tiddle had a run-in with a local lay-about; Thomas Nevin. Nevin was known to be really angry about the Tiddles bringing brown faces to this neck of the woods. And we have witnesses who claim they had a shouting match about eight weeks ago. On top of that, Nevin has a fresh scratch inside his right hand.'

'Nevin isn't a bloody killer, Quayle,' Tunstead said.

I held my index finger to my lips.

'I'm talking now, Tunstead,' I said, then I turned back.

'Kelly McAllister — the little Scottish lady who helps the Tiddles run their church — well, she knows all about the money the Tiddles had in the safe and… guess what? Her and Tommo know each other. They drink in the same pub—The Velvet Inn.'

'Jesus, Quayle. Half of Rathcoole and the surrounding area drink in The Velvet Inn,' Tunstead said.

'Half the folk don't drink in the Velvet Inn... there are four pubs round here smartarse, how does that even make sense?'

'Okay... then a quarter of the folk around here drink in The Velvet Inn. Two people who drink in the same pub is hardly a coincidence.'

The room fell silent. And I kinda squirmed a little.

'They were after the money in the safe,' I said, trying to compose myself. 'Kelly knows all about how that church is run. She benefits hugely from having Clive and Dorothy out of the picture. When Tommo Nevin had that row with Clive Tiddle, she must have got in contact with Nevin, asked him if—'

'Jesus Christ, Quayle,' Tunstead shouted, screeching his chair backwards and standing up.

'Calm down, Detective Tunstead,' Ashe said.

'Look, Quayle,' Riordan offered up in a soft voice; a voice not befitting his face. It was potted with acne scars; his nose looking as if it had been chewed on by a Jack Russell. 'We've been in discussion with Fairweather here. She talks very highly of you.' I looked at Fairweather and pursed my lips at her. 'Says you have been an almost perfect member of the force for twenty-five years. "Best I've ever worked with", were her exact words.'

'Wouldn't take much, she hasn't worked with many,' I said, laughing. 'We've run this station between us since 1995.'

Everybody laughed. Even Tunstead. And as he did, I

immediately recognised their laughs as sympathy laughs. My stomach turned itself over. I knew something was going on.

'We think it's time for you to retire,' Riordan said.

'What!' I screeched.

'Detective Quayle. For your brilliant service to the force you will receive your full pension *and* we are going to offer you a pay-off, just a little thank you for all the years you have protected the people of Rathcoole.'

'This is... this is...' I stood up and began to pace the small room.

'Rathcoole station has been under threat of closure, you have been made aware of that. Well... we're shutting it down and stretching Tallaght Station to cover this area. Fairweather has just announced her retirement, similar structure to the one we are offering you. The two uniforms... what are their names?'

'Johnny Gibbons and Olivia Sully,' Fairweather said.

'Yeah... Johnny and Sully. They'll be offered roles in Tallaght station. It's time, Quayle. Rathcoole is barely a police station anymore. It just doesn't have the resources, let alone the personnel. You know that yourself. We're going to let Tallaght's jurisdiction stretch into the mountains.'

'You can not be serious,' I said. 'Fairweather, what is—'

'It's time,' Fairweather said, looking at me. 'C'mon, Quayle. The package we're being offered is more than generous. We've worked here way too long. Let's do something else... you can join me on the golf course. You've always threatened to buy a set of clubs. Or, eh... what about all the travelling you've always said you'd do with Sheila?'

I pressed the butt of my palm to my forehead. Hard.

'And, eh....' Riordan coughed into his hand. 'We've also heard from a journalist from the *Irish Daily Star*, he, eh... he's asking about McDonalds. Says he has a witness that places you there with the twins a couple of hours after the murder. That doesn't look great, Quayle.'

I grunted, then took my hand from my forehead.

'You're letting me go in the middle of this case? The biggest case I've ever—'

'It's not the middle of the case,' Riordan said, standing up. 'It's the end. And we're going to let you sew it all up. As a last hurrah.'

I stared at him.

'It was the twins, Quayle,' Ashe said, mirroring Riordan by standing up too. Suddenly everybody but Fairweather was on their feet. 'Tomorrow morning we want you to charge them with double homicide to round up this case. It'll be your last act as a police officer.'

ALICE

My heart rate was definitely rising; practically thumping at my chest. I barely touched my ham; couldn't even stomach the fact that it was even sitting there under my nose for the best part of an hour. I pushed the plate forward and just sat back in my chair, waiting for everybody else to finish.

I literally went into that dining room confident we were going to end up as a hung jury, and left it absolutely petrified that Noel and Zoe were going to see that fucking video.

'Stay strong,' I whispered into Obese Guy's ear as we reentered the jury room. He looked back at me and nodded once. Then we all sat.

'Right... so... interesting,' Scarhead says when everybody has finally settled. 'We were told that this was a possibility, but the judge has now confirmed it for us. We don't need a unanimous decision, we need a majority of ten; and from what I can gather we have nine in favour of a guilty verdict. Am I right in thinking that... yes? Perhaps raise your hands if your verdict is guilty.'

Nine hands fly up. The fuckers. Quiff is keeping his stare

away from mine as he holds his hand aloft. He knows I'm pissed with him.

'So it's just you three,' Scarhead says, nodding to Obese Guy and then looking towards me and Red Head. 'I guess it'd be a good idea to ask you three for your opinion on why you feel the twins should be found not guilty, then perhaps if we could counter your arguments we may get a break through in all this.'

I didn't answer. But I didn't have to. The nodding of heads from Obese Guy and Red Head did my answering for me.

'Okay... so Gerry, would you like to start? Why do you think Faith and Grace should be found not guilty of these murders?'

Obese Guy slaps his hands onto his enormous belly.

'My opinion on it hasn't really changed,' he says. 'This case hasn't been proved beyond all doubt.'

'Aren't you taking that a bit literally?' Thick-rimmed Glasses says. 'I mean, we can't know with absolute certainty; we can't rewind the clock, go inside the Tiddles kitchen on August fifteenth two years ago and witness the bloody crime, can we? Beyond reasonable doubt doesn't mean *absolute* proof, it doesn't mean a smoking gun or a bloodied knife, as it would be in this instance. It just means did the prosecution prove the case? Well, given that the stab wounds came from children, given that the twins had the opportunity and the means to kill Clive and Dorothy. And given that nobody else's DNA — or any evidence whatsoever — was found at the scene... it all adds up to ample proof that the twins did this.'

Obese Guy brings his hands to rest on the table in front of him.

'I... I...'

'He's entitled to see the phrase reasonable doubt in whatever way he wants—'

'Shhh.' Thick-rimmed Glasses hisses at me. 'We will get to you, Alice,' he says. 'We are asking Gerry here for his opinion first.'

I grind my teeth. If Gerry breaks here, I'm screwed.

'I know what you're saying,' Obese Guy says to Thick-rimmed Glasses. 'It's just that in order for me to put those two children behind bars for years, perhaps even the rest of their lives, I would like much stronger proof than that. I'd actually like the bloodied knife. That'd help, wouldn't it? How come the prosecution didn't find that? I am not going to put these girls in prison just because a specialist says the stab wounds came from a child. There are a billion children in the world. And while I know Faith and Grace live with Clive and Dorothy and obviously had the, eh… means as you say… the stab wounds are not enough reason to convict. Do I think the stab wounds came from children? Yes. Do I believe those children were Faith and Grace? Well, it's very likely. But it hasn't been proven to me beyond doubt… so I am sticking to my verdict.'

Scarhead thumbs his scar.

'And is there anything that could sway you the other way?' he asks.

'I just… I just…' Obese Guy shrugs his shoulders. 'I don't think so, no. I'm sorry. I am. I'm sorry to everyone around this table who wants to get home, wants to get their life back to normal. But I am not sending two young girls to prison for decades just because us twelve have been put out for a couple weeks.'

He's argued well. But he hasn't filled me with confidence. I notice Scarhead look at Thick-Rimmed Glasses… I think they feel they can win him over. He opened himself up for targeting when he admitted it was *very likely* the twins may have done it. I've no idea how strong he's going to hold. I need to do something. I need to convince Obese Guy.

I become conscious of my breathing, only because I have to. If I don't slow my breaths down I'm going to collapse on to this bloody carpet again. The palms of my hand are much wetter than they were when I did collapse yesterday. I hold my eyes closed and see the video of me being taken behind by Emmet again. And then I see Noel's face. Watching that video. Jesus Christ.

'And you?' Scarhead says. I open my eyes to answer him. Then notice it's not me he directed that question to. It's Red Head.

'Well,' she says, 'I agree with Gerry. The prosecution didn't prove the case to every degree...'

'This is ludicrous saying the prosecution didn't prove the case... what else did you want them to do?' Thick-Rimmed Glasses says.

'Stop it,' Big Bust snaps at him. 'I thought we were giving these three a chance to talk.'

'Thank you, Gwen,' Red Head says. 'It's not just that... it's not just that I don't feel everything was proven, I... I genuinely don't believe they should even be here.'

'Huh?' Scarhead says, his brow all creased. 'What you talking about?'

'This is a court for adults. For crimes committed by adults.'

'Well, that's not true is it? Otherwise they wouldn't be here,' Thick-rimmed Glasses says leaning back in his chair all smug. He's becoming a bigger prick with every passing minute of these deliberations.

'They are only the second set of children ever to be tried for murder in these courts in the history of the legal system in Ireland,' Red Head says, in an effort to shut him up. 'And I didn't believe that first case should have been heard here either. Children's brains are only developing. They shouldn't be put behind bars for a considerable amount of time and then spending that time there as an adult for something they did when they were just kids.'

'Whoa, whoa, whoa,' Scarhead says. 'Are you saying you think they did it?'

My heart sinks. And my stomach rolls itself over. I rub at Red Head's arm, hoping she'll turn to me so I can nod my head at her in solidarity. But she doesn't turn back.

'It doesn't matter if I think they killed them or not—'

'Yes it does. Yes it absolutely does,' Thick-rimmed Glasses says. 'That's what your job is. Now it's a very simple question. Do you, or do you not, think the twins did it?'

'Yes.'

'No,' I say. Before I even knew I was going to say it; it just jumped out of my mouth.

I think the gasps coming from the far end of the table, from Scarhead and from Thick-rimmed Glasses, were more audible than my reaction.

Red Head turns to me.

'Don't worry, Alice,' she says. 'This is what's needed. The whole argument needs to be opened up.'

I rub at her arm again. But I get confused as arguments spark around the table.

'Calm down!' Scarhead shouts, shutting everybody to a silence. 'Sinead… let me get this straight. You feel Faith and Grace are guilty of this crime, but you will not find them guilty because you don't like the fact that this case skipped so many legal procedures in order to get the twins *here*… to Dublin's Criminal Courts?'

'But it *is* being held heard here,' Thick-rimmed Glasses says. 'And it isn't your bloody job to say where their case should be held. It's your job to say whether or not you feel Faith and Grace are guilty based on the evidence put in front of you during this trial. And I guess we all know where the evidence leads you. You think they're guilty.'

'I think we should hear from Alice,' Red Head says.

I pat my hand on top of Red Head's which is still gripping on to my bicep.

'I agree,' I say.

'What… that they did it and you are giving us a protest vote against the system?'

'No, no, no,' I say. 'I eh... agree with, eh…. sorry, what's your name again?'

'Gerry,' Obese Guy says, looking offended that I hadn't kept his name in my memory bank.

'Yeah... I agree with Gerry. I don't think the prosecution proved the case beyond reasonable doubt.'

Thick-rimmed Glasses stands up and begins to grip the back of his chair, his fingers whitening.

'There are alternatives,' I say. 'I know it's not our job to play judge or to play detective, but the money found in that safe tells me the Tiddles were not a very legitimate family. Somebody could have known about their money... we can't rule that out.'

'Ah, for fuck sake,' Thick-rimmed Glasses says. 'We're back to this bloody theory, are we? Accusing other people? Well, how the hell do you think Kelly McAllister benefited from killing Clive and Dorothy? She hardly got her hands on that cash at all, did she? The cops found it. So…' He shrugs a shoulder at me.

'Well, she got to run the church, perhaps all the money being generated through the church goes to her now. Or…' I pause. Because what I'm about to say doesn't really have any weight to it. 'Or Clive's sister Janet, who testified. I thought there was something dodgy about her when she was on the stand. She was so dismissive of her brother and sister-in-law. And now she has custody of the twins. Perhaps she feels they will bring her some money. Any idea what kinda money Child X and Y will get for their story once they're out of here?'

'Enough with the fucking conspiracies,' Thick-rimmed Glasses shouts, whipping off his glasses.

The sweat on my palms is getting ridiculous now, it's almost dripping from me. But I don't give a shit how many people shout. I certainly won't be changing my mind. And neither will Red Head. I'm certain of it. Her argument is moral. And moral arguments are as rock solid as arguments get. Besides, I'm still pretty sure she might be getting blackmailed just like I am. I look to Obese Guy. He seems shaken. I can't let him change his mind.

'I need to visit the toilet,' I say.

'Again?' Scarhead says, tutting.

'I just feel a little under the weather like I did yesterday. I suffer with hypertension. I, eh... Gerry,' I say, 'that trick you did for me yesterday with the cold water... could you show me how to do that again?'

Obese Guy wobbles his four chins up and down and then heaves himself from the chair before holding the bathroom door open for me. I purse a thin smile at him as I walk by and when the door closes behind us both we just stand there staring at each other.

'Gerry, please tell me you're not going to change your mind... please,' I whisper to him.

'Alice, I don't know what to think anymore.'

'Gerry! Stay strong.'

'Everyone thinks they did it. Even Sinead thinks they did it and she was saying they were not guilty from the start. And I... well, when she said that it made me really think if I genuinely feel they did it and... even though it wasn't proved beyond doubt, maybe I do believe they did it. I mean... I don't — and I mean no disrespect to you — but I don't believe in any of the other theories. Kelly McAllister? Janet Petersen? Nah,' he says, swaying his chins left and right. 'I don't even believe you believe those theories,' he says.

'Gerry, please. Please,' I say, taking a step towards him. I find myself leaning over his belly, my nose inches from his. 'Don't change your mind, Gerry,' I whisper towards his lips. Oh my God, the smell of his breath is disgusting; it's warm. But I need to do this. My life depends on it.

My lips meet his and I ever so slowly part them.

✝

Grace couldn't wait for them to go out... leave. Her legs were flexing with anxiety under the table.

'Okay darlings, we'll be back in a couple of hours, finish your breakfast,' Dorothy finally said. Then she and Clive shuffled down the hall way and out the door.

Grace turned immediately to her twin.

'Daddy climbed up a tree and hid a bag in the trunk last night.'

Faith looked up, then back down at her cereal bowl. But she immediately believed Grace. Because they both believed instantly and absolutely everything the other one said. She dropped her spoon into her bowl and then the twins raced each other to the back garden. After they'd juggled the stepladder over to the tree with a great deal of difficulty, Faith held the bottom while Grace climbed to the top. She knew what to do, had memorised it after watching Clive the night previous. She climbed onto one branch after stepping off the ladder, then felt for the hole behind the one above it; the one she was sure her father had dropped the money into. But it was just a normal branch. She was baffled. So she started to feel around the branch, until her finger tips patted their way on to a tiny switch hidden behind a twig. She pressed the switch downwards, then

i

yanked at the branch while trying to keep her footing steady. And the branch popped open; like a petrol cap on a car, leaving a gaping hole in the side of the trunk. Grace inched closer and, standing even more on her tip-toes, peered inside. Plastic bags. Bundles of them. All stuffed full. Maybe fifteen, twenty. There was no way she could ever get down far enough to get to them. If she had have climbed down, there was no way she could get back up.

She turned and informed Faith what she had found and then they both shrugged their shoulders.

'What you think is in them? Grace asked after she closed the branch tight shut.

'Dunno. You?'

'Secret files maybe?'

'Maybe.'

It was money. All the money coming in through the church. Three years prior Clive and Dorothy had built a secret safe in the floorboards of their bedroom, which could fit a small person inside of it where they to lie down flat. But it didn't take long for that safe to fill up with over five hundred thousand in used notes. That's how much money they were turning over. Clive came up with the ingenious idea of hiding it in the tree when he was outside in the garden literally trying to think of an answer to his dilemma. He was staring up through the branches as he was wondering how he could keep the money in a safe place... and then a grin slowly started to appear on his face. He told Dorothy it was a sign from God. And she believed him. He almost believed himself, in truth. He made the contraption in the space of a month. It was so simple. But it was genius. A real branch that bore into a large hole that had already existed in the side of the tree. It was a ten foot deep natural cavity that fed into the main trunk. He found a branch that he could ensure looked naturally part of the tree and built a mechanism that would pop it open when a tiny switch was flicked. Not in a million years would anybody have thought the branch was fake; even up close to it. You would only ever find the switch to pop open that branch if that's what you were actually looking for. If you didn't know about the tree, you'd never know about the tree.

Clive was pouring upwards of forty thousand into it every month. Sometimes the collections would come in close to a hundred thousand if they were running a fundraiser. At the point in which they were murdered, the Tiddles had almost five hundred thousand in used notes stacked in their bedroom safe of which they were living off day-to-day. And more than double that amount inside the trunk of that oak tree.

They were both into their fifties before they even sat down to discuss what they wanted to do with the money. Why they even needed it... If they even needed it... What they were actually collecting it for... After all, they weren't even spending any of it. Or rarely anyway. Not on themselves. They'd spend it on the church. Clive would update the bus every year or so. And they evolved the Community Centre into looking more and more like a modern church year on year. They'd spend cash on the latest sound systems; cushioned pews and the odd celebrity speaker.

The Tiddles never went on holiday, nor upgraded their home to anything bigger than the bungalow they were more than settled in. Even though they easily could have. They were literally lying on the money.

Both Clive and Dorothy were too busy collecting the cash that they genuinely never really got around to talking about how to spend it. They'd turned into robots, really; used to living day-to-day, running their 'family'. Thoughts of the future rarely consumed them. They never really thought of the cash as their reward, even though they had been obsessed about collecting it. Their main focus every day was to genuinely help people who were donating to them feel better. And, of course, to preach the word of the Lord Jesus Christ. That was always their main focus; preaching. They had been well and truly zombiefied into their own cult.

When they finally took the time to sit and discuss what to do with the money, they both agreed on a plan within a half an hour.

✝

They were going to start giving it back slowly to the people who had given it to them in the first place. They could redistribute the wealth as they saw fit. A few thousand here to Gertrude and Edin who were just about to get married; a few thousand to Brennan and Leanna who were expecting...

They made love the night they agreed to that plan, both feeling giddy from having a weight lift from their shoulders. It was the first time they'd had sex in eight years.

The Tiddles were the happiest they'd been in a long time as they dreamt up scenarios to financially help out their 'family' members. But what they were most excited about was what they had planned for the twins—even though it only put a tiny dent in the spend. As soon as they discussed the concept of holidays, Clive insisted on Florida first. For the girls. So they could have the time of their lives. They agreed to keep the tickets in the safe; and reveal them closer to the time, so they could record it on their phones and allow everybody to see the twins' reaction when they posted it on the church's Facebook page. It was all planned out. They both felt the twins were owed something really special. Clive and Dorothy discussed how much guilt they'd both been feeling having practically left them to look after themselves. And they both agreed they'd like to get closer to them during that holiday. No better place for a family to get closer than in the buzz of Disneyland.

The plan wasn't to give all of the money away. Far from it. Just a few quid to share around here and there, where and when needed. Dorothy was convinced Jesus had brought them to this destination; where they would have a lot of wealth to distribute amongst their 'family' as they saw fit—a bit like a mini Government. Clive genuinely just loved giving. Watching people's faces as they'd open up a gift or a donation from the Tiddles were the among the most treasured moments of Clive Tiddle's life. He truly was a giver.

Though he hadn't really given much to Kelly McAllister lately. Not in the way he used to give to her. They'd long since stopped their affair. Clive couldn't risk it. If Kelly was going to go all 'leave your wife for me' on him, he didn't want to know. He was actually quite relieved that he'd lost the stress of the affair as soon as it ended. Though he did miss the sex.

'What we meeting here for?' Kelly said. She was still unsure of them at this point. Dorothy hadn't really spoken to her since swearing at her. And Clive had been distant ever since he'd put a halt to their stay overs at the Ibis Hotel. Kelly had begun to fade into the background and genuinely felt as if she was just one of the regular 'family' members by this stage, not special anymore. Except she was *special. To both of the Tiddles. When they sat down to talk about who meant the most to them in their lives as they planned to distribute their wealth, they both felt guilty about how they'd treated Kelly over the previous year.*

'We bought it for you,' Clive said.

'Huh?' Kelly looked around herself.

'Well... we put down a large deposit it on it and have arranged a small mortgage for you. It's all yours. This is your home now.'

It was a terraced home in a tiny estate of six houses at the foothill of the mountains. About a twenty-minute walk up the hill to the community centre where she desperately wanted to spend most of the hours of most of her days. It wasn't that far from The Velvet Inn either. Walkable. She genuinely thought Clive and Dorothy had called her to meet them in that strange house to tell her she needed to find another 'family', such was her hurt of having been shunned. The Tiddles spent more money on Kelly than they did on everybody else combined. She was that special to both of them. They wanted to show their appreciation after she'd spent so many years dedicating herself to The New St Benedict's Church. Besides, she needed the stability. She'd never owned her own home; had jumped from one cheap rental flat or bedsit to another since moving to Dublin. On top of that, Clive and Dorothy had become aware that she was spending more time in the pub and they wanted her to get back to being the Kelly they had once sobered up and who was a joy to be around.

Kelly really wanted to ask them where they got the money from to put such a large amount down on a house for her—out of politeness more than anything. But she never did. Because she knew the answer. And she knew it wasn't to be discussed. Never again.

The one family member they didn't give anything to was actually a blood relative. Janet was furious when she found out Clive and Dorothy had bought Kelly McAllister a home. Grace had let it slip over the phone one evening. Janet had kept in contact with the twins ever since their communion night. Not regular contact; just a phone call every other month. But only because she was fascinated by them. The night of their communion had really opened up Janet and Eoin's eyes as to what they considered the delusion of the church. Catching up with the twins was pretty much a source of entertainment for them. It made a change from just watching the soaps while cracking open another cheap six-pack of beers.

'You cheapskate bastard!' Janet roared down the phone to Clive. 'I have nothing, barely two pennies to rub together and you are buying somebody a bloody house!'

'Now calm down,' Clive said to his sister. But Janet was off on one; likely drunk. Or high. Or both. Her and Eoin were the type who felt the world owed them something; the type of couple who'd sit on their arse all day and complain that they had nothing to do.

'You're a fucking freak. You're all freaks. In fact.... you're more of a freak than the rest of them. Because you don't believe any of that shit. I know it. And you know it.'

Clive held the phone away from his ear. His sister had always been an odd sort, but this level of bitterness and anger was about her peak. He knew why she was so upset. Because the argument was all about money. And Janet and Eoin were scroungers.

Dorothy and Clive had never even considered offering them any financial help. They weren't part of the church. They didn't deserve any riches if they didn't believe in Our Lord Jesus Christ. Even if they had been half-decent at keeping in contact with Faith and Grace over the past couple of years, they were still distant *family as far as Clive and Dorothy were concerned. Real family got down on their knees. And they thanked Jesus every day for giving them life. As far as Clive was concerned, Janet wasn't grateful for anything. There was no way she was getting a penny of that money; especially as she hadn't even put a cent into the pot.*

The twins were in their bedroom, unaware their father was having a row with his sister over the phone. In fact, they'd become so insular that they seemed to be unaware of almost everything that was going on. They only ever spent time in their bedroom, or at the community centre on Sundays, or quite often walking around their back garden.

Which is what Faith had been doing one afternoon before she raced as fast as she could through the kitchen, down the hallway and into her bedroom; slapping the door shut behind her.

She was panting heavily; disturbing Grace who was sitting up in bed reading passages from her Bible.

'Faith... you okay?' Grace said, dipping her eyebrows and slamming her Holy Book shut.

Faith was still panting. And she was pale. Very pale.

'You're not going to believe this,' she said.

DAY FIVE

Our heads were spinning; both mine and Sheila's. Though for different reasons.

She was reading over the paperwork Riordan had handed to me in a bright-white envelope, while I was sat on the floor of our bedroom, pouring over the CCTV footage on the small television that I'd managed to hook up to an old video recorder.

I watched Kelly sip on her vodka and coke; watched her scrunch up betting slips and toss them on to the table; watched her leave, presumably to visit the bookmakers next door, then come back in to sip on more vodka and coke just in time for the next race to start.

She did all this, practically on loop, for over four hours — up until just gone twenty past two that afternoon. And while she was doing that, Tommo Nevin was joking with his mates as he slugged back pint after pint of lager. Eight pints he sank in all the time Kelly was in that pub. He probably had just as many after I stopped watching the footage. But I didn't watch past the time Kelly left.

The only tiny suspicion I could find in the four hours and

twenty minutes of grainy footage that I'd watched occurred just gone midday, when Kelly and Tommo happened to visit the toilets at the same time. After tossing another betting docket onto the table, Kelly got up and made her way to the narrow corridor that led to the ladies room. A minute later, Tommo left his pint on the bar and headed down the same corridor. There was no CCTV camera covering that area of the pub. Tommo came back into the bar before Kelly; rubbing his right hand up and down his shirt. I hope he was drying excess water on his shirt having just washed his hands, but given that he was so quick in there I fear it may probably have been piss. A full minute later Kelly walked into shot. She ordered another vodka and coke without paying anyone around her any attention. Then she sat back down and waited on the next horse race to begin.

'They could have been up to something here,' I said to Sheila.

'Huh?' she replied, looking up from the paperwork.

'Doesn't matter.'

'I don't see any catch in this at all, Denis,' she said. 'One hundred thousand euro redundancy package, plus full pay for the next twenty years... what are you going on about... what catch?'

I sighed, then paused the tape and joined her sitting up in our bed.

'I don't know if there's a catch in the paperwork... it's just the whole thing seems really sneaky. Why now? In the middle of the biggest case I'll ever have...'

'Because this case has just made them realise that Rathcoole Garda Station doesn't have the resources for this type of investigation. They're going to let you tie up the case... arrest the twins. Then you can rub your hands with it all. Then me and you can go do—'

'I can't arrest the twins when I don't think they did anything,' I said.

Sheila rubbed at my shoulder.

'I'm excited about this,' she said. 'We can spend as much time as we want in Tuscany... And we might as well do it while we're young enough and our legs can still carry us up and down the vineyards.'

I leaned in to her to let her hold me and just about managed to stop myself from crying. It wasn't that I was upset about Faith and Grace, or the case in any way. It was the manner in which I was being dealt with. 'Thanks for your service, off ye go now.' Though in truth, the offer was a fair one. *Very* fair.

I fell asleep in my wife's arms that night—the first time in those four nights that I actually had a decent sleep. When my alarm beeped, Sheila turned in the bed.

'Did a night's sleep help you make up your mind?' she asked. I got out of bed and headed for the shower without answering her. I wasn't being rude. She knew what I meant. I didn't have an answer.

I grabbed breakfast on the go; munching on a banana and a cereal bar as I drove to the station. My mind was whirring; but for once it wasn't the dead bodies of Clive and Dorothy Tiddle that were consuming me, nor their cute little twins. It was my wife. Her eyes lit up last night when I showed her that paperwork. It was nice to have her back at the forefront of my thoughts. She'd gone missing from them over the previous days.

'You're here early,' I said to Fairweather. I noticed she was already dressed for the golf course; a pale green polo-buttoned shirt, navy casual slacks.

'Just getting the paperwork in order,' she replied. 'What about you... you signed on the dotted line yet?'

I took a seat opposite her and then pinched the bridge of my nose.

'Oh... I don't know about this, Fairweather,' I said. 'I just have a feeling I'm only being offered this because they don't want me working for the force anymore. They're giving Johnny and Sully new roles... why haven't they offered me and you one?'

'Well because we're old farts—near retirement age we are.'

'Speak for yourself,' I said to her. Fairweather was sixty-two, bang on the average age for a police officer to hang up their handcuffs. I was four years short of that, still firmly set in the routine and security my day job offered me.

'C'mon, Quayle. Hasn't Sheila's cancer made you think about what's most important in life? Don't you two want more quality time together, more adventures? You're not getting any younger.'

'It's not that,' I said. 'Of course the money would be good, spending more time with Sheila would be great...'

'Learning how to play golf...'

'Yes... golf,' I said, puffing out a laugh. 'But... but it's not about the advantages this pay-off gives me that I'm worried about. It's *why* they are offering it. That's what I want to know. It feels shallow, feels as if they just don't think I'm a good enough detective. They think I fucked up this case. I didn't. I'm the only one bloody working on it. Five hours I spent watching CCTV footage last night... The whole offer, it doesn't sit right with me. It just makes me feel like shit to be honest.'

'Quayle... don't be stupid. Take the offer.'

I pinched my nose again, more to stop the tears from falling than anything.

Footsteps shuffled outside Fairweather's door and then knuckles rattled against it.

'Come in,' Fairweather called out.

Ashe entered, his lips pursed at both of us.

'Hope you both slept well,' he said, 'given the circumstances.'

Fairweather entertained him with chit-chat about her acceptance of his retirement offer while I just sat there, pinching the bridge of my nose.

'You ready to visit the twins?' Ashe asked me.

I shook my head.

'I can't... I can't arrest them when I am not certain of their involvement in these murders,' I said. He didn't reply. He just perched his ass on to the corner of Fairweather's desk and folded his arms. 'I was pouring over footage of Tommo Nevin and Kelly McAllister last night. There's something really sneaky about those two...'

'And let me guess, you didn't find anything?' Ashe said. I stared at him, then at Fairweather. 'Faith and Grace are going to be arrested. You don't have to do it, of course. Tunstead can do it. We just thought it'd be nice for you to finalise this case before you retired.'

I stood up and paced the small square of Fairweather's office.

'I just... I can't... Kelly McAllister. There's something up with her. A Christian, a believer who loves to drink vodka and bet on horses during her day off?'

Ashe shook his head.

'You think Christians don't drink... don't have any bad habits? Jesus, Quayle, in my thirty-odd years of dealing with the dodgy people, I've found these Jesus freaks to be the dodgiest of the lot. Anyway...' he says to me, 'what CCTV footage were you pouring over?'

'Kelly McAllister and Tommo Nevin drink in the same pub.' Ashe glanced at Fairweather. 'They know something about these murders.'

'What was the footage of?'

'Them inside the pub, the morning of the killings.'

'And did you see anything of suspicion?' I sighed, then shook my head. 'What time was the footage from?'

'Half ten, around about the time of the killings.'

'Hold on... they were both in the pub at the time of the killings and you think they had something to do with it?'

'I don't know, I don't know,' I said, placing both hands on top of my head and clasping my fingers.

'If they were in the pub while Clive and Dorothy were being stabbed to death then that clears them… why were you watching that CCTV for hours if it is literally their alibi?'

I shrugged my shoulders.

'Maybe they are in it together, maybe they hired somebody to kill Clive and Dorothy while they used The Velvet Inn's CCTV as their alibi.'

Fairweather and Ashe shared another glance.

'Quayle,' Fairweather said, standing up. 'Listen to yourself. Do you really think Kelly McAllister and Tommo Nevin paid a hit-man to kill Clive and Dorothy Tiddle?'

I held my eyes shut when she said that. Because I knew it sounded ridiculous when said out loud.

The cringing didn't leave me, nor the frustration, for the entirety of the drive to Monaghan. Ashe drove in his car. We didn't talk much about the case at first; he just let me reflect on my twenty-five years as an officer; asking about my favourite colleagues over the years, my favourite cases.

When we eventually turned the conversation to the Tiddles, a lot of what he was saying made sense. Gerd Bracken taking over the twins' case spoke volumes. It was a siren that should have sounded for me yesterday. But it didn't. Bracken taking over Faith and Grace's case meant they *needed* defending.

He beamed his bright-white veneers at me again when we finally arrived at the Petersen house. He was a strange looking man, but magnetising in some way. His skin was orange, not light brown or tanned, but dusky orange. Like a Wotsit. Yet despite that, he was handsome in a weird way.

Ashe allowed me to enter the living room first, into the sound of the cartoons.

Grace glanced over at me, then stood up from the sofa. I think she was anticipating another hug. But I remained upright.

Ashe picked up the TV remote control to press at the standby button. And that's when Faith noticed, for the first time, that we were all in the room.

I hunched down to a bended knee position, just as I had the first time I'd met them.

'Faith and Grace,' I said, really slowly. 'I am arresting you on suspicion of the murder of your parents Clive and Dorothy Tiddle.'

ALICE

I can feel him against my stomach. Hard. Clammy. And oddly round. Like a potato. I'm not sure what's worse; his bulge pressing against me or his saliva inside my mouth. I can actually taste his ham lunch.

I pull away from him, and as I do, he brings a fingertip to his mouth to mop up the saliva that's about to drip from his bottom lip.

'Wow, Alice,' he says, grinning at me.

I want to turn around, run into the cubicle and vomit all of the disgustingness away. But I can't. So I just stand still. And swallow.

'You, eh... you won't change your mind, Gerry, right?' I say.

He wobbles his chins from side to side, then beams a huge smile at me. And as he does, I glance down at his pants and notice his bulge is still sticking towards me. Jesus, it *is* shaped like a bloody potato.

'Right, well, let's just get out of here and—'

'Whoa,' he says, reaching a hand either side of my waist.

'Let's have another…' His face pushes down to mine and I allow our lips to touch. But I lean back almost instantly.

'Enough, big boy,' I say. 'You need to calm down.' I point at his bulge. He places a hand over it and chuckles like a teenage boy. 'You need to put that away and compose yourself before you get back around that table. We just need to stay strong.'

'But can we… eh… can we do this again?' he says.

I nod.

'Sure… if we win, if we hold out and this is a hung jury, you and I can celebrate in style.' I wink at him.

He chuckles again as I turn to the tap to rinse my hands. I'd rather be rinsing my mouth.

After I've dripped my hands dry, I turn the latch in the door.

'See you out there, big boy,' I whisper.

I leave him standing with his potato boner still stretching towards me, and when I get back to the jury room I purse my lips at the jurors before I sit.

'All better now?' Red Head asks.

'Much better,' I say. Which is the truth. Obese Guy ain't going to change his mind. This jury's going to be hung. I know it.

I stare directly at his crotch as soon as he returns from the bathroom. I think he's still hard. Or maybe he always has that bulge. I wouldn't know. I'd never looked in that area before it started to stab at my stomach while we were kissing. As soon as he sits down he eyeballs me and curls up one side of his mouth. Uuugh. I can't believe I've just let him snog my face off. I feel filthy. As if I wanna take a scrubbing brush to my tongue. But that kiss has pretty much just saved my life. So I need to just suck it the hell up.

'Okay… well are we sure we're all set to continue our deliberations?' Scarhead says. We all nod and then he shuffles his paperwork again. 'Alice, you do look better. Whatever trick it is Gerry has for stopping anxiety, it sure works. Now... please listen you two,' he says slowly. 'We didn't discuss the trial when you were in the bathroom, I promise. But we did discuss where we should take deliberations next. As you know, we are sitting on a fine line between giving the judge a verdict or not... some jurors feel we should discuss the investigation again, does that sit okay with you two?'

I turn my lips downwards and shrug my shoulders.

'Whatever you guys wanna do,' I say.

Gerry mumbles a 'yes', then eyeballs me again to offer another half-smile. He's revolting.

'Lisa here...' Scarhead says, would like to discuss something she thinks is quite significant.

Braces sits more forward in her chair.

'It's just....' she says, 'don't we all think it's rather strange that everybody who took the stand in this trial feels as if the twins are guilty? From the two representatives of Tusla, the detectives, the stab wound experts, the forensics experts, Kelly McAllister, even the twins' dance teacher Claire Barry. Doesn't this tell us all something? Even people who are close with the twins feel they did it. Anyone investigating the case thinks they did it.'

'Not true,' I say.

'Well... I assume you are talking about Detective Quayle,' Braces says to me.

'Uh-huh,' I say, 'he is on record as telling the girls' own defence lawyer that he didn't think they did it. He practically said it in a press conference too. So you can't go around saying *everybody* involved in the case says they did it, especially when the lead detective himself—'

'He arrested them, for crying out loud, Alice,' Thick-rimmed Glasses says.

I shrug, trying to match the prick with his own level of pretentiousness.

'Please... continue,' Scarhead says to Braces.

'I actually don't think Quayle feels they're innocent. I think he did, initially, think that. During the investigation. But now I believe he thinks they're guilty—but was just too damn proud to admit he was wrong on the stand.'

'It seems to me as if this is arguing second guesses,' Red Head says. 'That's how you think you'll win a guilty verdict?

'No, it's not that...' Braces seems more intimidated by Red Head's response compared to mine. She shuffles in her chair, then rings her hands.

'Listen, I've already admitted to you that I think the twins are guilty of this crime but that I disagree with how the legal system has handled this case from the beginning,' Red Head says. 'But you're gonna need better arguments than that to win a guilty verdict.'

Thick-rimmed Glasses lets a frustrated gargle erupt from the back of his throat, then tosses the pen he'd been fidgeting with on to the table.

'Do you not understand how stubborn and arrogant you sound, Sinead?' he says before he presses his two palms against his face. When he removes them, he sighs. 'I'm trying not to get too frustrated, I don't want to shout,' he says. 'But we've been the best part of two days deliberating this trial. I'm sure you can appreciate that all of us who are in no doubt that the girls are guilty are rather frustrated by the fact that you agree with us... yet you disagree with the system. Well, we're not here to judge the system. We are only here to judge the case put in front of us. Now, if you continue to suggest that you feel the girls are guilty of this crime, yet you refuse to find them guilty of this crime, I am going to suggest that our Head Juror makes Judge Delia McCormick aware of your opinion. I'd be very interested to see what the judge has to say about that.'

Another eerie silences washes across the table. Red Head looks to me, and I, very nonchalantly, shake my head at her.

'Don't let him bully you,' I whisper, though it isn't a well-disguised whisper. I know he heard me, the whole table could hear me in that silence.

'This is getting like a football match, or American politics,' Scarhead says. 'Everybody taking sides and refusing to acknowledge anything the opposition are saying. It's actually getting quite pedantic and, may I say, immature. From both sides.'

Everybody shuffles in their chairs. I don't give a shit if he thinks I've acted immaturely or pedantically. I just want to save my marriage, save my relationship with my daughter. Jesus, I've even gone to the lengths of snogging that grotesque-looking fat fuck at the other end of the table. Being seen as immature or pedantic is more than fine by me. Once we're a hung jury, I don't give two shits what anybody around this table thinks.

'It's now coming up to half-past three,' Scarhead says, flicking his wrist to glance at his watch. The judge has let us out at four-thirty every day of this trial, so I imagine it'll be the same today. We have one hour left to sort this out... or we come back again on Monday morning.

'Might not have to return,' I say, my arms crossed under my breasts. 'Judge might call a hung jury by the end of proceedings today, this could be all over in an hour.'

Ripples of chatter reverberate around the table. Gerry seems to instantly get into a heated discussion with Big Bust.

'I don't care!' he shouts. 'I won't be changing my mind!'

He looks down at me and nods slightly after arguing his point. And I cringe inside.

'Okay, okay... enough. Enough already,' Red Head

shouts above the chatter, shutting everybody up instantly. She places her two hands wide across our side of the table. 'Thank you,' she says as she sits back down. 'If you could all please give me a minute to explain myself. I think you'll find what I have to say somewhat important.' I notice a number of jurors lean forward on the table. I think, although she has been not guilty from the start, they kind of respect Red Head in some way. I guess she's argued every point sensibly and, dare I say it, *maturely* from the beginning. Especially compared to me and Gerry. I've just come off as some mad woman; disruptive and arguing and fainting. And poor Gerry's just come off as the absolute buffoon around the table. 'They are only children,' she says. 'It is totally unfair that their case has made it to these courts. Not only that… the exposure of this case was so magnified and so sensationalised by a media we have been conned into thinking is unbiased. All media outlets in Ireland are biased—biased towards sensationalism. They only care about *a* story; they don't care about *the* story.' Two jurors remove their forearms from the table. 'The twins, in my opinion, were practically convicted by newspaper headlines two years ago. And the media has never let off since.'

'Why are you fixated on the media? We weren't supposed to be privy to anything about this case before it came to court,' Big Bust says.

Red Head shows the palms of her hands.

'C'mon, Ireland's tiny. We all know it. I didn't research the case. I didn't know everything about the case in any detail until I was put on the jury. But did I read headlines and see bulletins on the TV? Yes. How could we escape that?' she says.

I hold my breath and ever so slowly glance around the table.

'Well I didn't read anything. I just maybe heard the odd thing about Child X and Y,' Big Bust says.

'Exactly,' Red Head says. 'That's all I'm saying... that we all knew about Child X and Y in some capacity. We couldn't escape it.'

'It's just you seem to know an awful lot about it, Sinead,' Thick-rimmed Glasses says. 'You have said you even have opinions on what court this case should have been heard at.'

'Well, hold on, let me stop you there,' she says, 'because I think you're going to like what I have to say.'

Red Head places a hand on my arm, grasping my elbow lightly. I look up at Obese Guy and squint my eyes at him. What the fuck does she mean by saying Thick-rimmed Glasses will *like* what she has to say?

'I was so hopeful that this case would get the fair trial and the fair hearing it deserves. For the children. Those poor children. Can you imagine? Nine years of age, your parents have just been killed in cold blood and you are arrested for their murder? Imagine if they didn't do this... just think about that for one second. I came onto this case as balanced and as open-minded as you can be as a juror. I wanted those children to have the fairest of trials. Because this court... it really only should be for adults, no matter the crime. This case needed a fair investigation. From what I understand, it didn't really get one. Not just because Detective Quayle fumbled, but because of how the girls were treated from the off. Arrested, then rearrested. Questioned initially without actual legal representation. Silly press conferences. Statements made to Gerd Bracken by Detective Quayle the first night they met... No matter what angle you look at it from, the investigation was a circus.'

I form a ball with my fist under the table and punch some air. Relief more than anything. I wasn't sure where she was going with this initially.

'This case also needed a fair trial. But with Gerd Bracken taking over the defence pro bono, just to get the exposure he knew this case would bring him, I've never felt this trial was going to be balanced. He was as likely to sensationlise this trial as much as the media. But thankfully, the case got a fair judge. And, I must say, it also got a fair jury. I was really, really intent, when I was appointed to this trial, to make sure this jury was as fair as it could be. I wanted us to argue every nook and cranny of this case; discuss the investigation, the treatment of the children, the witnesses, the DNA — or lack of it — the timeline... and we did. We argued the shit out of it all until we started to repeat ourselves.'

I place my hand on her knee. And she puts her clammy hand on top of mine.

'No,' I say. Out loud. Something about her touch has really unnerved me.

'I wanted to hold out,' she says.

'No,' I say again. More panicked this time. 'Tell her, Gerry, tell her.'

Gerry bolts upright, finally clocking what's going on.

'No, Sinead,' he says. 'Don't give in.'

'I'm not giving in, Gerry,' she says. 'I had my mind made up the moment this trial finished. I've been holding out. Because I wanted to give our deliberations the best shot. As soon as the trial finished yesterday morning I said to myself that I'd give it until close of play on Friday.'

'No. No. No. Sinead,' I say. I claw at her, gripping her shoulder. 'You're not... are you?'

She nods her head once at me, then turns to the table.

'The twins are guilty. I just wanted to give them the best possible argument they could get—'

'No... No... Gerry, convince her, convince her,' I say. And as soon as I say it I hear myself. I sound like one hell of a desperate bitch. Probably because I am a desperate bitch.

I sit back in my chair, my mouth wide open, my hands flopped to my side.

'So… so you want me to ring it in?' Scarhead asks, in what sounds like slow-motion.

'Well, that's ten:two now, right?' Thick-rimmed Glasses sounds as if he's miles away, talking at us through a tiny tunnel.

'Yeah, let's just confirm it,' Scarhead says. 'Can I have a raise of hands from those whose verdict is now guilty?'

I squeeze my eyes firmly shut, because I can't bring myself to see the number of hands in the air.

TODAY

Sheila nudges me as soon as the jury's door snatches open, and we both immediately sit more upright on our bench.

I'm not sure how to feel sitting here now. Though the cannabis always seems to keep my heart rate at a steady pace and my mind in a happy place. Most experts on the TV this morning were saying that the longer the jury were out, the more likely it was that they would acquit. Me and Sheila spent much of the day talking about it—she disagrees with the experts; is adamant the twins are going down.

None of the twelve jurors look out to the court as they enter; every single one of them keeping their stare straight and focused.

After they're all seated, the door to our left opens and I lean forward, just to get a look at them. Sometimes Grace looks up at me, but not always. And not today.

'All rise,' a call shouts. And then Judge Delia McCormick enters from the back door and strides her way to her throne.

She flicks through some paperwork on the desk, then clears her throat to signal that she needs everyone's attention. Though she didn't need to do that; all eyes were glued to her already, every ear poised.

'I understand you have reached a verdict,' she says looking over her glasses at the jury.

'We have, Your Honour,' the Head Juror says.

Then Judge McCormick falls silent as she shuffles her paperwork around some more; as if she's teasing us... holding us all in suspense.

I look to Gerd Bracken. He seems nervous. I've never observed him like this before; holding a balled fist to his mouth and gnawing at it.

'I speak to every occupant of this court room,' the judge says, her voice booming. 'Regardless of the jury's findings, I am warning that *any* overreaction to the reading of their verdict will see you held in contempt of this court.'

The courtroom falls silent again; nobody even daring to whisper while Judge McCormick shuffles through her paperwork. Again.

'Okay,' she says, finally. 'Can the Head Juror pass the jury's verdict to the foreperson.'

A young woman dressed all in black takes a sheet of paper from the juror with the scar and then trots her way to the centre of the court-room and unfolds it.

'In the case of the state versus Grace and Faith Tiddle, charged with the double homicide of Clive and Dorothy Tiddle,' she says, 'we, the jury, find both of the accused guilty.'

Gasps are sucked in from all directions around us. But that's it. No overreaction. No screaming. No cheering. No sobbing. Just audible, sharp intakes of breath. Then silence.

I lean more forward to stare down at the crowns of Faith and Grace's heads. They don't move an inch. Not until Bracken's assistant leans towards Grace to whisper something into her ear. And then Grace passes on the message by turning to her sister. Faith's shoulders heave slowly up and down, and then both twins sit still and silent again.

'Told you,' Sheila whispers, nudging her knee against mine.

I spin around to take in the reaction of some of the faces behind me; Kelly McAllister wiping a tear from her eye with a folded handkerchief, and Janet Petersen staring down at her lap before her husband Eoin cups her face to bring it towards his.

'C'mon you, turn around… it's all over now,' Sheila says, placing a hand to my knee.

I face her, kiss her, and as I am doing so, I hear the judge dismissing Faith and Grace from the courtroom. Both of them are handcuffed in front of the gallery — which hadn't been done through this trial even though they spent all of it behind bars — before they're led back out through the side door they had both just entered five minutes ago.

Bracken and his assistant are in animated conversation below me; clearly not happy.

The judge coughs again, silencing the slight murmur of chatter that is threatening to grow in volume.

'I want to thank everybody in this courtroom for their cooperation in what I can at best describe as a unique court case,' she says. 'Thank you to the witnesses who took to the stand for their expertise and honesty,' Sheila nudges her knee against mine again, 'and to both the defence and prosecution teams. There were strong arguments and strong disagreements from both sides of this courtroom, but I am glad to say I feel both the defence and the prosecution behaved in the manner this courtroom demands… Even you, Mr Bracken.' The judge holds her smile closed, but some members of the court chuckle. Bracken just remains still, a fist still held to his mouth. 'But I would most of all like to thank the jury who had the biggest decision of all to make. I am truly grateful you took your time to argue this out—even though I did suggest to you at lunch-time today that a unanimous verdict was not a requirement.'

The judge pauses to glance down at her notes and as she does I hear the door behind me sweep open. I stare back, to see Janet and Eoin sneaking out before the judge has even completed her summoning up.

'I, too, now have a big decision to make,' the judge says. 'I, like you jurors, will not take my decision lightly. I am going to give myself ample time to research and think this through. I note in my diary I have an available date exactly four weeks from now. So that is when I will recall Faith and Grace Tiddle to the courtroom to hand down sentencing. I can ensure you that it will be a sentence pertinent to the courts in which they were tried. But I will take my time to ensure all procedure is followed and that justice is served in the proper manner. This case has been as unique for me as it has been for you all. This day four weeks is May 26th. Court dismissed.'

Everybody seems to stand at the same time. And suddenly we're all trying to crush our way out of the double doors at the back of the courtroom.

'Think we can get a flight out on Sunday?' Sheila whispers to me as we get enveloped in the crowd.

'I'm sure we can... I need to get my hands on some of that sun cream I like... the spray-on one.'

'Don't worry,' she says. 'I've already bought it. It's packed in the suitcase.'

I'd love to have my mind in Tuscany right now, just as Sheila has. Just as I promised Sheila I would have as soon as this trial was over. But my mind is whirring with the case still, even though we've just heard the full-time whistle. Ever since I retired, myself and Sheila decided we were going to live out our remaining years just as we'd always dreamed we would. Since I took retirement we've begun to split our years into quarters. We spend January to March in Florida. We love it out there. But American policy says we can only stay in the country for up to ninety days a year. So we do. Literally ninety days every time. Then we head off to a rustic villa in Tuscany, only this year that trip was delayed because of the trial. We don't mind. We've lots of years left. Sheila has shown absolutely no signs of illness since she started on the cannabis. She still has a tumour, but it seems to be reducing in size every time it's measured. For the end of the summer — from July to September — we aim to visit a different country each year. Last year we spent most of our time in southern Portugal. This year we plan on going to the south of France. And then from October until the New Year, we stay at home. In Dublin. Some of our friends have said we're crazy coming home for the winter; that if they had our freedom and our money, they'd go somewhere nice and hot for Christmas. We tried that the first year. It doesn't work. It's not supposed to be hot at Christmas. Besides, there is something so warm about Dublin in the winter months.

I relax my shoulders when my wife holds my hand just as the crowd separates before us to make it through the main entrance.

'Excuse me, Detective… eh, *Mr* Quayle, Faith and Grace have requested to speak with you. Do you mind?'

A middle-aged man I'd never laid eyes on before points his whole hand in the opposite direction of the oncoming crowd.

I look at my wife, and she nods her head.

'Sure,' I say. Then I take Sheila by the hand and we begin to slalom through strangers to follow the middle-aged man. Eventually we turn left into a quiet corridor and make our way to the bottom of it, stopping outside a large brown door.

'They're in there, Mr Quayle.'

I stare at the door and shake my head with wonder.

'Thank you, but do you know—'

I stop talking. Because the man has disappeared. It's just me and Sheila. And that brown door. Sheila shrugs her shoulders at me. Then I shrug one of mine back at her before I push gently at the door.

'Won't be long,' I whisper to her.

It's a long, skinny room. Not unlike the corridors we just strolled down. I shuffle quietly towards the familiar frame of Gerd Bracken in the distance perched on a desk, his back to me.

'I could fuckin' kill her,' a lady's voice says.

'Relax, Imogen,' Bracken replies. 'We only had one juror this time… we usually have three or four, that's why we never get beaten. We just didn't get enough jurors with dirt this time.'

'That's my fuckin' record gone up in the smoke,' Imogen says. 'Losing doesn't suit me.'

My eyebrows raise. I can't believe that when this girl eventually speaks, she's full of vulgarity.

'You're not going to send that text are you?'

I stand there, unsure whether or not I should step in on their conversation. I'm not sure what they're talking about. Sounds to me as if they've just found out only one juror voted not guilty; it must have been an eleven-to-one loss.

'Ah… I don't fuckin' know,' Imogen says, snatching at a pen. 'I'll see what mood I'm in when I finish this shit.'

She clicks at the pen and then begins scribbling on some paperwork. Bracken spins off the desk and almost baulks when he sees me.

'Detective Quayle…. I, eh, hope you, eh…' He looks shaken. The fucker's not used to losing.

'Sorry for creeping up on you,' I say. 'I didn't mean to…

you, eh... didn't hear me come in and... a man told me the twins requested I drop by.'

Bracken looks over his shoulder at Imogen who has strangely re-transformed into the little bookworm I always assumed she was.

'What, ehm... what did you hear us saying, Detective Quayle?' Bracken asks.

'Not much. You were discussing the jury... you only managed to win over one juror, is that right?'

He laughs. And slaps his hand on the desk.

'That's exactly it,' he says. 'The twins... they are just in here. Officer Coulter!' he calls out.

Another door at the end of this room opens and I hear the click of their shoes before they appear. They're both handcuffed, and both wearing the same expression they have done ever since I first met them almost two years ago. An expression that says absolutely nothing.

'We just wanted to say thanks anyway, Detective Quayle. Thanks for trying.' They say it in unison. As if they've rehearsed it.

I raise an eyebrow at them.

'I wish you both the best,' I say, and then I turn to leave.

'Detective Quayle,' Grace calls after me. I stop, and spin slowly. 'We, eh... we were wondering, because you never said so in the trial. But... did you ever stop believing in us?'

I huff out a small laugh and then move towards her before crouching down to bended knee.

'Course I stopped believing you,' I said. 'It just took me a little longer than everybody else.'

'Hey!' Bracken calls out, placing a palm to my shoulder. 'You will not engage with my clients in that manner—'

'Shut the hell up, Bracken,' I say, shrugging him away from me. 'I've heard enough of your voice over the past two weeks. You lying toad. The truth never seems to leave your lips, does it? I've had more than a lifetime of hearing your voice.'

I turn and pace towards the brown door and when I snatch it open, Sheila's smile stops me in my tracks.

'That was quick,' she says. 'Did they not have much to say?'

I shake my head.

'Not really.' Then I close the door tight behind me and grab at my wife's hand. 'Now, my love,' I say, 'let's go home and see if we can book those flights for Monday, huh?'

ALICE

I peer from the top of our street, resting a hand to Mrs Balfe's garden wall. I'm looking for any unusual movement from my house. Not that I'd expect Noel — if he had been sent the video — to be stomping around the front garden ranting and raving like a madman. Yet for some reason I've been standing here staring at my house for at least five full minutes… just waiting. Pausing. Gazing. Hesitating more than anything, I guess.

I hear a cough and glance over my shoulder.

'Ah hello, Mrs Balfe,' I say.

She smiles her gums at me. A slightly warmer response than I got from her two days ago. Though I guess that time I was keeled over, trying to puke anything out that would come up from my stomach. I'm not sure why that's not what I'm doing right now. Perhaps my stomach's on strike from rolling itself over. Because that's all it's done the past forty-eight hours. Bizarrely enough, after Red Head outed herself as the moral compass of our jury, my stomach, for some reason, stopped spinning. Not sure why. Maybe because there was nothing I could do about it anymore. It was out of my hands from that moment onwards. My life was now all in the hands — or at the finger tips to be more precise — of the bitch who hacked into my phone. All she has to do is tap at her screen once and my life is over.

I've dialled her number ten times since I got out of court about half an hour ago. But her phone's dead. I've also texted twice; both times pleading that she doesn't send the video to Noel or Zoe. I was adamant as I could be in the texts that I had done the best I could; that I was really impressive in arguing for not guilty.

The keys jingle in my shaking hands as I attempt to slot one into the keyhole.

When it finally goes in, I turn the lock, sneak quietly inside and take off my coat to hang it over Noel's on the butt of our bannister. Then I sniff.

Stir fry. Noel's usual Friday evening dinner. Things are running as normal. I let out a grateful breath and then head for the kitchen, passing the shouting voices and guns shooting from Alfie's video games in the back room.

Noel's back is to me as he shuffles at the pan. But he's whistling. So I don't have to see his face to know he's in good form.

'Evening,' I say.

He spins around, his eyes narrow. Then he unties the apron from around his waist and strides over to me. He leans closer, kisses my cheek.

'I heard it on the news... Must have been a tough day,' he says.

'Long,' I reply, sighing.

'Least it's all over now, and those crazy twins are behind bars. You called guilty practically from the start of this trial. I'm proud of you. Sit down... I'll have dinner ready in a few minutes. And a nice bottle of red. Then you can tell me all about it.'

I scan the countertops of our kitchen after he's turned back to the frying pan.

'Where is, eh… where's your phone?' I ask.

He pats at his trousers pockets, then nods towards the hallway.

'Must be still in my jacket,' he says.

He hasn't checked his phone since he got home… that must be an hour or so ago now. Maybe she *has* texted him. Maybe he just hasn't bloody seen it.

'What ye need it for?' he asks as I make my way back towards the hall.

'I thought I had Debra and Paul's number in my phone but it seems to have disappeared. I just want to store it again…'

There's tension music playing from Alfie's game as I walk past… hitting my current state of mind right in the fucking bullseye. I lift my coat and then tug at Noel's, and feel weight in the inside pocket. I grab for the phone and immediately tap into it.

One text message alert.

My shoulders arch up to my ears.

Then I let out a slow exhale.

It's only Shay—Noel's friend from the quiz team… bantering about a question they got wrong last night.

'What you smiling at?' Alfie says, startling me.

'Oh… nothing,' I reply, and then he pulls open the door to the downstairs toilet, walks inside and slams it shut behind him.

'Alfie!' Noel shouts, startling me again.

I palm his phone into my trouser pocket.

'He's in there,' I say.

'C'mon,' Noel says to me, holding the kitchen door open. 'Dinner's ready.'

I kiss my husband on the lips as I walk by him and then take a seat.

Chicken stir fry in soy sauce. He knows that's my favourite.

Alfie bundles out of the loo and into the kitchen without, I bet, washing his hands. But I'm sick of telling him and am too way tired for that conversation again.

'Another stir fry?' he grunts.

Little shit.

'Why don't you make dinner for us tomorrow instead, huh?' I say. He doesn't answer that. Never does.

Noel pulls out a chair and sits into it, then he pours us both a glass of red.

'Would you rather not talk about it then?' Noel asks.

'Eh...' I shake my head. 'I, eh... the stir fry looks delicious... is this a different soy sauce?'

He laughs. And so do I.

Alfie looks up at us and rolls his eyes.

'Well, even if you don't want to talk about it, I just want to say we're proud of you, aren't we Alfie?'

'Yes, Ma,' Alfie replies. 'I am... seriously. What ye did, it was, eh... brave.'

I'm taken aback. Alfie hasn't so much as paid me a bit of notice, never mind a compliment, in years.

'Brave? Thank you,' I say, taking a sip of wine.

'How long do you think they'll go to prison for?' Alfie asks.

'Hold on, son... your mother doesn't want to talk—'

'It's okay... it's fine, Noel. It's nice to have you involved in our conversation at dinner, Alfie,' I say, rustling at his hair. 'Truth is, I don't know how long they will have to spend in prison. There's never been anything like this kind of case in Ireland before. Could be twenty years... could be life. I mean, it's unlikely they'll ever be children again, not in the outside world.'

He scrunches up his face and then shovels a forkful of stir fry into his mouth.

'How long do you think they should go to prison for though?' he asks, chewing.

I blow out my lips.

'Life,' I say. 'They don't belong in society, these girls.'

'Wow,' Noel says, laughing with his mouth full.

'Does that sound really harsh?' I say.

He nods his head and as he does, Alfie laughs. And I feel something I haven't felt in way too long. Happy. So I laugh too. Out loud. Until I see the hall door swing open behind Noel and in that instance I am certain my life is about to end. It's Zoe. And she's stomping straight towards me.

'How did you get on, Mam?' she says, holding her arms out to me. I stand up and take her hug, my heart resetting.

'Well... this is nice,' I say. 'All four of us together for dinner, huh?'

'Ah sure I've been thinking about you all day. Especially how ill you looked the other night. Guilty it was, anyway. Just what you wanted. It must have been so tough. I'm proud of you, Mam,' she rubs the blades of my shoulder. And as she does, I laugh out loud. Again.

'Ah, so your Dad ordered you both to turn up for dinner this evening and for you to say you were proud of me, huh?'

Alfie's the first to laugh, and then everybody follows.

'We're just here, cos we love you, Mam,' Zoe assures me as she pours herself a glass of red. 'Be nice for you to get back to normal, but I bet you have a story to tell, after all that, don't ya?'

'Oh yeah,' I say. 'Too fucking right I do.'

And everybody laughs again. Alfie particularly loudly. Because I rarely let him hear me swear.

'I'll get you a bowlful,' Noel says to Zoe.

'Lovely stuff, Dad,' she replies. And as she says that, she removes her phone from her jeans pocket and places it on the table beside her wine. I stare at the screen. It's blank. The smile drops from my face and my heart begins to thump. But I don't think it needs to. I really don't believe that bitch is going to text. She would have done it as soon as the case was called in court. Why would she wait?

Zoe teases Alfie about being locked in the downstairs back room, asking what he *really* gets up to in there.

'I hear what boys your age do,' she says, trying to embarrass him. Noel looks at me and grins.

'So how are you feeling now, Mam… overall?' Zoe asks.

I puff out a laugh that is almost a cry, too; my eyes instantly watering.

'I just... I just feel grateful,' I say.

Then Zoe's phone vibrates on the table at the exact same time Noel's buzzes against my thigh. And I know. I know right now in this moment that my life is fucked.

I drop my fork to my bowl as Zoe picks up her phone. And then, as soon as her thumb taps against the screen, I hear it...

My heavy panting.

Followed swiftly by my loud squeals of ecstasy.

✝

'We have to kill mammy and daddy,' Faith said, cramming her words in between heavy breaths.

Grace got to her feet and rubbed at both of her eyes.

'Huh?' she said.

Faith first tried to steady her breathing, then her body, by gripping the magazine she was holding in her hands even tighter.

'We have to kill mammy and daddy. Jesus needs them. It says so... it says so in this,' she said, throwing the magazine on to her own bed. Grace bent down, picked it up and stared at the two-page spread her sister had left it open on. It was an article about the Menendez brothers—two young men who took the lives both of their parents' in cold blood in America.

Grace looked up over the magazine spread and stared at her sister.

'But... but...' Grace stuttered. Then she tossed the magazine back on to her sister's bed. 'But it's just a story in a magazine.'

Faith shook her head.

'No it's not. The magazine was open on that page in our garden. Jesus left it there.'

✞

Grace squinted, then picked up the two-page spread again and cast her finger down the side column.

'But, sure, there's a small article on this page about a butterfly too, one with four wings. A conjoined butterfly it's called; look, it says how rare they are. You sure Jesus is not sending us a message about butterflies?'

Faith shook her head again.

'No. It's about the main story—the killings. Killing parents. He wants us to do it.'

'No he doesn't. He can't. He can't,' Grace said.

Then she chicaned herself around the bed and reached an arm to her sister's shoulder.

'Why would he want us to kill Mammy and Daddy, Faith?'

'Cos maybe he wants them... maybe they're needed in Heaven. With him.'

'But then who'd look after us?'

Faith shrugged. Then she mirrored her sister by placing a hand to Grace's shoulder.

They both stood there for a moment in silence, forehead to forehead.

'Trust in the Lord with all thine heart; and not lean unto thine own understanding. In all thy ways acknowledge Him, and he shall direct paths.'

Faith whispered the verse, practically into Grace's mouth.

Then they both sat slowly down on their own beds, knees up to their chins and tried to talk it through. Twenty minutes later they were on those knees, pleading with Jesus. Begging that if he was asking them to do what they think he was asking them to do, then they'd need another sign. They prayed for the lamplight in their bedroom to flicker; for the conjoined butterfly to flap its wings on the page of the magazine; for a roll of thunder to rumble in the sky; for a knocking sound outside their bedroom window. But nothing happened. Except silence. And stillness.

They were both in the garden the next day, still stewing over the magazine when it appeared from out of nowhere.

Faith stopped dead in her tracks.

Grace fell slowly to her knees. As if she'd been shot in the gut and the realisation of mortality was ever so gradually dawning on her.

They didn't say anything. Not for ages. They just replayed what they'd witnessed again and again... over and over in their minds. It flew over their heads and landed on one the protruding roots of the oak tree. A butterfly. A conjoined one. Two black and white wings, and two yellow ones with thin red stripes. It stalled there on the root for a short while, looked about itself and then flew upwards through the branches and out of sight.

Grace eventually went back inside without saying a word. But Faith lasted another two hours; frozen in the same spot.

She did eventually follow her sister into the safe haven that was their bedroom. Neither of them came out all night, except to take dinner from the kitchen to eat on their beds.

'We are practising a new prayer,' Faith said. 'Can we eat dinner in our bedroom tonight, please... please?'

They knew they could get away with this sort of thing. All four Tiddles eating dinner at the kitchen table had long since stopped being a routine that must be adhered to.

'Sure,' Dorothy said. 'But don't get any dinner on those bed clothes.'

They took their plates from their mother and then trotted to their bedroom to plan how they would kill her... and their father.

'When are we going to do it?' Grace asked.

Faith chewed on her dinner. And then swallowed before answering.

'Tomorrow.'

'Tomorrow. Why tomorrow?'

Faith took another bite, then shrugged back at her sister.

'We can do it while Daddy's having his Saturday mid-morning nap. Just before we go to dance class.'

Grace looked down at her dinner, before tossing the fork onto the plate and pushing it away from herself.

'How are we going to do it?'

'Knife; one of those big black sharp ones in the kitchen,' Faith said.

'You've been thinking about this.'

'I knew,' Faith said, still chewing. 'I knew as soon as I saw that magazine.'

The day before had been still. Real still; the sun blazing high in the sky as it had done all that week. Faith decided to have a walk in the back garden while Grace was taking a shower. It was lying there next to the bush that ran along the side of the garden. A magazine. Wide open on the two-page spread about the Menendez brothers. She knew instantly it had been sent by Jesus. This was the second time he'd left her a message via magazine. The first magazine she'd found in the back garden — almost two years previous — had actually blown from a neighbour's bin who lived half a mile up the slope that led to the Tiddle bungalow. It was open on a feature about dying plants. And so Faith simply saw to it that she had to water her father's plants. They did need watering—Clive had begun to neglect his hobby as the church evolved into his only obsession. And so Faith saved the plants' lives thanks to Jesus through the medium of magazine. The second magazine — the one with the article about the Menendez brothers killing their parents — had been placed there by Eoin. For a laugh more than anything. When Janet was fuming; literally kicking the walls of her tiny flat all up in a rage about her brother and his 'tight-ass dirty cunt of a wife', Eoin happened to be flicking through the magazine that had come free inside the midweek tabloid newspaper.

'Hey...' he said turning to his wife and snorting out a laugh. 'Why don't you leave that for Faith to find? She might think it's a sign from God and actually do it.'

They were driving to Dublin the next day to see a friend and to do some shopping anyway. Eoin genuinely only brought the magazine for the laugh. To stir some shit. The twins had informed their aunt and uncle, on the night of their Holy Communion, that Jesus communicated with Faith. And since that revelation both Janet and Eoin began to ring the twins every now and then when they were bored and drunk, just to see what crazy Jesus shit they had been up to recently. Faith had told them over the phone once that she'd found a magazine in their garden that had a story in it about saving dying plants, and went on to proudly detail how she managed to bring her father's roses back to life, thanks to Jesus. Janet and Eoin often had to pinch their noses to stop their laughter from being heard down the line during those phone calls.

Janet dismissed the joke of leaving the magazine for the twins to find as 'fucking stupid'. But Eoin still brought it with him for the drive to Dublin because he had nothing else even close to being regarded as fun or exciting to do. And so rather than spend an hour shopping with his wife, he took a drive out to Rathcoole to toss the magazine over the bush that separated the Tiddle's garden from a large expanse of yellow field. He laughed to himself as he did it. Then popped himself back in the car and drove back to the shopping centre; hoping his wife was done with her browsing.

He had nothing to do with the butterfly. Nor did Janet. That, appearing the following day in the Tiddle back garden and flapping its four wings, was pure happenchance.

'Won't we go to Hell... I mean what about Thou Shall Not Kill?' Grace asked.

Faith shook her head.

'Not if Jesus asked us to do it. He'll forgive us.'

'But sure... won't the police know it was us?' Grace said. 'Is Jesus telling us we have to spend our lives in prison?'

Faith shrugged.

'We'll just follow Jesus's plan... wherever it leads us. The police won't have to know it was us. That's why we do it before dance

class, because we can tell the police we were at dance class when Mammy and Daddy were killed.'

Grace puffed out her cheeks, but she was still wide-eyed and blood was gushing inside her veins. Faith was much more relaxed. Much more calm. Her face may have been a little on the pale side, but she was taking everything in her stride.

After all, Jesus's plan is what it is; no need to ever feel any emotion about it whatsoever. If he's the one in control, all will be okay.

'We can do this,' Faith said. 'We kill them with the knife, wash our hands real quick, change our clothes, and get to dance class as soon as we can. When we come home, we can ring the police, tell them we found Mammy and Daddy just lying there.'

'Yeah but what do we do with the knife? And the clothes that we use when we kill them? And the magazine? The police will find them all. They'll know it was us.'

'They won't find them,' Faith said.

'Huh?' Grace replied, her fingers fidgeting. 'Where we going to hide them?'

Faith threw her legs over the side of her bed and stood. Then she made her way slowly to their bedroom window and pulled back the curtains; revealing, to her sister, the silhouette of the oak tree as it stood tall in front of a blood orange sky.

The End

WANT TO KNOW WHAT HAPPENED TO THESE CHARACTERS NEXT?

- How long did Faith and Grace get sentenced for?

- What happened after Alice's daughter viewed the video?

- How Denis and Sheila Quayle are getting on in their travels?

Please click the link below to watch an exclusive interview with author David B. Lyons in which he answers all those questions and discusses this book in more detail.

www.subscribepage.com/faithgrace

DAVID B. LYONS' NOVELS?

ACKNOWLEDGEMENTS

This book — about two *very* odd sisters — is very aptly dedicated to my very own odd sister; Debra Boland (née Lyons).

I'm not sure why. Perhaps I'm just running out of people to dedicate books to.

For the very brief moment in our lives when I thought my sister was cool (she 17, me 14) because she was hanging around with older guys and drinking warm cans of beer, I stressed a desire to hang out with her. She refused. She didn't want her little brother ruining the street cred she thought she had.

But now that we're adults, all she does is pester me to come hang out with her.

Your lil brother cool enough for you now, huh?

Anyway, thanks for, eh… for, eh… hmmm... I'm trying to think what you've ever done for me in life... Thanks for, eh…

Acknowledgements

oh yeah, thanks for introducing me to *Dirty Dancing*. It's a fuckin' great movie. Oh yeah, and thanks for my nephews; Ben and Adam. I adore them. And I adore you, too. And your husband, Paul.

Thank you Mam, also. Unlike Debra, you always let me hang around with you and your friends. S'probably why I have a tendency to act like a sixty-year-old Dublin housewife at times.

To my wife, Kerry, and our daughter Lola: you know how much of a struggle this book was for me to write through my own illnesses in late 2019 and into the fucked up world that is/was COVID-19 and Lockdown in the spring/summer of 2020.

Your patience is a virtue. Your belief in me is immeasurable.

I owe a great deal of gratitude, as always, to Margaret Lyons, Hannah Healy and Barry O'Hanlon whose eyes are always the first to read my works. I know you three will always give it to me straight. Thank you also to Livia Sbrabaro and Rubina Gomes who read early drafts of Faith & Grace and who gave me some fantastic pointers.

I owe a huge debt of gratitude to lawyer Phelim O'Neill who helped me iron out the plot of this court case and to the super-impressive Liza Young whose knowledge of the investigative processes in Ireland proved invaluable.

The final salute and thank you goes to my editor in chief; the always impressive Brigit Taylor.